THE **SHADOWS** OF **MISKATONIC**
BOOK THREE

Shadow Zone

BARBARA COTTRELL

DEDICATION

To all the writers and readers who keep
the world of H. P. Lovecraft alive

The true work of art is born from the "artist": a mysterious, enigmatic, and mystical creation. It detaches itself from him, it acquires an autonomous life, becomes a personality, an independent subject, animated with a spiritual breath, the living subject of a real existence of being.

—Wassily Kandinsky, painter

I have been fighting the temptation to go back, if only to convince myself that the thing really occurred. But why shouldn't I go back? The wonders I shall see, the secrets I shall learn, are beyond imagining.

—Clark Ashton Smith,
The City of the Singing Flame

Chapter One

The creature's jackal-like face twisted in triumph as it raised its sword above its head. A crowd gathered at the altar's base. They leaned forward in anticipation, ears pricked, teeth bared. They waited for the blow to land, for the deed to be done.

Gerard Caron held his breath as he studied the painting that rested on an easel in front of him.

"Is it real?" the man beside him blurted.

"There's no way to know for sure," Gerard admitted. "The artist we're talking about is a legend, a myth—"

"A boogeyman," the stranger added.

Gerard glanced at the man beside him. He rarely met people after hours at his gallery. Dark art was a risky business, especially in Arkham. Miskatonic University was a magnet for kooks. Most of them were harmless, but some of Gerard's encounters were disturbing enough for him to lay down a set of rules. He always worked in well-worn channels, with people he knew. Even though he hated cell phones, he clung to his electronic tether. He told his friends where he was going, texting them before and after every meeting. But when this man called and hinted at what he had (*what he might have,* Gerard corrected himself), he relaxed his rules.

Just this once, he promised himself. *I'll do it just this once.*

The setting sun popped out from behind a ragged line of clouds, all that remained of a fierce summer storm that swept through Arkham. It hit the canvas with a glancing blow, illuminating two figures in the painting's corner. They were females, *human* females, wearing long robes. In the arms of one—

The other man shifted in the gloom. "It *is* real, isn't it?" he breathed.

Gerard said nothing. He wanted to kick the man out, to return to his normal routine. Two words held him back.

What if?

"There might be a way of identifying it," Gerard decided after a long silence. "The artist never signed his work, but there are rumors he marked them in other ways."

Gerard moved closer to the painting to get a better look. An odor rose from the canvas. Leaning forward, he took a deep breath, like a connoisseur appreciating fine wine. The smell was complex—dry, dusty, undercut with the unmistakable smell of rot. A contradiction. Just like the man who painted it.

The man who supposedly painted it.

Gerard struggled to stay professional, but as his eyes drifted across the painting, his excitement grew.

At the bottom of the canvas, he spotted a single word. He raised his reading glasses to examine the spidery writing. "*Al-Uqdah,*" he read.

"What?" the man demanded.

"I'm not sure, but I think it's Arabic. I have a translation app on my—"

Out of the corner of his eye, Gerard saw a blur of motion. He was hit by a burst of rapid, rabbit-like punches.

Pain shot through his body, and something warm and wet trickled down his spine.

Blood, Gerard thought. *I've been stabbed.*

He dropped his phone and spun to face his knife-wielding attacker.

The next blow hit him in the chest. He gasped, feeling the snick of metal on bone. When his attacker yanked out the knife, Gerard lurched forward, falling into the man's arms.

His attacker lowered him gently to the ground. "I'm sorry. It's nothing personal, but I need to keep this a secret," he explained.

The man stepped over him to reclaim the painting.

Gerard rolled onto his stomach, crawling in his own blood to stop the man from taking it from him. "No, please," he gasped. "Wait, wait—"

A sharp, popping sound pierced the gallery. The man who stabbed him collapsed at the foot of the easel. Gerard stared up at the canvas. The creature at the altar loomed over them both. The gallery owner watched in disbelief as the figure in the painting stirred. The terrible thing flexed its jaw, preparing to devour both men. The wooden floor vibrated with an angry, insect-like buzz.

Blood loss, he thought vaguely, *I'm seeing things because I'm bleeding to death.*

Another man stepped into the room, his gun flashing in the sunlight.

The painting stilled and became two-dimensional again.

The intruder slipped on white cotton gloves and lifted the painting off its easel, carefully handling it by the edges.

Gerard moaned his approval.

This man is a professional, he thought.

He tried not to look at the evidence of the man's other talent, at his attacker lying still beside him, blood leeching onto the floor.

"It is real, isn't it?" Gerard gasped.

The stranger said nothing.

"Can I have a closer look?"

The intruder's lips twisted into a smile. "Do you think that's wise? I mean, look what's already happened to you."

"I don't care. I must . . ." His words ended with a wheeze.

The man picked up the painting and held it in front of him. A fresh wave of agony ripped through Gerard as he strained for a better look. The pain didn't matter. *It's him. After all these years, I'm finally seeing something by him.* It wasn't what he expected. The artist's legend was so much larger than life that Gerard assumed the work would be big. He expected a Rembrandt, a masterpiece measured in feet. The work was modest in size, but the scene bristled with energy. He could practically hear the snarl of the creatures, the crackle of the altar fire. His nose filled with the sour stench of unwashed bodies. From the bottom of the painting, a creature glared at Gerard, eyes red and fierce, as if caught by a camera flash.

Gerard closed his eyes, recording the image in his mind. "Thank you," he said to the shadowy figure.

The man chuckled. "Not words I usually hear in my profession."

"I mean it. I never thought I'd see one." Gerard kept his eyes shut, waiting for the gunshot.

The man's footsteps retreated.

Gerard blinked, confused. "What? What are—?" he spluttered.

"Good luck, Mr. Caron." The man punched the keypad on the wall, and the burglar alarm howled in distress.

The gesture saved Gerard's life.

Chapter Two

WHERE IS SOLOMON REYE?

The words, spray-painted on a wall at Miskatonic University, bit into Ellen Logan. The oppressive summer heat faded, and her mind returned to a cold basement in the Pine Barrens of New Jersey. Five months earlier, in the dead of winter, she'd escaped the clutches of a serial killer named Calvin Leonard. A man she claimed had a partner in crime, Solomon Reye. A demon from the Dreamlands.

The police dismissed the demon angle. "Trauma," they told her. "That's just the trauma talking."

The reality was horrifying enough—ten bodies discovered in an abandoned farmhouse—many mere piles of flesh. Only Ellen Logan had survived. Bloody Ellen Logan, clutching a baseball bat. She'd killed Calvin Leonard. Solomon Reye . . .

"He's the one who got away," she whispered.

In his absence, the legend grew. Spawned in the dark heart of the internet. Questions swirled around her. Why did she survive? Why did she emerge from the basement unharmed? What made Ellen Logan so special?

She remembered the moment when it all changed. A reporter thrust a microphone in her face and demanded, "How did you get out alive? Did you make a deal with Calvin Leonard?"

A few days later, a headline blared from the local paper:

"The Pine Barren Blasphemies: Was There a Second Killer?"

The article didn't mention Ellen by name.

It didn't need to.

That's when the whispers started. The sideways glances.

Even now, she could feel people watching her, their eyes boring into her back.

WHERE IS SOLOMON REYE?

Ellen backed away from the spray-painted accusation, turned, and headed off-campus to the place she considered her refuge from the world: Edgewood Manor Retirement Home.

She first visited the Victorian house when she interviewed Harold Graham about an old abandoned mine. The conversation had grown heated. Intense. A few weeks later, Graham was dead. Ellen knew the man had a constellation of health problems—that he was living on borrowed time. Still, questions burned in her mind. *Did I push him over the edge? Was he another one of my victims?* After the funeral, Ellen returned to Edgewood to check on his widow, Lily. And something remarkable happened. What started as an obligation blossomed into a friendship.

Ellen arrived at Lily's room just as the older woman returned from her yoga class. She plopped down on her friend's couch and snatched chocolate from a candy dish. "Sorry I'm late."

"You know, you don't have to keep visiting me," Lily replied. "I'm sure you're a busy girl."

"I enjoy visiting you."

"You like visiting my sweets."

Ellen smiled and reached for another piece of candy.

Her friend arched an eyebrow.

"Are you sure you want to do that? You don't want to get pudgy your senior year."

"Lily!" she protested as she dropped the truffle.

The comment stung. After her ordeal with Calvin Leonard and her wild tales of how she "escaped" into the Dreamlands, the doctors at Miskatonic had medicated her. They put her on a potent mix of antipsychotics and mood stabilizers. One of the side effects of the medicines was weight gain. Ellen never considered herself vain, but the weight gain was one of the reasons she stopped taking them. As soon as she went cold turkey, the extra pounds melted away, but the insecurity lingered, clinging to her like a storm cloud.

"Oh, don't misunderstand me. There's nothing wrong with you now," Lily chirped, patting a spot on her love seat. "But why don't we have some iced tea instead?"

Ellen cleared away the newspapers on the cushions. A headline glared at her:

"One Man Dead,
Gallery Owner Critically Injured in Bold
Daylight Robbery"

Her friend shook her head. "Can you believe it? All that violence. Over *art*."

Ellen couldn't ignore the sneer in her friend's voice. Ellen's uncle Joshua was an art dealer. Their lives revolved around art.

"Art is big business," Ellen pointed out as she took her iced tea. "Do you know how much they think the *Mona Lisa* is worth?"

"I can't imagine."

"Half a billion dollars. For something small enough to slip into a duffel bag."

"Nothing but nonsense." Lily dismissed the thought with a wave of her hand.

A nurse entered the room before Ellen could respond. He was young and good-looking in a boy-band way. His fresh face made her feel old.

"Oh, Justin. Again?" Lily lowered her voice to a stage whisper. "He can't keep his hands off me."

The man blushed to the tips of his ears.

"Would you give us a moment alone, dear?" Lily cooed.

"Yell if you need help," Ellen told Justin as she left the room to wander the halls.

Edgewood Manor had changed since her first visit. She read somewhere that a corporation recently bought it. "Nothing will change," a spokesperson insisted. He claimed their goal was to make the place more efficient without sacrificing quality.

The threadbare furniture and chipped linoleum floors told a different story. Edgewood hadn't just reached a tipping point. It had blown right through it. And then there were the rules. Residents must not . . . residents will not . . . residents are forbidden . . . One rule plastered on the front door bothered Ellen the most.

Residents are not allowed on the porch unless family or staff is present.

The first time Ellen came to Edgewood, the porch was full of residents. They napped. Read books. Argued. Watched people on the street. No one supervised them back then.

What had changed? she wondered. *Was someone snatching old people off porches?*

A resident joined her and gazed longingly out the bay window.

"Would you like to go outside with me?" Ellen offered.

The resident looked at her, her eyes filling with tears.

"Yes. Please," she whispered.

Ellen escorted the woman to the porch and helped her into one of the Adirondack chairs. She perched on the railing a few feet away and tilted her head back, letting the sun warm her skin.

"You're not a staff member," a voice declared.

Ellen groaned.

Great, she thought as she opened her eyes, *Edgewood's resident rule enforcer.*

A man sat in the porch's corner, smoking a cigarette, his legs splayed in front of him. He had stringy gray hair and a lanky body. He looked vaguely familiar. Ellen was sure she had seen him before, but she had seen a lot of guys like him. He was straight out of the movies. The aging cowboy. Tommy Lee Jones in *Lonesome Dove.* Jack Palance in *City Slickers.*

"You're not a staff member, either," she pointed out. "Where's *your* babysitter?"

The stranger took a deep drag off his cigarette and flicked the ashes into a coffee can.

"You're that girl."

"Excuse me?" she blurted, even though she knew what was coming.

"You're that girl. The one who escaped from that serial killer in New Jersey. God, what was his name?"

"Calvin Leonard." She hated to say his name, but her psychiatrist insisted on it.

That's how you rob him of his power.

"The Tailor. Isn't that what he called himself? He sewed body parts onto his victims. Tried to transform them into divine creatures."

Ellen gave him a hard look.

"Are you one of his fans?"

The man stared at her with intense blue eyes.

"No, I'm one of yours," he replied. "You ended all his nonsense with a baseball bat."

A nurse marched onto the porch, hands on her hips in a classic battle pose.

"What the hell are you doing?" the woman barked at Ellen. "I've seen you around, so I know you're familiar with the rules. No one is allowed on the porch without family or staff."

"This is my daughter-in-law. And we decided to add Mary to our little family," the man chimed in, nodding at the woman Ellen had brought outside. "Is there a problem, Miss Worden? Or is the god of liability against random acts of kindness?"

Miss Worden hissed. "*You.* I should have known you were involved."

The man flicked his cigarette into the coffee can. "What can I say? I'm diabolical."

Ellen stifled a giggle.

A moment later, Lily popped her head out the front door. When she saw the man on the porch, her expression cooled. "Robert."

"Lily," he replied in a neutral voice.

Lily grabbed Ellen by the arm and yanked her off the railing. "You can come back. I'm done flirting with the new boy."

Robert raised an eyebrow. "You mean there's a time when you're *not* flirting?"

"When I'm with you," Lily cooed.

His lips twisted into a crooked smile.

"It was nice to see you again, Ellen," he offered as Lily yanked her inside the house.

Ellen tensed at the sound of her name, at the familiarity in his voice.

A chill spread through her body.

How does he know my name? Have we met before?

Suddenly, her refuge from the world felt a lot less secure.

The other residents only added to her unease. As Lily escorted her back to her room, she could feel their eyes on her, their whispered thoughts a low, anxious murmur.

That's the girl. The girl with the bat. The one who killed . . .

Ellen turned her back, hoping to shield herself from their piercing words.

When they finally reached Lily's room, her friend scolded her. "You shouldn't talk to Robert."

"What? Why?" Ellen blurted, grateful for something else to concentrate on.

"He's not a nice man."

"A lot of people around here fit that description," Ellen joked.

Lily grabbed her arm and squeezed. "I mean it. Don't talk to him."

Ellen studied her friend. "What's with you, Lil?" she demanded as a terrible thought bloomed in her head. She moved closer and lowered her voice. "He's not taking advantage of you, is he?"

Lily almost choked. "*Him?* That scarecrow? I'd tear him apart if he tried." Lily hesitated for a moment. Then she moved to her nightstand and picked up an envelope.

"He's been bugging me. He wants me to give this to you. To pass on to Dr. Carter."

Andrew Carter.

Ellen sighed. She hadn't thought about Andrew Carter in a long time. What was the point? He had been warned about her unhealthy "obsession" with him. Now, with the rumors about her spreading . . .

He wouldn't touch me with a ten-foot pole.

Still, Ellen took the letter, if only to relieve her friend of the burden. "I can't promise he'll get it," she warned Lily as she stuffed it into her bag. "Not that it matters. It's probably just fan mail."

"Fan mail?" Lily echoed.

"People give me stuff for Carter all the time. They think that since I worked with him in the past . . ." She let the sentence die.

"Are you sleeping with him?" Lily asked.

Ellen stiffened. It was a familiar question, but one that caught her off guard every time.

"I have a boyfriend. And he is *not* Andrew Carter."

Lily gawked at her. "Wait a minute. You have a boyfriend? Why haven't I met him?"

"And have you steal him from me? I don't think so!" Ellen quipped.

"I wouldn't stand a chance against you, my dear."

Ellen looked at the floor, hiding a smile. Her happiness didn't last long. "Tom went home for the summer," she explained. "His mom has cancer."

"Oh! I'm so sorry to hear that."

Ellen nodded and looked away, her eyes locking on a spot above Lily's head.

A purple light pulsed at the junction between the wall and the ceiling.

The glow spilled down the wall like liquid, making Ellen's skin prickle.

It reminded her of the gateway Solomon Reye used to kidnap her and pull her into the parallel world of the Dreamlands. A moment that forever divided her life into two parts: before and after.

Ellen blinked, hoping the image would go away with a quick power cycle of her eyes.

The spot continued to grow, spreading like a stain.

She jumped off the couch, panic coursing through her body. "Lily, you need to leave. Now!"

Lily turned, looking toward the opening Ellen knew she couldn't see.

"What? Why? I don't—" her friend spluttered.

Ellen stepped between Lily and the ever-widening hole. Heat blasted her back, making her feel like she was standing in front of an open oven. She put her hands on her friend's shoulders.

"Please. Trust me," she pleaded, squeezing hard enough to make her friend wince. "Leave."

Lily Graham was a tough woman. She didn't like being told what to do, but the look on Ellen's face was enough to make her flee.

Leaving Ellen alone with . . .

What exactly?

Ellen took a deep breath and gazed into the abyss.

She found herself looking into the same room, at a mirror image of the place her friend called home. A strange man dominated the space. He stood in front of a chalkboard, clad in a robe and pajama bottoms. He filled the slate with scribbles that looked like equations. Books covered every surface of the room. Papers littered the floor.

Ellen moved closer, hypnotized by the pounding of chalk. *Bam, bam bam bam, bam bam, ba-bam.*

It sounded like an irregular heartbeat.

She took a step forward, passing through the wall without being aware of it.

"Who are you?" Ellen whispered.

The man at the chalkboard paused in his work and stared at her with glowing eyes. Except he wasn't looking at her. His eyes locked on a spot behind her. They widened as he stared at something impossibly tall. He yanked off his glasses and rubbed at his face, leaving chalky war paint on his skin.

"You're here," he breathed in a voice thick with wonder. "I-I can actually *see* you."

Out of the corner of her eye, Ellen saw movement, heard the swish of what sounded like a robe. Her spine stiffened, turning into hard, immovable steel.

Even if she wanted to move, her body wouldn't let her. Her mind also refused, reminding her of all the people who destroyed themselves by looking. Orpheus, who lost the wife he worked so hard to rescue from the Underworld. Lot's wife, turned into a pillar of salt because she couldn't resist watching the destruction of Sodom and Gomorrah.

A humorless chuckle filled the room.

The shadowy presence behind her moved closer, its breath singeing the hairs on Ellen's neck. A strange smell enveloped her, the not-unpleasant aroma of sawdust and wet plaster.

My sweet, misguided child, a voice slithered in her head. *Refusing to look at me doesn't make me any less real.*

"You're not here," she insisted in a clear voice, using the words her psychiatrists gave her for when her "visions" started.

"Oh, but I am. Do you want to feel?"

Chalkboard Man leaned forward, his face bright with fascination.

"Yes," he croaked to the figure behind her. "Show her."

A pair of leathery hands seized her. Sharp nails sunk into her shoulders.

Ellen screamed.

"Girl!" a voice growled above her. "Snap out of it!"

Ellen's eyes fluttered open, and she found herself on the floor of Lily Graham's room. The cowboy from the porch knelt beside her. Lily fluttered around him like an anxious bird.

Ellen's eyes darted to the wall.

The purple light was gone; the passage between the worlds had closed.

"What happened?" she croaked.

"Lily barged into my room. Said something was wrong with you," Cowboy Man replied.

Robert, she remembered. *The man's name is Robert.*

"When I got here, you were mumbling and clawing at the wall. Then you screamed and hit the floor."

"I fainted?"

Robert's eyes flicked nervously to the wall. "I didn't say that."

A jolt of energy pulsed through Ellen.

Did he see the portal, too? she wondered.

"You're lucky he caught you. It could have been much, much worse." Lily shot Robert a grateful look that seemed to annoy him.

"Are you going to get off the floor?" he barked at Ellen. "Or do you want to keep making a scene?"

Ellen looked up.

A crowd of people filled the doorway, jostling each other for a better view.

"Oh, oh, no," she whispered.

You just gave them more grist for the rumor mill, she thought.

The group parted for Nurse Worden. She fixed Ellen with a level gaze. "You, again! What have you done now?"

"It's my fault," Lily blurted. "I teased Ellen about needing to lose weight—she's been skipping meals. I guess it caught up with her."

"I got dizzy. That's all," Ellen insisted as she moved to her feet.

Nurse Worden shot her a skeptical look. "You should go to the hospital. Get yourself checked out."

"What she needs to do is eat," Robert offered. "And some old lady needs to stop telling her she's fat."

"I was only giving her some advice," Lily protested.

"Yeah, Lily. We're all familiar with your 'helpful' advice," he replied.

Several people in the crowd tittered.

"All right, you two. Enough," Nurse Worden snapped. "I'm not going to referee another fight."

Ellen looked closely at Nurse Worden. The woman's face was tight, lined with exhaustion. She wondered how much of Nurse Worden's staff had been cut in the name of "efficiency."

"You sure you're okay?" the nurse asked.

Ellen nodded.

"And you'll get something to eat?"

"Yes, and if I still feel strange, I'll go to the clinic on campus," Ellen assured her.

Nurse Worden nodded, satisfied. She turned to dismiss the crowd.

"Why do you have to be such a bastard, Robert?" Lily spat.

He ignored her and turned to Ellen. "Take care of yourself," he said, departing with a nod.

"That man. That man," Lily hissed as soon as Robert left.

Her words barely registered.

Ellen stared at the wall, her eyes drifting to the corner where the two worlds met.

The blank surface offered her nothing.

"I should go. I've caused enough trouble for one day." She grabbed her backpack and headed for the door.

"Oh, no. Please don't! Don't leave," Lily urged. "Robert's right. Don't listen to an old lady. You're not fat. You can have as many of my sweets as you like."

Ellen smiled at her friend. "I'm sorry, Lily," she replied. "My uncle will want to eat soon, and dinner's not going to make itself. Well, it would if he let me get takeout, but Joshua's not the kind—"

"He pushes you too hard. *You* push yourself too hard."

Ellen squirmed under the weight of her backpack.

"Is it because of the others?" her friend asked.

The others. No one ever called the Tailor's victims by their names. They were always lumped together in a homogenous mass, their identities consumed along with their bodies.

"Ellen?"

"Hmm?"

"Do yourself a favor. Don't let the dead rule your life."

Ellen's breath hitched in her throat. She felt like she was being pulled into the icy depths. "I don't think I have a choice," she whispered.

"What?"

"Nothing." Ellen offered her friend a smile she didn't feel. "I should go. Let you get back to your flirting."

"I wasn't flirting with Robert!" Lily protested.

Ellen cocked her head.

"I wasn't talking about Robert. I was talking about that young nurse, Justin," she replied, grateful to have something "normal" to distract her. "My, my. Isn't this an interesting development?"

Her friend flushed. She grabbed Ellen by the shoulders and spun her around, pushing her toward the door.

"You're right. You should be going. Off you go, bird. Flap, flap, flap."

The front gates to the house were open. That was unusual. Ellen and her uncle lived in a notorious house in Arkham. People loved to vandalize it. With the gates closed, the attacks were limited to bottle throwing and the odd piece of graffiti. With the gates open . . .

"Shit!"

Ellen ran down the driveway, her mind churning with grim possibilities.

Broken windows. Toppled statues. Cut cables.

A portal to another world.

Ellen skittered to a stop.

In the driveway sat a silver Mercedes.

Her uncle bought and sold art, but most of his business was online. Their visitors were usually UPS and FedEx drivers.

Ellen couldn't remember the last time Joshua entertained a buyer at the house.

The headline from the paper popped into her head: *One Man Dead, Gallery Owner Critically Injured in Bold Daylight Robbery.*

She reached into her bag and grabbed a can of mace.

The door to Joshua's study was closed. Ellen sighed at the sight. Joshua had shut her out of his life over the past few months. She wasn't sure why, but she had her suspicions. After all, why should her uncle be any different? Why shouldn't he believe all the stories about her? Still, his rejection hurt. Of all the people she knew, she thought he would be the one to defend her, to know she would never partner up with a serial killer, not even to save her own life.

The sound of angry voices greeted her in the hall. The voices became heavier, thick with the threat of violence.

Joshua's in a wheelchair. If someone wanted to overpower him, it would be trivial.

Ellen raised her can of mace and headed for the study.

A man burst out the door just as she reached it. He threw his hands in front of his face when he saw her weapon. "Whoa! Whoa, whoa! Don't shoot," he pleaded.

"It's all right, Ellen," a disembodied voice reassured her.

Ellen tried to look past the man to glimpse her uncle. "Are you okay, Joshua?"

"I'm fine."

She lowered her weapon.

"Ellen?" A cautious smile spread across the man's face. "Little Ellen Logan?"

Ellen studied the stranger. He had a lean, foxlike face with grayish-blond hair buzzed business short. He had a regal, almost European bearing. The way the man held himself reminded Ellen of stories she read as a child, of royalty trying to pass themselves off as regular people.

"Who are you?" Ellen demanded.

"A colleague of your uncle's. Galen Erso." He offered her his hand.

Ellen crossed her arms and shot him a skeptical look. "You're the man who designed the Death Star? I don't think so."

The man laughed, the sound warm and rich. "Still crazy about *Star Wars*. You haven't changed a bit. Well, except for the mace."

His familiarity, and the fact that Joshua was safe, made Ellen relax a little. Even if the stranger was hiding behind a fake name.

She tossed her weapon back into her bag. "Sorry about that."

"Understandable. Especially after what you've been through." The man then called out to Joshua, "We'll talk later, yes?"

"Not if I can help it," her unseen uncle growled.

Ellen walked the man to the door. He paused on the threshold and offered her his hand again. This time, she took it. His skin was soft, like the leather of a reading chair.

"It was good to see you again. I hope you're well," he said.

"I am." *All things considered,* she silently added. "Would you do me a favor?"

His expression flickered before he smiled. "Perhaps."

"Would you close the gates when you leave?"

The man smacked his head. "I knew there was something I forgot to do!" he exclaimed, then leaned forward, eyes twinkling. "Locked gates? Passwords at the door? When did Joshua get so dramatic?"

Dramatic?

The word echoed in her head as she watched the man drive away. The crunch of tires on gravel filled Ellen with a deep sadness. She knew it would be a long time before they had another visitor.

"You certainly made an impression on him," Joshua grumbled when she returned.

"It's called being polite. You should try it," she replied as she perched on the edge of his desk. "Who is he?"

"A colleague."

"Uh-huh," she replied. "Have you been following the news? There was a robbery at one of the art galleries in town."

"I don't do any business locally," he grumbled, flashing her a sour look. "Don't you have homework to do?"

Ellen pursed her lips. Joshua always brought up Miskatonic University when he was mad. He had resisted the move to Arkham. He didn't want her to attend the university. He certainly didn't want her accepted into the advanced program. But Andrew Carter made it happen. He'd arranged it after she escaped from the Tailor.

Joshua resented her for "forcing" him to return to Arkham, for using his dependence on her care as a bargaining chip.

She couldn't imagine how he felt about Carter.

"I was wondering if you knew the owner who was hurt," Ellen continued. "His name was Gerard Car . . . Car-something."

Joshua frowned. "Car-something? Doesn't ring a bell." His hand dropped to his wheelchair, and he toggled the brake.

Liar, she thought.

Ellen hopped off the desk and headed for the door. "Well, when you're ready to tell me the truth, you know where to find me."

Chapter Three

Summer school.

For most people, the words were a curse, a sentence to be endured. But Ellen was happy as she sat in the food court of Miskatonic University, cramming between classes. She had a lot of catching up to do. Her late entry into the advanced program put her behind the other students. *Way* behind. But she didn't mind the pressure. Summer school kept her grounded. Focused. It kept her mind off Edgewood Manor. She visited Lily a few times after her strange vision. She even smuggled in some ghost-hunting equipment to check the walls in her friend's room. But she found nothing strange—no purple light. No man at the chalkboard. No shadowy presence.

Not even a lousy rat in the wall.

Her psychiatrist warned her this might happen, that as Ellen recovered, she might experience some "instability." *Instability* was a polite way of saying *hallucinations*. Now that she was off her meds, that seemed the most likely explanation. But the man at the chalkboard . . . he had nothing to do with what happened to her. He wasn't part of her "trauma."

Why on earth would I imagine him?

"Hey, are you okay?" a voice asked, interrupting her thoughts.

Ellen opened her eyes. It took her a moment to remember where she was—eating lunch at Miskatonic University.

The woman at the next table was watching her. Ellen forced a smile. "I'm fine. I just came up with the right answer *after* the test."

The woman grimaced. "God, I hate when your brain does that to you! I mean, why even bother?"

Good question, Ellen thought.

Once she finished eating, she returned to her homework. Even though there were subjects that needed more urgent attention, she pulled out her astronomy textbook. Dr. Kaku required only one book, a collection of images from the Hubble Telescope. He taught his class the way Andrew Carter did, showing them the objects in the universe—nebulas, star clusters, gas clouds—and teaching them how to search for the things lurking behind them. Ellen wasn't sure what humanity could do if they spotted something hiding behind a star. Still, she enjoyed the class.

"Hey, you dropped this."

Ellen looked up from the Horsehead Nebula.

The woman from the next table held out an envelope.

Ellen flashed her an embarrassed look. "Thanks," she said as she took it. "It's been one of those days."

The woman glanced at the book. "Has Dr. Kaku gotten to Drake's equation yet?" she asked.

"Not yet."

"Well, be prepared. That day will be a doozy."

"Thanks for the warning." Ellen watched the woman walk away and then glanced at the envelope.

It was addressed to Andrew Carter.

She groaned. "Oh, God. More fan mail."

Still, Ellen opened it, curious what this woman's "pitch" would be.

I have no right to ask you for your help. You and I have a difficult relationship, even in the best of times. And in the worst? Well, I'm sure you remember the bad times. You have been generous, kinder than I deserve. I wanted to leave you alone, but . . .

Something strange is happening at Edgewood Manor. I don't know what it is. People see things at night. Yes, I know. It's all part of getting old. But there *is* something here. I don't know what it is. I'm hoping you might figure it out and put an end to it. Nothing's happened yet, but it feels like it's only a matter of time before someone gets hurt. Or worse.

If you don't do it for me, do it for the others.

Your father,
Robert Carter

At first, Ellen didn't understand what she was reading. It took a moment for things to click. This was the letter Lily gave her to pass on to Andrew Carter. After everything that happened in Edgewood Manor, she had forgotten all about it.

And the man who wrote it . . .

"Robert Carter. Robert . . . Carter."

The man on the porch, her mind offered. *The aging cowboy. Robert Carter.*

"Andrew's father," she murmured, her voice barely audible above the pounding of her heart.

Now she knew why he seemed so familiar. When she and Andrew interviewed Lily's husband, Robert Carter ambushed them in the halls of Edgewood. Harsh words were exchanged. He punched Andrew in the face and had to be restrained by orderlies.

No wonder I didn't recognize him, she thought. *The last time I saw him, he was in a bathrobe and raving like a lunatic.*

She wanted to dismiss Robert Carter's letter, to turn her attention back to studying.

Her eyes kept snagging on the same spot.

Something strange is happening at Edgewood Manor.

Not just at Edgewood Manor, she thought. *In Lily's room.*

Where I saw the man at the blackboard. And the shadowy presence behind me.

Ellen shivered as she remembered the thing's touch, the nails that dug into her skin.

She scrambled to her feet and shoveled her things into her bag.

"Are you sure everything's okay?" Ellen demanded into the phone as she paced outside Dr. Andrew Carter's office.

"Things are fine," Lily Graham assured her. "Why? Do you know something I don't? Do Miskatonic students have a direct connection to the Grim Reaper?"

"Not funny, Lil!" Ellen scolded her.

Her friend fell silent, then said, "You opened the letter from Robert, didn't you?"

Ellen looked at the floor. "He thinks something is going on at Edgewood."

"What kind of something?"

"I don't know. He didn't say."

Lily dropped her voice. "Listen to me, Ellen. The man is crazy. I don't know what's wrong with him, but he sees things. Honestly, he belongs in an institution, not Edgewood."

Ellen's stomach lurched. *I see things, too,* she wanted to say. *Does that mean I belong in an institution?* She rubbed at the headache brewing behind her eyes. "Nothing strange is going on?"

"The house makes weird noises at night, that's all. The place is old. It has creaky bones."

Ellen perked up. "You're hearing noises?"

"Ellen." Lily's voice was stern.

"Okay, okay," she relented. "It's probably just as well. I can't find him."

"Who?"

"Dr. Carter."

"Oh, honey, don't bother him. I told you everything is fine. Robert is just a crazy old man."

"But he's . . ." Ellen bit down on the next words. Lily didn't know Robert was Andrew Carter's father. Andrew Carter went to great lengths to hide his family connections. And did it really matter? Did being a Carter give Robert any special powers?

"If it makes you feel any better, drop in on him the next time you visit," Lily suggested. "You'll see what I mean."

"I might just do that. I'll talk to you later, Lil, okay?"

"Take care of yourself, my dear."

Ellen ended the call and stared at Carter's office. A cutout of Lucy Van Pelt hung from the door. The Peanuts character sat proudly at her booth. Above her, there was a familiar sign with a movable slider.

It informed her the doctor was out.

She knocked on the door just in case. Pressed her ear against the wood. Nothing stirred. His office was as still and lifeless as a tomb. Ellen had no idea how to reach Andrew Carter. She didn't know where he lived. She didn't have a phone number or an email address. He wasn't on social media. All Ellen had was an office phone and address. Since he wasn't teaching summer classes, they were useless.

I might as well be sending smoke signals, she thought.

She suspected Carter preferred it that way. It wasn't just the rumors that kept him away. When she returned from her ordeal, he asked her what happened. She told him everything. How she slipped into the Dreamlands with a demon hot on her trail. How she met a king in a mystical city who helped her.

And Randolph Carter, a voice nagged her. Don't forget about Randolph Carter.

Ellen's cheeks flared. She told him she had sex with Randolph Carter, escaping Solomon Reye's grasp by being with another man first.

Not just another man, the voice chided her.

His grandfather.

You told him you slept with his grandfather.

And you wonder why you can't reach him?

"Honesty is the best policy. What a crock of shit." She turned to leave and slammed into someone. Hard.

"Oh my God, I'm so sor—"

The apology froze in her throat.

Randolph Carter stood in front of her.

The blood rushed from Ellen's head. For a moment, she thought she would pass out. "W-what are you doing here?" she stammered.

"I work here, remember?" Andrew Carter growled.

The familiar voice sent a wave of relief through Ellen.

Andrew Carter had grown a beard over the summer. That was all.

Still, the resemblance between him and his grandfather was uncanny.

Carter's eyes narrowed. "Are you drunk?"

"I need to talk to you," she blurted.

"I don't have time."

"Please. It's important, Andrew."

"That's Dr. Carter to you."

A woman stepped out from behind Carter. Elegant, with perfect hair and a crisp business suit that screamed bureaucrat. As she approached, Ellen was assaulted by a wave of perfume. It reminded her of a resident at Edgewood who bathed herself in Chanel No. 5 to hide the spread of her cancer.

"Who are you?" Ellen asked.

"Catharine Strauss. Head of University Relations," she replied, her eyes sweeping over Ellen like a cold wind. "And you must be Ellen Logan. Miskatonic's final girl."

"Cathy," Carter called out.

Cathy? The familiarity made Ellen's skin crawl.

"You're not supposed to be here. Dr. Carter has been informed about you."

Informed. Another polite word. It meant Ellen was a stalker.

She kept her eyes fixed on Andrew. "I just need a minute," she pleaded. "You know I wouldn't bother you unless it was important."

"Do you know how much trouble you've caused Dr. Carter?"

Ellen glanced at the woman. "No, but I suspect you're going to tell me."

Miss Strauss continued as if she hadn't heard the snarky remark.

"When you vanished, Dr. Carter became the prime suspect. The police dragged him into the precinct and interrogated him for twelve hours."

Ellen's gaze settled on the bureaucrat.

"Twelve hours? They interrogated him for twelve hours, and you let them?"

Miss Strauss blinked. "Excuse me?"

"Why didn't Miskatonic bring in lawyers the moment he was taken into custody? Why did you leave him on his own for twelve hours?"

"Good question," Carter muttered.

The woman looked at Ellen, stunned. She had a script in mind, and Ellen wasn't playing her part. "That's not the point," she insisted once she recovered. "And it wasn't my decision."

"It never is," Ellen said softly.

The bureaucrat turned to Carter. "Listen to me, Andrew. You need to stay away from her. She's unstable. The doctors have diagnosed her as schizophrenic."

Ellen stiffened. Her condition was the last thing she wanted him to know. The last thing she wanted anyone to know.

"I'm not schizophrenic," she insisted, hoping to salvage the situation. "The doctors think I have schizoaffective syndrome."

"Schizoaffective syndrome?" Carter echoed. "What the hell is that?"

"Schizophrenia means you're mad," she explained. "Schizoaffective means they're waiting for you to go mad. I'm in the bullpen but haven't been called in to pitch yet."

"You are on medicine. You're not going to deny that, are you?" the woman purred.

Ellen studied the bureaucrat. "Miss Strauss, have you heard of something called HIPAA? Not sure what all the letters stand for. Health Insurance Accountability something-something.

All I know is that you looked at my medical records, and now you've shared them with Dr. Carter. That's a violation of federal law."

Miss Strauss's lips curled into a sneer. "I'm a university official. I have a right to look at your records."

"I think I'll let a lawyer decide that."

"You don't have a lawyer."

"Miskatonic may not be able to find lawyers, but I'm sure I can."

The color rose in the bureaucrat's cheeks.

Carter snorted.

Ellen looked at him. They had shared a psychic connection in the past, but she didn't want to reach out to him that way. Not with Miss Strauss around. No point talking to him, anyway. There was nothing Andrew Carter could do. "I'll do this on my own," she murmured.

"Do what?" he demanded.

"I'll do this on my own," she repeated, more firmly this time.

"Do what?" Carter called after her. "Ellen, do what?"

"For God's sake, Andrew. Don't encourage her!" Miss Strauss snapped as Ellen walked away.

She barely heard them.

She was already making plans.

Chapter Four

Ellen stood in the hall outside Robert Carter's half-opened door, a few doors down from Lily's room. Her friend's room was bright, the walls a testament to a life well lived: her husband, children, grandchildren, students, community groups. Robert Carter's walls were bare. There were no pictures of Andrew or Andrew's siblings (*did he even have brothers or sisters?*). No pictures of Andrew's mother. Nothing to suggest Robert Carter had a life before Edgewood Manor.

Ellen lingered, trying to figure out what she could say to make him go along with her plan.

"Are you going to keep standing there, or are you coming in?" Robert Carter yelled.

Ellen entered the room. It had a faint institutional smell. She thought again of Lily's room. Her friend's space was always scented with a strategically placed candle, one that changed with the seasons. This time of year, it was summer garden, a flowery brew that made Ellen's eyes water.

Andrew Carter's father lay on a narrow, rumpled bed.

"Is this a bad time?" Ellen asked.

"That depends. Do you have my painkillers?"

"It's a bad time." Ellen turned to leave.

Robert squinted at her. "Wait a minute. You're Andy's girl, aren't you?"

Andy's girl. Ellen snickered. She could imagine no situation where Carter would allow himself to be called Andy. She grabbed a chair and sat next to the bed.

"My name's Ellen. Ellen Logan," she announced as he struggled to sit up. "Do you have a headache?"

"Headache?" He echoed, making it sound like the most ridiculous thing he'd ever heard.

Ellen dug into her bag. "I have some Tylenol if you need it," she offered.

"The only thing that makes a dent in a headbanger like this is Vicodin," he glanced at her backpack. "You wouldn't happen to have any in that Bag of Holding, would you?"

A Dungeons and Dragons joke. Not what she expected from Andrew's father. "Sorry. They won't let me have any hardcore drugs. Except the ones I don't want to take."

He waved off her apology. "Doesn't matter. Tell me why Andrew isn't here." He looked over her shoulder. "He's not here, right? Lurking outside, making you do all the dirty work?"

"It's just me, I'm afraid."

"You failed."

Failed. The word grated. "I didn't fail. I didn't even get a chance," she insisted. "I tried to give him the letter, but the moment I approached him, someone from the university came between us. She refused to let us talk. Refused to leave us alone, even for a second."

"And Andrew let her?"

"There's been a lot of fallout about the whole serial killer thing. I'm toxic right now." Ellen shook her head. "Not just toxic. I'm radioactive."

"Blaming the victim," Robert Carter offered. "Miskatonic is good at that."

Sympathy. Another thing she didn't expect from Andrew's father.

"They think I'm delusional. That I see things." Ellen sighed. "Andrew's been told to stay away from me."

A ghost of a smile passed over Robert Carter's face. "They say the same thing about me."

"Miskatonic?"

"Everyone." He fell silent, drifting away from her.

Ellen was considering asking him about the note when he returned.

"It's the thin place," he murmured.

"What?" Ellen blurted, convinced she misheard him.

"Thin places always give me headaches." He grimaced as he rubbed his face. "I was in and out of the Dreamlands a lot as a child. Looking for my lost father."

Thin place. Dreamlands. Lost father.

Robert Carter offered her a grim smile. "Still think you're delusional?"

Ellen glanced at the wall, half expecting to see a glowing purple light.

"Who was that guy at the chalkboard?" he asked.

She gasped, her hand tightening into a fist. "*You saw him?*"

"I pulled you away from him. Didn't you feel it?"

Did you see what was behind me?

Ellen wanted to ask the question, but a shadow passed across the old man's face.

"You remind me of my father. Oblivious. Absent."

"I'm sorry."

He fixed her with a flat stare. "Are you?" he demanded.

"Yes. I am." Ellen held his gaze. "It sounds like he let you down."

"More than a few times." He sighed, looking away.

"What's going on in Edgewood?" she asked after a few seconds had passed.

Another grim smile spread across his face. "You opened the letter."

"Of course I did! Did you really expect me *not* to?" she shot back. "What's going on in Edgewood?"

"Nothing you can do anything about."

She leaned forward. This wasn't the right time, but Ellen wasn't sure there would ever be a good time.

"Look, Mr. Carter, you're an honest man. A brutally honest man, so I'm going to be brutally honest with you. I'm the closest you're going to get to your son. I may be radioactive, but you . . . no chart exists for how far you are from him."

Robert Carter said nothing.

"Let me investigate this, and as soon as I reach Andrew, I'll bring him in." Ellen held her breath. She waited, afraid to move, to do anything to break the mood.

"This is humiliating. Having to ask a teenager for help," he said, plucking at the bedsheet twisted around him.

"Well, consider yourself lucky. I'm not a teenager."

"Might as well be," he grumbled.

"'If you don't do it for me, do it for the others.' Isn't that what you wrote in your letter? Well, pardon the expression, but suck it up, old man."

Robert Carter fell silent for what felt like a lifetime. "What I'm about to tell you is ridiculous."

Ellen smiled. "That's okay. I'm used to ridiculous."

Chapter Five

The wheeze of the espresso machine greeted Ellen at the door, misting the air with the potent promise of caffeine. Unhallowed Grounds was a popular coffeehouse located just outside the gates of Miskatonic University. Even in the summer, the place was packed. Ellen had to wait several minutes for a table to open.

As she slid into her seat, a boisterous crowd passed by on their way to one of the big tables in the back. Ellen kept her head down and pecked at her cell phone. The last thing she wanted was to be recognized.

"Miskatonic's final girl," she whispered, shaking her head in disgust.

"Summer school," a voice announced. "I never thought I'd see you in summer school. Don't tell me the mighty Ellen Logan flunked a class."

"Screw you, Greg." She rose to greet her friend, pulling him into a tight hug. She had known Greg since they were first-year students. He was one of her few surviving friends.

Greg turned to the young man standing behind him. His companion had pitch-black hair and porcelain skin and looked like he hadn't seen the light of day in a long time.

Classic Miskatonic pallor, she thought as Greg introduced them.

"This is Joseph Turner. He helped me research Edgewood Manor."

"Ellen Logan," she offered.

Joseph Turner juggled a poster tube to shake her hand. "I'll get us something to drink," he said to Greg as he leaned the poster tube against the wall. "Iced tea, right?"

"*Sweet* iced tea," Greg corrected him.

Joseph Turner's gaze shifted to her. "Ellen?"

She nodded at the iced coffee on the table. "I'm good, thanks."

Once Joseph was gone, her friend moved closer. "You know, the big guy is here."

Ellen frowned. "Big guy?"

Greg nodded at a spot over her shoulder. "Dr. Carter. He's watching you. I'm surprised you haven't noticed."

Ellen followed her friend's stare. Andrew Carter sat at the head of a large table, part of the boisterous group that just walked by her. She had no idea who he was performing for this time—students, wealthy alums . . . circus troupe? All she knew was that he was miserable. He didn't bother to hide his boredom. His eyes were fixed on a spot in the middle of the room. Even though his group was still getting settled, his leg bounced in frustration. Ellen shivered. The beard, glazed eyes, hostile posture . . .

Carter looked *way* too much like his grandfather.

"He's not looking at me. He's just checked out," Ellen insisted. When she moved to sit, his eyes followed her. Ellen nodded at him, testing the waters.

His eyes darted away.

Toxic, toxic, toxic, her mind chanted.

"Do you want to go somewhere else?" Greg suggested.

Ellen scanned the group for Miss Strauss.

"No. We're good. I don't think there's a restraining order on me yet."

"What?"

"Nothing. Nothing." She waved him to a seat.

"Carter's an asshole," Greg muttered as they settled.

"Carter's not an asshole," Ellen replied. "He's always surrounded by people who want a piece of him because of who he is. That would make anyone hostile."

Her friend shrugged. "I don't know. Being surrounded by admirers? That doesn't sound so bad."

"That's because you're a loser."

Ellen and Greg locked eyes for a long, weightless moment, then dissolved into laughter.

"Fuck you, Logan. Fuck. You."

Joseph Turner returned, drinks in hand. He gazed at them uncertainly. "Um, is everything okay?"

A titter escaped her mouth.

"Everything's fine," Greg reassured him. "Just two friends catching up."

Friends. A warm glow spread through Ellen. *I need to slow down,* she reminded herself. *Get my head out of the books sometimes.*

Joseph put down the drinks and swiped a chair from a nearby table.

"So, what's this all about?" Greg said as he settled back with his drink. "When you called, I thought you were joking. You want to bug a nursing home?"

"A retirement home," she corrected him.

"Why the hell do you want to bug a retirement home?" He glanced at Joseph. "I don't even want to think about the noises that come out of that place at night."

"No worse than what your neighbors hear," Ellen shot back.

Joseph Turner grinned into his cup.

Greg grimaced. "Funny, Logan. Real funny."

"I have a friend who lives in Edgewood. A few days ago, she gave me a note from one of the other residents." Ellen felt a crawling between her shoulder blades. This time, she *knew* Carter was watching her. "He says something is going on at night. That the place is being invaded."

"Invaded? By what?" Turner demanded.

Robert Carter's words came back to her: *What I'm about to tell you is ridiculous.*

"Dogs. He says packs of dogs roam the halls of Edgewood at night. Big, upright, white dogs. Like *Hound of the Baskervilles* big. They walk down the halls at night. Jump on beds."

"Strange," Turner murmured.

"There's more," Ellen replied. "My friend thinks it's intentional. That someone is letting these creatures in."

Greg frowned. "Why would they do that?"

She shrugged, even as her thoughts drifted to the man at the chalkboard. "No idea."

They fell silent.

Ellen resisted the urge to look at Andrew. She studied the walls of Unhallowed Grounds, where the latest student art exhibit was on display. A lumpy creature leered at her from one of the paintings, its needle-thin teeth dripping with green saliva.

"Sleep paralysis," Greg blurted.

"Excuse me?" she replied, tearing her eyes away from the strange creature.

"It's probably sleep paralysis. I learned about it in psych class," her friend said. "Have you ever woken up and been convinced something was in the room with you, and you couldn't move?"

"Are you kidding? That's the only way I dream," Joseph Turner joked.

"That's sleep paralysis. Every night, your brain shuts your body down so that you won't hurt yourself when you dream. When you wake up too fast, your brain doesn't have time to react. You wind up in that twilight zone between being asleep and being awake. You lie in bed. Paralyzed."

"And since you can't move, you think someone or something is holding you down," Joseph Turner added.

"Like big *Hound of the Baskervilles* dogs?" Ellen asked.

"Or witches. Or ghosts. Or aliens. It depends on what you fear." Greg paused. "Is your friend scared of dogs?"

"I don't know," she admitted. "And to be fair, Rob—the guy I talked to—doesn't have the best reputation. But here's the thing. I talked to the other residents. They described the creatures the same way my friend did."

Greg snorted. "So what? Stories spread like wildfire in places like that."

Ellen stared at her iced coffee, fighting a wave of anger. She remembered how scared Lily was when she finally admitted something was wrong.

"They wouldn't talk to each other, Greg. Not about that."

"How do you know?" he pressed her.

"Put yourself in their place. You're getting older. Your senses are failing. Maybe you're having your first brush with dementia. And you see dogs running in the halls? Jumping on your bed? Is that something you'd share with people over breakfast?"

"Is there even such a thing as mass sleep paralysis?" Joseph Turner asked.

Ellen glanced at Greg's friend, annoyed. The question came out of nowhere. *And just when I was gaining some ground.*

"One person having sleep paralysis and seeing a demon dog, I'll buy that," he continued. "But has there ever been a case of mass sleep paralysis? When everyone has it at the same time and in the exact same way?"

Greg's face fell when he realized what Joseph was saying. He smacked the table in frustration. "Goddamn it!"

"I'll take that as a no," Joseph drawled.

Ellen leaned forward.

"Look, I started from the same place you did. When this guy told me his story, I didn't believe him. I mean, it's crazy! Then another person stepped forward. And another. And another. And there came a point when I had to doubt too many people."

Greg slumped in his chair. "Dogs in a retirement home. Seriously, Logan?"

"You know, there might be something to this," Joseph announced.

Greg gawked at his friend. "You're kidding, right?"

Joseph Turner kept his eyes on Ellen as he uncapped the end of the poster tube.

"I'm an architecture major. Just transferred from Chicago," he informed her. "Arkham is a great place to be an architect. The houses are old—some of the oldest in the country. Prime examples of adaptive reuse."

Ellen and Greg stared at him blankly.

"It's when a building is transformed from one set of functions to another. Like when you take a private residence and transform it into a bed-and-breakfast."

"Why didn't you just say that?" Greg grumbled.

Joseph ignored him and spread a blueprint out on the table.

"The place you call Edgewood Manor has a long, deep history."

"The place we *call* Edgewood Manor?" Ellen repeated.

"It started as the Vanderschluss house. Built by Thijmen Vanderschluss in the 1600s."

"Thijmen Vanderschluss? That's a mouthful. Dutch?" Greg asked.

"You think?" Joseph smirked. "I could go into its history, but that would take an entire book. The house has changed a lot over the years. Additions. Demolitions. Remodeling. What interests us is here."

He stabbed a spot on the blueprint.

"The basement," Greg groaned. "Why does it always have to be in the basement? Why can't there be interesting places in the kitchen? Or the sunroom?"

"Because you can't hide a tunnel in a sunroom."

"What?" Greg and Ellen said simultaneously.

Joseph smiled.

"In the 1980s, the owners of Edgewood applied for a building permit to put an addition on the house. During a routine inspection, the city realized the basement dimensions didn't quite add up. After a little poking, they found a hollow spot on the wall. A hidden door that led to a passage."

"Where did it go?" Greg asked before Ellen could.

"Arkham Grove."

Greg grimaced and put his head on the table. "Terrific. That's just terrific!"

Ellen nudged him. "Oh, come on. Where's your sense of adventure?"

Turner looked at them. "Okay. I'm missing something."

"You said you're from Chicago, right?" she asked.

"Yes."

"Arkham Grove is right up there with Resurrection Cemetery."

"Haunted?"

"Extremely haunted. Infamously haunted," she replied. "More witches and wizards are buried there than any other graveyard in the country. Don't ask me how they know that. Wizards and witches usually avoid being counted."

Greg brought up a map of Arkham Grove on his computer. The cemetery was on the other side of the Miskatonic River in New Arkham.

But there was no New Arkham in the 1600s. Only wilderness.

Ellen studied the satellite map.

"I didn't realize how close Edgewood is to the cemetery," she murmured as she gnawed on her lip. "How far do you think that is? A couple of hundred feet?"

"If that," Joseph offered.

Greg frowned at the location on the map. "A tunnel between Edgewood and Arkham Grove? Probably a smuggler's cave or something."

"It was, in a way."

Joseph threw down a piece of paper. A photocopy of an article from *The Arkham Inquisitor*: "Local House a Stop on the Underground Railroad."

Ellen clapped her hands. "The Underground Railroad! Oh my God, how cool!"

Greg chuckled. "You want to say that one more time, Logan? I don't think everyone at Carter's table heard you."

Joseph Turner swiveled in his chair. "Dr. Carter? Dr. Carter is here?"

"I forgot all about this," Ellen murmured as she scanned the article. "There's a historical plaque on the porch. I walk by it all the time."

"Nice to know there's a place in Arkham that actually did some good," Greg muttered.

Joseph sighed. "I'm afraid that might not be the case anymore," he continued, raising his voice to be heard over the sudden blast of the espresso machine. "The owners of Edgewood were ordered to wall up the tunnel for safety reasons. My guess is they didn't. It would have cost a fortune. Probably paid an inspector to look the other way."

Greg raised a fist in salute. "All hail the mighty bribe."

"The old tunnel might explain how something could get into Edgewood." Joseph Turner paused to gather his thoughts. "Do you know if Arkham Grove has a problem with wild dogs?"

"Wild dogs? In the middle of town?" Ellen frowned.

"My sister lived in Romania for a few years," Joseph replied. "They had a huge problem with feral dogs in Bucharest. Especially in the abandoned parts of town."

She turned to Greg. "Is Arkham Grove abandoned?"

Greg consulted his computer. "No burials since the 1980s, so I'm going to say yes."

People trickled past the table.

"Hide your stuff," Greg hissed. "Dr. Carter's coming. Hide your stuff."

Ellen rolled her eyes. "Oh, please! Andrew's not a cop. And we have nothing to hide."

"Well, that doesn't sound suspicious at all," Carter announced.

He stopped beside her, tapped his fingers on the table, then peered at Greg's computer. "Arkham Grove? You're not planning on digging up bodies, are you?"

"We're not sure. We'll see how things go," Ellen replied.

Greg and Joseph snickered like naughty schoolboys.

"Where's Miss Strauss?" Ellen asked.

Andrew Carter gave her a cool, measured stare. "Out terrorizing someone else, I suspect." His eyes drifted to the blueprints on the table. "What's going on, Ellen?"

Before she could answer, Joseph Turner jumped to his feet and thrust out his hand, his words coming out in a long, exuberant rush. "Dr. Carter, I just wanted to say what an honor it is to meet you."

Andrew Carter paled and backed away like a spooked horse.

Ellen frowned. She had seen admirers ambush Carter before. He'd never reacted like this.

"Andrew, are you okay?" she asked.

"I'm fine," he insisted. He turned and walked out of the coffeehouse.

Ellen rose to follow him.

Greg grabbed her arm. "Not now, Logan."

"But—"

"Trust me. Not now."

Ellen sunk back into her chair. "Thanks a lot, fanboy!" she sniped at Joseph Turner.

"What was that all about?" Greg asked.

"I don't know," she admitted, then cursed herself. *Close,* she thought, *you were so close. All you needed to say was there's something wrong at Edgewood. But you had to be a smart-ass, didn't you? You had to make a crack about Miss Strauss.*

"So, what do we do now?" She sighed.

"About what?" Greg asked.

She smacked the blueprint of Edgewood Manor. "This! People being terrorized! Hidden tunnels! Wild dogs!"

"The possibility of wild dogs," her friend corrected her.

Ellen nodded, yielding the point.

"We need to bug the place. See what's really going on in Edgewood," she suggested.

Greg sat back and took a sip of sweet tea. "Planting recording devices is illegal. If we're caught, we could go to jail."

Ellen watched the ice settle in her drink. "Does that mean you won't do it?"

"You know, my grandmother lived in a home like Edgewood," Joseph said softly. "She always complained about things running over her face. Every night, she said, things ran over her face. My mom ignored her. We all did. We thought she was loopy. After she died, the staff cleaned out her room. They moved the bed and found a rat hole in the wall."

Greg's lips curled in disgust.

"My mother never forgave herself. And if there's a chance, even the slightest chance, this is happening to someone else's grandparent . . ." His clear eyes settled on Ellen. "I'll help you. Even if Greg won't, I will."

Greg raised his hands in surrender. "All right. I'm in. I'm in." He shot Joseph a sharp look. "Way to lay on the guilt, Joe!"

"What do we do next?" Ellen asked.

"*You.* What do *you* do next," Greg corrected her. "I'll give you the equipment you need. You have to find a way to sneak it into Edgewood."

Chapter Six

Ellen waited in the shadow of Edgewood Manor. It had taken her a couple of days to devise a plan to plant the microphones and another day to convince herself it would work. Everything depended on Joseph Turner. That alone made her uneasy. She didn't know what to make of Greg's new friend. Part of it was the way he looked. Ellen hated judging people based on their appearance, but Joseph Turner seemed off. As they walked toward the house, she was struck by how pale he was. He was dressed for the summer in a short-sleeve shirt and khaki pants, but nothing about him suggested heat. Whenever Ellen looked at him, she thought of cold places—dark water and black sand.

"Something wrong?" Joseph demanded, his gaze sharp beneath his sunglasses.

"No, it's just . . . the last time I was here, I had a horrible experience," she admitted as they climbed the front stairs to the patio. It was a half truth, but half a truth was better than a lie. "Thanks for agreeing to do this."

"Are you kidding? I'm dying to see the place."

"A little advice? Don't use the word *dying* around here."

Joseph winced. "Yeah, right. Sorry."

Edgewood's front door opened as they approached. Lily emerged with Robert Carter at her side.

"There you are! Right on time!" Lily called out.

Ellen elbowed Joseph. "Watch out for this one. She's a heartbreaker."

"Oh, don't listen to her. She's just jealous because the boys pay attention to me." Lily looked up at the man looming over her. "I'm Lily Graham. You must be Mr. Turner."

Joseph removed his sunglasses. "Yes, ma'am."

"Such a tall boy. Do you play basketball?"

Robert Carter groaned. "No filter at all between her brain and her mouth."

Joseph Turner came to her rescue. "I'm not a basketball player. I'm an albino."

Albino, Ellen thought. *Pale skin. Light eyes. Dyed black hair. Everything made sense.*

Turner shot Ellen a sideways look. "What did *you* think I was?" he demanded.

Lily intervened before Ellen could reply. "Would you excuse us? Joseph and I need to prepare for his big presentation," she announced, threading her arm through his.

Robert Carter watched them walk away. Ellen could only describe Carter's expression as . . .

A smile spread across Ellen's face.

"Lily likes you," she blurted.

Robert Carter ignored her. "Where's Andrew?"

"I'm still radioactive, I'm afraid."

"And they say he's in love with you. That he runs after you like a puppy."

Ellen snorted. This was a new twist. In all the rumors she heard, the chase went the other way.

"Can you honestly imagine your son fawning over *me*?"

Robert Carter stared at her for a long time. "It's possible," he decided. "Though you're not his usual type."

What's his usual type?

Ellen clamped down on the words before she could say them. Before she could betray any interest in Andrew Carter's "type."

She dug into her pocket and pulled out what looked like a handful of LEGO pieces.

"Are those the microphones?" he asked as she counted them out.

"Yep." She hesitated before she put them in his hand. "The guy who gave me these wants you to know this is illegal. And that by using these, you assume full responsibility for what—"

"Oh, please. I'd be dead before they got around to prosecuting me. Besides, I could blame you. A clear case of elder abuse."

Ellen shook her head.

"What?" he asked as she dropped the microphones into his hand.

"For a moment there, you reminded me of Andrew."

"I'll make sure to tell him that the next time I see him."

"Just put these where you think they'll work best," she instructed. "You don't have to do anything. There are no switches to throw and no buttons to push. We remotely activate them."

"You don't think the nurses will notice me planting these things?"

"Not if Joseph plays his part." Ellen frowned as her eyes drifted to the porch corner where Joseph chatted with Lily. A bubble of doubt surfaced.

He says he's a transfer student from Chicago. How many people arrive at school in the middle of summer break?

After a few minutes, Lily walked back toward Ellen, her face glowing with pleasure.

"You're really looking forward to this, aren't you?" Ellen said.

"Are you kidding? She's been talking about it all week. Got everyone all riled up," Robert offered.

Lily straightened. "I do not *rile* people up."

When Ellen entered Edgewood Manor, she realized Robert was right. Lily had riled people up. The event drew a large crowd. Everyone seemed to be there. The residents. The nurses. The nurse's attendants. Even some of the higher-functioning patients with Alzheimer's. Most of them stared into space, but a few struggled to engage. Ellen shivered. A friend had once asked her to use her psychic abilities to explore the mind of a woman with Alzheimer's. One moment, she was in a clear, crisp landscape. The next, a fog bled over the hills, engulfing her in a shadowy world. As Ellen fought her way out of the woman's mind, she could think only one thing. *Disease. I can feel the disease all around me. Swirling in my head.* For months afterward, every memory slip, every moment of forgetfulness terrified her. She was convinced it was still with her, stuck like gum to a shoe.

"This is quite a turnout," Joseph Turner mumbled as he surveyed the crowd gathered in the common room.

Ellen blinked. She didn't realize she had drifted off.

Was that another thing to worry about?

"May I have your attention?" Lily called out over the buzz of conversation.

When the crowd refused to settle down, she put her fingers in her mouth and whistled.

"Wow," Joseph whispered in the silence that followed.

Ellen felt a rush of pride. "She's a tough old broad."

"I'm surprised they let her organize this," he said, nervousness leeching into his voice.

She smirked. "Oh, they know better than to get in the way of Lily Graham when she sets her mind on something."

"May I have your attention?" Lily called out again. "Today, we have a unique opportunity to learn more about Edgewood Manor. Mr. Turner is a student at Miskatonic University—"

Someone in the audience hissed.

Lily's eyes swept the crowd. "Mr. Turner is a student at Miskatonic University," she repeated, daring someone to interrupt again. "He is an architecture major. Edgewood Manor is the subject of his senior thesis."

"Is that true?" Ellen whispered.

Joseph chuckled. "No."

She smiled and looked at the ground.

"Mr. Turner will take us on a special in-house field trip. So, without further ado, I'll step aside and let him lead the way."

Joseph handed Ellen his satchel.

She pulled out a clipboard and nodded at Robert Carter.

"Thank you, Ms. Graham. And to all of you for showing up," Joseph began.

His greeting was met with stony silence. He took a deep breath.

"Look, I could bore you. I could *really* bore you." He gestured to Ellen. "Miss Logan is carrying a bag stuffed with documents about this place. They're full of architectural jargon. Words like *programmatic roots. Entablature. Fenestration patterns.* That's not what Edgewood Manor is. That would be like saying I know you because I've read your medical records. It's not only absurd. It's arrogant."

"Damn straight," a voice in the crowd muttered.

"The history of a place is the story of the people who lived there. Their hopes. Their dreams. Their heartbreaks and tragedies. And Edgewood is full of emotions. It's bursting at the seams with emotions." He scanned the audience. "If you'll follow me, we'll start our journey with Edgewood's founder, the man who built this place."

Joseph led the party down the hall to the first stop on their tour. As the nurses, attendants, and patients filed out, Ellen and Robert lingered. Andrew's father planted some microphones in the room, and she marked the locations on a map she had on her clipboard.

She and Robert rejoined the group at the back of the house, where the residents with dementia lived. Having never been there, Ellen watched as a nurse punched in a code to open the door. Lily joked that the unit was a one-way trip. Now, added to her Alzheimer's fears, Ellen had a terrible vision of people being trapped, locked in place while a fire raged around them.

Safety violation? She scribbled in her notes.

Joseph stopped in front of the nurses' station. "This is where it all begins—the footprint of the original house. The home of Thijmen Vanderschluss." Joseph winced as he pronounced the name. "Yes, you heard correctly. His name was Thijmen. *Theud*, meaning 'people.' And *men*, meaning well . . . 'men.'"

"Wait a second. His parents named their son 'People Men'?" someone asked.

"I don't think his father put too much thought into his name. You see, Thijmen's mother died giving birth to him, leaving his father alone with five children. A merchant in Amsterdam, the father was financially secure, but . . ." Joseph let out a huff of air.

"Look, I have nothing to support this, but I think Thijmen's father abused him. He blamed the child for his wife's death. As soon as he was old enough, Thijmen boarded a ship and left for America. He never looked back.

"The New World wound up being a good choice. He apprenticed with a local physician. Or at least the man who passed for a physician in those days. He took the teenager under his wing, and Thijmen inherited the land when the doctor died. The property was on the edge of an old-growth forest at the time. That's how Edgewood got its name. He used the wood to build his house."

"Well, what do you know? You learn something new every day," a woman beside Ellen muttered.

It took Ellen a moment to recognize Miss Worden, the nurse who scolded her for being on the porch. The nurse had come in on her day off and was in street clothes.

She and Ellen nodded at each other.

"Thijmen didn't have very long to enjoy the place. He was a successful doctor. *Too* successful. His neighbors were suspicious of his prosperity. In 1692, when the Salem witch hunt hit Arkham, he was the first suspect. In fact, he was the ideal suspect. What people used to call 'cunning folk.'" Joseph paused, ticking the points off on his fingers. "He was a bachelor who lived alone on the edge of a forest. He dispensed folk medicine. There were rumors he 'consorted' with the native tribes. When times are stable, men like him are tolerated. When things get tough . . ." He let the words trail off.

"What happened?" Ellen asked.

Joseph gave her a sad look. "A mob dragged him out of his house and lynched him."

Murmurs passed through the crowd.

"He was killed? Here?" Robert Carter exclaimed.

"The tree they hanged him on has been cut down, but yes, he died here." Joseph let the news sink in. After a long pause, he added, "But here's the thing. The mob may have been right. Thijmen was probably a witch."

Ellen gawked at Joseph. This wasn't how the story was supposed to go. Victims of witch hunts were always innocent, caught up in a system gone mad.

"For years after his death, people saw strange lights. Glowing orbs that lured villagers into the forest. Many people disappeared."

"*Feu follet*," a man next to Lily breathed. "That's what my mom called them."

"We called them *luz mala*," another resident offered.

"The place fell into ruin," Joseph said, continuing the sad story. "The villagers eventually set fire to Thijmen's house. Then they salted the earth for good measure."

"A promising start to this place," Miss Worden muttered as the group followed Joseph out of the dementia ward.

Robert Carter joined Ellen, and she checked off the locations of more hidden microphones.

The group drifted down a long hall that led to the main house. To the left was the kitchen, where the staff prepared all of Edgewood's meals. To the right, the dining room.

Joseph stopped in the hall that linked them.

"Fast forward to 1841. A Quaker named Samuel Shields decided to build on the property that had been abandoned for almost two hundred years. He had no time for tales of witches and cursed land. In this dining room, he met with his fellow Quakers to plan ways to fight slavery. He met Adele Robinson at one of these meetings. She was a smart, independent woman and passionate about the cause. And when Sam laid eyes on her—"

"Love at first sight," Lily cooed.

Robert Carter rolled his eyes.

"The attraction was mutual. After a few months, they were engaged. Samuel expanded the house in preparation for their life together. She loved to cook, so he built a grand kitchen for her."

Joseph pointed to the kitchen, where staff members were making sandwiches.

"I knew the kitchen was a relic, but Jesus," Miss Worden complained.

A few residents chuckled in sympathy.

"She didn't live to see it." Joseph sighed. "Adele was trying to get a family to the next stop on the Underground Railroad. The last one before they reached freedom in Canada. A bounty hunter surprised them on the banks of the Miskatonic River. He killed Adele and sent the family back to slavery."

Stillness descended on the crowd.

Misery, Ellen thought as her eyes climbed the walls. *This place is steeped in misery.*

"Samuel was devastated. Crushed. No one would have blamed him if he abandoned the cause. But he did something amazing." Joseph moved over to Ellen. As he fished a blueprint out of his bag, he whispered, "Keep an eye out, okay?"

"For what?" she replied.

"I'm not sure, but you'll know when you see it."

He unrolled the plans and turned to the crowd. "I'm not sure exactly where it is. The plans I have are sketchy, but Samuel Shields built a tunnel under this house. So people fighting the good fight wouldn't suffer the same fate as his dear Adele."

Robert Carter gasped.

Ellen could see him making the connection between the tunnel and the wild dogs.

"So, where's the tunnel?" someone in the crowd demanded.

Joseph shrugged. "Like I said, the plans are unclear, but I think the entrance is around here."

That's when Ellen saw it. Miss Worden, the head nurse, glanced at the floor. Then her eyes flicked to a small door next to the kitchen—a door hidden behind a strategically placed plant.

Subtle, Ellen thought.

"Where does the tunnel go?" Lily asked.

"Arkham Grove."

"The cemetery?"

"Oh, terrific. Express service," Robert Carter said with a snort.

The residents roared with laughter.

"Can people still get through it?" a man asked.

"It was walled up long ago," Joseph reassured him.

"I'm glad." Lily shuddered. "Can you imagine all the spiders and nasty creatures crawling around in that tunnel?"

Robert Carter shot her a pointed look. "And I thought you *liked* nasty creatures, Lily."

Lily turned bright red.

Miss Worden stepped between them. "Miss Logan, would you be so kind as to wait here with Robert?" she cooed.

"Hey, wait! What did I do?" he called after her.

"Honestly. Is that what you call flirting?" Ellen muttered once they were alone.

Now it was Robert Carter's turn to blush.

She smiled, her mind teeming with plans to get them together. Ellen forced her thoughts back to the task at hand. To the cursed house that surrounded them. "Miss Worden knows."

"What?"

"Miss Worden knows where the secret passage is. When Joseph was talking about it, she glanced at the door."

Robert Carter stepped around the plant and jiggled the doorknob. It was locked.

"I think we should put a garden spike in this plant, don't you?" he suggested as they knelt, and he pushed a microphone into the soil. "The thing doesn't look like it's been watered in a decade."

Ellen saw a flash of color out of the corner of her eye. She glanced up at the intersection that led to Lily's room.

A man stood in the passage, staring into space. At first, Ellen thought a patient with Alzheimer's had wandered off. Then she noticed the tattered bathrobe—the young face, the fingers dusted with chalk.

Ellen's breath hitched in her throat.

Chalkboard Man.

Suddenly, she felt weightless, suspended over a bottomless abyss. The man turned and wandered out of sight. An ominous black shadow followed in his wake. Trailing him like a robe.

Robe.

The smell of sawdust and wet plaster filled her nose.

Ellen shoved the clipboard at a bewildered Robert Carter and ran after the figure in the direction she suspected he was headed.

Back to Lily's room.

I must get to him, she thought. *I must get to him before . . .*

Before . . .

Before . . .

Before what?

What was Chalkboard Man trying to do?

She burst into her friend's room. As she entered, she passed through a black cloud. A strange taste coated Ellen's tongue—a sickly mix of sweetness and rot. *Is this what a curse tastes like?* she wondered as she coughed, trying to spit out the foulness. The room was hot, claustrophobically hot, but there was no sign of the figure. No sign of a thin place. Ellen looked everywhere: under Lily's bed, in her closet. She even peeked behind the shower curtain in the bathroom, the classic place where a boogeyman would lurk.

Nothing.

The man had vanished into thin air.

Ellen plopped down on Lily's bed and buried her face in her hands.

"You're losing it," she murmured to herself. "You're fucking losing it, girl."

Through the screen of her fingers, she saw a pair of worn slippers sticking out from behind the main door. Ellen scurried to her feet just as the man jumped out of his hiding spot and slammed the door behind him.

She reached in the bag for her mace before remembering, *This is not my bag. It's Joseph Turner's.*

"Who are you?" the man thundered. "What are you doing here? Why are there people everywhere? Tromping through my house?"

"*Your* house?" she echoed, trying to hide the fear in her voice. "Are you Thijmen?"

The man frowned as he swiped his hand across his face, leaving more white streaks on his skin. "Thijmen? Who the hell is Thijmen? My name is Sloane. Michael Sloane." He paused, waiting to be recognized. When Ellen stared at him blankly, his frown deepened. "Why are all those old people here? Following that man?"

The hair stood up on the back of her neck. *He's been watching us.*

"That man's my friend. He's giving a tour of the house to the residents."

The man scowled. "Residents? I don't understand. They're all old. Why—?"

"This is a retirement home," she offered, then added, "You know, a place where old people live."

His expression paled. "Oh, no. Oh, no, no, no. It can't be. Old people in Edgewood? This is Edgewood, right?"

"Yes."

"You have to leave. Everyone has to leave. You're in the way!" he spat as he paced the floors. "Oh, he won't like this. He won't like this one bit!"

Ellen frowned. "Who won't like this?"

"There's no time to explain. Come with me. *Now!*" He reached for her. His fingers only brushed her wrist, but the pain that shot through her was intense. Strange shapes swam in front of her eyes. Jagged shapes punched into her skull.

Ellen staggered backward as Joseph Turner's bag slipped off her shoulder. Papers spilled across the floor.

Michael Sloane stared at them, mesmerized.

"That's it. That's. It." He looked up at her. "I'll show you. The proof is in the pudding, right? Then you'll see."

"What are you talking about?"

He held up his hands, motioning for her to stay. "I need to get something. Don't go, okay?"

"Okay," she agreed.

"Okay, what?"

Ellen blinked. She was alone in Lily's bright summer room with a pool of paper at her feet. Joseph Turner was watching her from the doorway.

Ellen ran to the wall and pounded on it. "Hey, are you still there? Can you hear me?" she shouted at the wallpaper. "I'm here. I didn't leave. I'm right here!"

Joseph advanced carefully into the room. "Who are you talking to, Ellen?"

"Michael. He was here. He was right here." Ellen cringed at her own words. They sounded . . . *Crazy,* she thought. *Just say it. You sound crazy.*

Off your meds.

Joseph dropped to his knees to gather his papers.

Ellen was about to join him when he pushed photos into her hands.

"Look at these," he demanded.

They were old, from the early twentieth century. Ellen flipped through endless pictures of Miskatonic students. They were arranged in fraternities. Debating societies. Religious groups. Even temperance organizations. She frowned. Ellen wasn't sure what she was looking for. Then, like the hidden door, there it was. There *he* was. Standing behind a rowing banner, beaming so brightly he was almost unrecognizable.

Chalkboard Man.

She stabbed the picture with her finger. "That's him!"

Joseph Turner gave her a sideways look. "That's the man? The one you saw?"

"Yes."

"The man who was just here?"

Irritation crept into her voice. "*Yes.* Who is he?"

"His name is Michael Sloane. And he disappeared from Edgewood in 1928."

Fueled by a new sense of urgency, Ellen marched toward her uncle's study. Michael Sloane had finally convinced her she wasn't mad. For months, her psychiatrist had said that her journey to the Dreamlands was a delusion, a response to being held captive by Calvin Leonard. But the vision of Michael Sloane made no sense. *Why would I make him up? Of all the places in the world, why would I imagine things happening in Edgewood? In the one place that's my sanctuary? My refuge?*

Then there was the photo. The flesh-and-blood man staring back at her had a history. And like everyone else at Edgewood, it did not have a happy ending.

She pounded on the door to her uncle's study.

"What do you want?" a distant voice responded.

Ellen gritted her teeth.

"Let me in."

"What do you want?" Joshua repeated.

He sounded closer this time.

"I need to talk to you."

"I'm busy," he insisted.

"You're always busy."

The door opened. Joshua wedged his wheelchair in the doorway, blocking her view of the study.

Ellen was stunned by his appearance. His clothes were rumpled, his cheeks rough and unshaven. Dark circles ringed his eyes.

She felt a stab of guilt.

There's something wrong with him. Why haven't I noticed?

"What do you want, Ellen?" His steely voice interrupted her thoughts.

"I need to get in touch with Andrew. Do you have his phone number?"

"Andrew Carter?"

Ellen stifled the urge to scream. *How many Andrews do we know?*

Joshua shook his head. "You and Andrew."

"What's that supposed to mean?"

He rubbed his eyes.

He looked worn down. Ancient.

"You're not good for each other, so just don't, okay? Just. Don't."

She knelt in front of his wheelchair.

"You're sick, Joshua. Let me call a doctor."

"Me, sick? That's rich, coming from you."

Ellen felt like a rogue wave had smacked her. The kind that came out of nowhere and swallowed ships.

"Why aren't you taking your medicine?" he asked. "Risperdal and Depakote. That's what you're on, right? Or *supposed* to be on."

"How—?"

"Your refills are piling up."

A clammy hand squeezed her heart. The house's second floor was hers, out of her uncle's reach.

For a moment, Ellen had an absurd image of Joshua abandoning his wheelchair and crawling up the stairs. Heading to her room. Rifling through her things.

No, that's not Joshua's style. He would have someone else do it. Ellen straightened.

The man, she thought with a flash. *The man who was here the other day. With the silver Mercedes and his smooth manners.*

She jerked to her feet. "*You fuck!*" she erupted. She tried to push her way past him, to get into his study and see what he was up to.

Joshua rammed her with his wheelchair.

Ellen stumbled backward and crashed to the floor. Searing pain shot up her leg.

He looked at her in disbelief. As if she was the one who crashed into him.

"Ellen," he called out. "Oh my God, Ellen."

She struggled to her feet, tears streaming down her face.

Joshua's cell phone played the cheerful sound of "Walking on Sunshine."

Joshua glanced at the number and winced.

"I need to take this. Just stay here, okay? I'll give you Andrew's number as soon as I'm done."

He fiddled with the brake on his wheelchair.

Liar, Ellen thought.

"Yeah. Sure." She sniffled as she retreated.

She was packed and gone by the time he finished the call.

Chapter Seven

Three a.m. The witching hour. The time when super-natural creatures roam the earth. When black magic is most potent. Ellen felt none of its mystical force. Wedged between Greg Linley and Joseph Turner, both snoring like bullhorns, she listened to more snoring coming through the microphones in Edgewood Manor. The stakeout wasn't as exciting as she expected it to be. She was bored. Her fingertips were numb from playing solitaire on her phone. She wanted to use the time to study, but Greg wouldn't let her turn on the van lights. He was afraid of being spotted and having to explain why they were there.

Ellen leaned her head against the sliding door.

Two days had passed since she'd moved out of Joshua's house. She took refuge in the attic room she rented in Old Arkham, the secret place where she hid when things got too intense. The converted Victorian, home to ten students, was also where she conducted research on her family that she didn't want Joshua to see.

Joshua.

Ellen sighed.

She had expected her uncle to notice her absence, to at least try to call and apologize.

Nothing.

Not that it mattered. Ellen wasn't ready to forgive him.

Her hand drifted to her bruised shin. Everything about that day, about him, felt wrong. Something had come between them, a shadow she couldn't see. A shadow she *needed* to see.

Her cell phone buzzed. Ellen glanced at the screen, half expecting to see Joshua's face.

Her boyfriend, Tom, popped up on the display.

Finally, she thought.

She hadn't heard from Tom since he went home to Oregon to care for his sick mother.

Sick mother.

He's calling you in the middle of the night, and he has a sick mother.

Ellen opened the sliding door and hopped out of the van.

"Oh, God, Tom. Is this about your mother? Please don't tell me this is about your mother."

"What? She's . . . um . . . I . . . I . . . I didn't expect you to answer," Tom stammered before he caught himself. "What time is it there?"

"A little after three."

"Pulling an all-nighter?"

Ellen smiled. She couldn't resist. "I'm on a stakeout," she replied.

"With Dr. Carter?"

"No, not with Dr. Carter," she replied. "We're not allowed to play with each other anymore."

"What?"

The word sounded sharp, laced with suspicion.

Ellen frowned. She didn't think Tom had a problem with Andrew Carter. His tone suggested otherwise.

"What's going on?" she asked, desperate to change the subject. "Is it your mom?"

A ragged breath greeted her question. "I'm afraid so. She's going downhill. The cancer's spreading faster than the doctors expected."

Ellen looked across the street.

Edgewood Manor blurred.

"I'm sorry to hear that, Tom," she said, dabbing at her tears.

"The doctors don't know how long she has. My family wants me to stay. *I* want to stay."

"Of course you do," she replied. "It shouldn't be a problem. You can take a personal leave for a quarter or two."

"I'm not coming back to Miskatonic. I'm transferring to Oregon State," he announced. "There's more. I've been seeing someone. An old friend. She's been helping me with my mother. And . . . well . . ."

Ellen felt something inside her snap, the sensation so strong she expected it to make noise. *Andrew. Uncle Joshua. Tom. All the people who matter in my life, who held me in place . . . gone.*

"Mary isn't the only reason I'm leaving," Tom continued. "Miskatonic is a dangerous place. Maybe you get your kicks out of risking your life. Especially with Carter."

This time, his jealousy came through loud and clear.

"It's not about kicks, and it's *not* about Carter," she snarled. "And I can't believe you're judging me when you're the one who's cheating!"

"I'm not cheating on you!" he protested.

"Not from where I'm fucking standing!"

Greg got out of the van and joined her. "Um, Ellen."

"Not a good time!" she barked at her friend.

"I know. And I'm sorry," Greg replied in an unfamiliar voice. "Something's happening."

Ellen followed Greg's wide-eyed stare.

A purple light bathed Edgewood in a sickly hue. The trees beside the house shook, their leaves quivering in the still summer night. The movement was wrong. It reminded Ellen of an old silent movie. Everything looked speeded up. Out of sync.

"What's going on?" Greg asked.

"I don't know," Ellen breathed.

"What's going on?" Tom asked from Oregon.

"I said I don't know!"

A scream pierced the summer air. It was so loud Ellen thought it was Greg. It wasn't until he jumped that she realized the sound was coming from Edgewood.

Greg vaulted into the van.

Joseph stirred, jolted out of sleep by the commotion.

Greg shoved Joseph aside and took his place at the listening post.

"What the hell is going on? Who's screaming?" Tom's voice buzzed in her ear. "Where's Carter? Put him on. Now."

"I told you, he's not here!" Ellen punched the speaker button on her phone. "Greg, will you please tell Tom that Carter's not here?"

"Dr. Carter's not here. And I think you're a real shit for breaking up with her!" Greg snapped as he twisted the controls.

Ellen groaned. *So much for privacy.*

Another scream shot through Edgewood.

"Microphone three," Greg announced.

Joseph thumbed through the maps, but Ellen knew where it was. She'd planted the microphone herself. "That's Lily's room." She scrambled over Greg to grab her things.

"Wait a minute! Wait, wait!" he protested. "You don't know if there's anything wrong. Your friend might be having a bad dream."

"*HRRRRR.*" The growl reached for her through the speakers. The sound, guttural and low, hit the curve of her back and slithered up her spine. Ellen's brain stalled. Only one thought filled her head. *Get out! Run, run, run! Now!*

She looked at Greg. "Does that sound like a bad dream?" she whispered.

"Microphone five. The sound's moving down the hall." Joseph's voice was tight with panic.

This time, when she reached for her bag, Greg didn't stop her.

"What the hell is that?" Greg asked as she pulled out a small black object.

"A Taser."

"A *Taser*?" Greg looked like he was about to get sick. "This isn't what I signed up for, Logan."

"Things have changed," Joseph Turner replied grimly.

"You stay here, Greg. You're good at the surveillance thing. I'll go in," she volunteered.

"I'll come with you," Joseph added.

Greg fixed her with a sharp, defensive gaze. "I'm not a coward, Logan," he declared.

Ellen put her hand on his shoulder.

"I never said you were," she reassured him. "We need you right where you are."

Her friend nodded and let out a deep breath.

"We'll keep in touch over our phones. Do you have an earbud?" he asked.

Ellen cursed. She had one. She could picture exactly where she'd left it when she rushed to meet them.

"I might have something," Greg muttered. "Give me your phone."

Greg snorted when she handed it to him. "Do you realize you've been live for the last few minutes?"

He held up her phone. It was still on speaker. "Do you have any last words for Tom?" Greg asked.

Ellen wanted to say something nasty, something cruel and biting. *How long?* she wondered. *How long ago did he decide? He called her at three a.m. Was he hoping to break up by leaving a message? Take the easy way out?*

Before Ellen could work up her anger, a vision appeared in her mind—a gaunt woman in her late forties in bed, trying to summon the energy to live another day.

"What's your mother's name, Tom?"

"Huh?"

"Your mom. What's her name?"

"Abby," he replied after a long pause.

"Tell Abby to fight. Fight hard. And you and your . . ." The word *girlfriend* stuck in her throat. "Help her, okay? The two of you. Help your mom."

"Ellen, wait. I—"

Greg cut Tom off mid-appeal and stared at her. "That was classy, Logan. That was seriously classy."

As he rummaged for an earbud, the phone buzzed again with Tom's face.

Greg silenced it.

"I'm putting your phone on Do Not Disturb. At least until you're done in there, okay?"

She nodded.

Greg handed her the earbud and clapped her on the back. "Go out there and save the world, Supergirl."

Ellen and Joseph slipped out of the van and into the warm summer night. She felt like a diver plunging into the ocean. The atmosphere felt thick. Alien. There were no more strange noises coming from Edgewood, but she didn't trust the silence. It was like someone, or something, was holding its breath.

Ellen glanced at her phone.

Her cell phone dropped to no bars, then rebounded.

"What the hell?" she whispered.

Something's messing with me.

"What's the plan, Ellen?" Joseph barked, startling her out of her paranoid thoughts.

She shook her head in the hopes of clearing it.

"Robert said he would leave a door open for us, just in case we needed to get in," she replied. "Let's see if he did."

As she and Joseph crept around the house's perimeter, Ellen glanced nervously at the looming structure. She had never been to Edgewood at night. Her skin tingled as they snuck around the house, a psychic sensation that Andrew Carter snidely called her "Spidey sense." She couldn't help but think about Edgewood's grim history—the persecuted witch, the murdered fiancée, the missing mathematician.

This place devours people.

"This is awful," Joseph announced, bringing her back to reality.

"What's happening?" Greg demanded from his post in the van.

Joseph nudged the cinder block that held open a side door. "Someone's propped open a door on the west side of the house."

Ellen frowned. "This isn't right. Robert shouldn't be able to do this. No one should be able to do this."

"We should report it," Joseph Turner said.

She looked up and nodded.

"We will once we're done," she replied. "Let's get through this first, okay?"

Ellen stepped over the cinder block.

Joseph bent down to remove it.

She stopped him.

"Let's get through this first," she said again.

The moment she walked through the door, Ellen knew there was something different about Edgewood Manor. She was familiar with the house's normal sounds, its smells, its moods. As she crept down the hall, she was greeted with the same sickly stench she'd experienced in Lily's room. The smell assaulted her senses. Made her eyes water.

It's getting stronger, she thought, *spreading like cancer.*

Cancer.

Ellen gasped.

Did the house eavesdrop on my conversation with Tom?

"Logan?" Greg called out.

Her eyes drifted to a painting on the wall. It was a picture of a sailboat on a bay—a generic piece of institutional art. She touched the picture, and the surface rippled beneath her fingertips. The image morphed into a picture of a demon sitting on a woman's chest. A famous painting, a classic depiction of . . .

"Sleep paralysis," she whispered.

"Ellen, what is going on?" Greg's voice sounded in her ear.

"This house. It's, it's . . . responding to me."

"What do you mean *responding to you*?" Her friend's voice was shrill.

Joseph popped up in front of her, making her jump.

She hadn't noticed he had wandered off.

Ellen shivered.

That's because the house distracted me.

She touched the painting again. This time, her fingers pressed into solid canvas.

Joseph frowned. "What are you doing?"

Before Ellen could respond, the door to Lily's room flew open. Purple light leaked into the hall as Michael Sloane was tossed through the doorway. He crashed into the opposite wall and collapsed in a lifeless heap on the floor.

"*HRRR.*"

Edgewood Manor shook with the same growl they'd heard in the van.

A figure stepped out of Lily's room. It was huge, even taller than Joseph. It stood upright, but its shoulders were hunched as if it had spent a lot of time in confined spaces. Ellen studied its worm-white skin, the canine snout, the large bat-like ears.

Her knees buckled. "Dogs. They're not dogs," she whispered.

The thing turned to her and sneered, saliva dripping from its mouth.

Greg's voice buzzed in her ear. "What did you say? I can't hear you."

Joseph pulled himself to his full height and locked eyes with the creature, his face twisted with rage. He looked fierce, completely unlike the mild-mannered man she thought she knew.

"Joe?" Ellen called out.

Joseph was still for another moment. Then he shrieked and charged the nightmare.

Ellen's scream joined Joseph Turner's battle cry. The walls around her buzzed with the sound. She thought she saw the walls buckle and move, as if Edgewood were absorbing her fear. She could only watch as Joseph closed on the creature in the hall. Ellen waited for the beast to attack, for Greg's friend to be torn apart limb by limb.

Instead, the beast turned and fled.

Joseph ran after it, his war cry echoing down the hall.

Ellen's shock came out as a chant. "*Oh my God, oh my God, oh my.*"

"Logan, you talk to me. *Now,*" Greg ordered, his voice sharp as a spear.

"There's something in Edgewood. It just came after us." Ellen's voice quivered.

"What was it?"

Ellen knew what it was. She didn't want to say it. She didn't want to believe it. "I don't know. Joseph just rushed it, and the thing ran. The thing turned around, and it fucking ran!"

"You're telling me he *chased* it?"

A giggle escaped her lips. "Crazy son of a bitch."

"And he left you there? Alone?"

Her eyes fell across the body of Michael Sloane, still crumpled in the hall. "Oh, no. No, no, no."

She rushed to the man's side and rolled him over. His eyes fluttered open. He grabbed her hand and pressed it between his. There was no pain this time, no jagged images stabbing at her skull.

"This isn't what I expected. I thought it would be more. So much more," he groaned. His eyes locked on a spot above her head. "I never wanted this."

"*HRRR.*" A deep growl came from behind.

A pair of powerful arms seized Ellen, lifting her off the ground. The creature tried to bring its arm to her throat to put her in a chokehold, but Ellen blocked it with her arm. She kept the thing from crushing her windpipe, but its other arm wrapped around her waist, squeezing her in a tight, python-like grip. The pressure it put on her was incredible. Ellen's eyes bulged, and her senses flickered, threatening to plunge her into darkness.

She did everything she could to break free. She struggled. She thrashed. She kicked.

Nothing worked.

The Taser, her dazed mind blurted.

Her fingers groped for her weapon, but the thing shook her like a rag doll. The Taser fell out of her pocket and skittered across the floor. Out of the corner of her eye, she saw Michael Sloane lunge for it.

"Use it. It's a gun," she croaked. "Shoot it!"

The creature tightened its grip around her, and Ellen's vision dimmed. *I'm running out of time . . . and oxygen.* Her mind fixed on the last time she saw Andrew. How bored he looked surrounded by his admirers at the coffeehouse. Leg bouncing, desperate to be free. Desperate to be with her.

Strange, she thought as she began to slip away. *So strange Andrew Carter means so much to me.*

"Help me," she pleaded with Michael Sloane.

The floor in front of her rippled and became liquid, like the painting down the hall. A form erupted from the linoleum tiles—a huge figure swathed in a black robe. Its body was a construct made of all the house's parts. Its head was old and wooden, its body a jumble of stone, plaster, and brick.

Dark, intelligent eyes burned from deep holes in its face.

Michael stirred beside her.

"Master," he breathed in awe.

The thing threw out its arms, and a crackle of electricity arced around her.

The creature shrieked and dropped her. Ellen tumbled to the floor, retching and coughing, gulping cold fistfuls of air. When her vision finally cleared, everything was quiet. Michael Sloane stood over her, waving a piece of paper at her.

Figures swam off the page, dancing before her eyes.

"This will show you the way." He dropped to his knees, offering her the paper, but Ellen was too dazed to take it.

He stuffed it into the pocket of her jeans.

"Hey, you! Get away from her!" a voice thundered.

Greg had abandoned his post in the van. He charged down the hall, snarling at the man beside Ellen, his eyes blazing with anger.

Michael Sloane jumped up and scurried away like a startled deer.

"Don't, don't. Be careful," she gasped when Greg reached her. "The creatures! Watch out for the creatures!"

Greg scowled. "What are you talking about, Logan?"

"There's a guy in a big black robe. I think he . . ."

Ellen propped herself on her elbows and looked around. The hall was empty.

"The creatures," she murmured. "Where are the creatures?"

Greg picked up her Taser and offered it to her.

"Listen to me. We need to get out of here. One of the residents called 911," he informed her. "I don't know about you, but I'd rather not be here when the cops arrive."

Ellen looked at the Taser.

It hadn't been fired.

Strange, she thought as she took it back. *I thought I saw electricity . . .*

"Did you hear me? The cops are coming. We need to get out of here. *Now!*"

No matter how hard she concentrated, she couldn't move her body. She felt vague—as if her mind was stuffed with cotton.

"Okay, okay," she murmured.

Greg grabbed her and hauled her to her feet. Ellen's body screamed in protest, and for a moment, her vision dimmed. She was sure Greg was going to accomplish what the creature hadn't.

"What are you doing to her?" a voice demanded, piercing through the haze that threatened to engulf her.

Ellen recognized the voice.

Her eyes opened, and she focused on Robert Carter. "They're not dogs," she spluttered. "They're not dogs, Robert!"

Robert spat out a curse, his foul words drowned out by the sound of approaching sirens. "Follow me. Quickly," he commanded them.

Even in the darkness, Ellen could see the trail Joseph and the monster had left behind. They had blown through Edgewood, toppling furniture and knocking pictures askew.

The path ended with an upended plant. A cinder block held the basement door open.

Just like the door outside, she thought as she turned to Robert.

"Did you do that?" she asked, nodding at the door.

Powerful fists pounded on the front door. "Police!"

In the distance, the residents cried out. Down the hall, Ellen heard the anxious scuffle of feet.

"Go," Robert commanded them. "I'll take care of this."

Ellen hadn't been in a basement since Calvin Leonard had abducted her. This room was nothing like the dank, dungeon-like space where Calvin held her hostage. Light illuminated Edgewood's basement, and a clean concrete scent permeated the area.

That this space was different didn't matter. The moment Greg closed the door behind them, Ellen saw death. Bodies piled on the floor like wood stacks. The odor of rotting flesh filled her nose.

Somewhere in the basement, a machine stirred.

THUNK.

The sound hit Ellen hard.

Like a baseball bat.

Heat spread through her body as she remembered killing Calvin Leonard. How his head split open like a piñata—bones and brain spilling onto the floor. His death infuriated her. It was too quick. Too easy. After everything he had done, he deserved more. He deserved to suffer. She kept hitting him with the bat—each swing harder than the last. As if that would punish him. As if that would make up for what he had done to his victims. And when someone tried to stop her . . .

An image swam out of the depths. A man with delicate, childlike features grabbed the bat and tried to wrestle the weapon away from her. She swung the bat at him and . . . heard the sharp crack of metal on bone. Felt the impact of the blow ride up her arms.

The man crumpled at her feet.

Ellen sunk to the cold, concrete floor, whimpering.

I killed one of the people in Calvin's basement. One of the victims.

Her hand fluttered to her mouth. "Oh, God, no. Please, no."

It's a false memory, her rational mind insisted. *You would never . . .*

But I did, Ellen thought. She could feel the memory etched in her muscles.

Greg's face popped into view.

Ellen screamed and scurried backward.

"I'm sorry. I'm sorry, I'm sorry," she babbled, her eyes hot with tears.

Her friend crouched beside her. "Logan, I don't know what the hell is going on with you, but we need to keep moving. We're almost there." He nodded at the jagged opening in the wall.

"The tunnel," she croaked. Her voice sounded strange and smoky, but saying the words drove away the nightmare. It cleared the fog in her head.

Upstairs, she heard a flurry of voices.

Greg helped her to her feet, and they hurried through the passage.

The Miskatonic River had risen in the century and a half since the tunnel was built. Water oozed up from the ground as they made their way through the passage. A dense network of wet tree roots brushed their heads, tickling them with dampness. The walls looked like they were about to crumble. But with each muddy step, Ellen felt better. The dark energy that surrounded her in Edgewood faded. It was replaced by cautious wonder. *I'm traveling through the Underground Railroad.* Ellen could feel the energy of those who'd passed through. The excitement of the people who risked everything for a different future.

She glanced at Greg, wondering whether his ancestors had taken a similar path.

"Fuck!"

Greg's curse cut through her thoughts. "What's wrong?"

His cell phone light illuminated a stone wall. "Dead end. I guess the people at Edgewood fixed it, after all." Greg shot her a grim look. "Logan?"

"Yeah?"

"Have I told you I'm claustrophobic?"

Now it's my turn to be strong, Ellen thought.

"We're not trapped, Greg," she reassured him. "We can always go back. Even if the door to Edgewood is locked, Robert is on the outside. He'll help us. And if Joseph could get through . . ." Ellen studied the wall, her eyes drifting across the grimy surface.

They came to rest on some long horizontal marks where the mud and grime had been scraped clean.

"I thought the passage to the graveyard would be open," she murmured.

"They must have walled it off when the inspectors found it," Greg offered.

"I don't think they did." Ellen could feel the answer coming, bubbling beneath the surface. She talked herself through the problem. "An open passage from Edgewood to the grave-yard? That doesn't make sense." She turned to Greg. "If you were doing something illegal, would you want people to find you by going straight through a tunnel? Especially when the woman you loved was killed?"

"A hidden door. This wall has a hidden door," Greg announced. "That means there's a way to open it."

Ellen's eyes returned to the clean spot on the wall. When she shone her cell phone light on it, a thin metal rod winked at her. She tugged on it, and a fake wall slid open with a teeth-grinding rasp. Ellen reached for her Taser as she peered into the space.

Stone surrounded her on all sides.

"A tomb," she whispered. She took a cautious step and crossed the threshold. "I think we're in Arkham Grove."

Greg tried to follow, but she waved him off.

"Let me make sure there's a way out first."

"Um, Logan?" Her friend pointed at the ceiling.

The cover to the tomb had been pushed aside. A set of worn stone stairs led out of the grave.

Ellen's skin crawled. *Too easy,* she thought. *This is way too easy.* She crept up the stairs, her hands gliding along walls etched with decades of graffiti. The strange markings hinted at dark rituals, of people violating the dead.

A puff of fresh air teased her hair.

A draft, she thought in disbelief. *This is the way out.* "Greg, I think—"

A mountain of white flesh fell between her and Greg. She heard her friend yelp as the door started to close.

Creature, Ellen thought, *it's another one of those goddamn creatures.*

Jesus, how many of them are out here?

"Logan! *Logan!*" Greg screamed as he lunged, trying to keep the door from closing.

The stone entrance ground shut, trapping Ellen alone with the creature.

The thing didn't attack her. It cocked its head and leered, as if it was savoring the moment. Ellen got her first good look at it. She could see why the people in Edgewood thought it was a dog. The thing in front of her had a canine face—pointed ears, long snout, pointed teeth. But it was a dog in the same way she was a Neanderthal.

The thing flashed her a brown, rotten smile.

"*Mouqabbilat,*" it rasped.

Ellen gasped. The word was familiar. She heard it in the Dreamlands when a creature very similar to this one spoke. She couldn't deny what it was anymore. The memories were too strong for her to ignore. "G . . . g . . . ghoul," she stammered.

The creature charged her.

She threw up her hands in a feeble defense.

The cell phone light hit it in the eyes, and it turned away, blinded.

Ellen took advantage of the moment and grabbed her Taser. The metal prongs leaped out as she fired, thumping into the monster's chest. The creature froze. Ellen watched as its body jittered and danced, hitting the floor with a satisfying *whump.*

As she turned to flee, the hidden door opened.

"I'm coming, Ellen! Hang on!" Greg shouted as he clawed at the narrow space.

"Greg! No! *Don't!*"

Her eyes darted to the ghoul. She wasn't sure how long the effects of the shock would last. For humans, it was anywhere between five and sixty minutes. For this thing . . .

Ellen shuddered.

God only knows.

Greg pushed the door open and rushed into the room. His foot caught on the fallen creature. He plummeted, belly flopping onto the cold, hard earth.

The ghoul twisted and grabbed her friend, sinking its teeth into Greg's leg. His high-pitched scream echoed off the walls.

Ellen clapped her hands over her ears. She was seized by a sudden urge to run—to do anything to escape the sound. Even if it meant leaving behind a friend.

The creature looked up, leering at her with its bloody mouth.

The ghoul's arrogance burned through her fear.

A deep, primal anger rose inside her, flooding her body with adrenaline. She punched the button on her Taser, delivering another potent shock.

The creature seized more violently this time. It was paralyzed long enough for Greg to crawl away. Ellen rushed to his side. She hooked her arms under him and dragged him toward the stairs. Blood poured from the bite. It wasn't a clean wound. Infection wasn't just possible. It was inevitable.

Assuming we both live long enough to get out of here.

"Ellen," Greg called out. His head lolled.

She shook her friend. "Don't you dare pass out on me," she hissed at him.

Thump!

Another creature dropped down in front of them.

Ellen saw a glint of steel. *Weapon,* she thought numbly. *This one has a weapon.* Ellen pulled Greg against her, doing her best to protect him.

The ghoul ignored her. It approached its fallen comrade, raised its weapon, and struck. One moment, the ghoul's head was there; the next, it was a spurting stump. Ellen watched as the ghoul kept hitting the body.

THUNK. THUNK. THUNK.

Do something! Her mind screamed. *You're next! Do something!*

"Ellen," Greg groaned, stirring in her arms.

The attacker whirled to face them. "Greg?"

Her mind stuttered in disbelief. *No, it can't be. He . . . he . . . just . . .*

Joseph stepped out of the darkness and knelt in front of Greg. "What the hell happened?"

Ellen nodded at the pile of meat on the floor. Her stomach churned, and she choked down a hot rush of bile. "*That* happened. It bit him," she whispered.

Joseph hissed, the sound amplified by the silence of the tomb. He set down his weapon and tore off part of his shirt. As he applied a tourniquet to Greg, Ellen studied Joseph's weapon. A long sword. A huge, gore-spattered sword that buzzed with a strange energy.

Like that dagger in Lord of the Rings, *she thought. The one that protected Frodo from goblins.*

Ellen reached out to touch it.

Joseph's head jerked up, and he roared, "Leave it alone!"

She withdrew her hand as if she had been burned.

His eyes instantly softened. "I'm sorry, but we can't waste any time. We need to get Greg out of here. Now."

⁘

You're not planning on digging up bodies, are you? Andrew Carter's words came back to Ellen, taunting her as she and Joseph fought their way out of the brambly depths of Arkham Grove. With Greg dangling between them, they looked like grave robbers.

Ellen looked down at her friend's feet, at the untied laces of his Converse sneakers.

He hadn't stirred since he called out her name in the tomb.

Let him be okay. Oh, dear God, please let him be okay.

"Turn left. Then another left at the stone angel," Joseph Turner commanded her.

Ellen did what she was told. She was more than happy to let someone else take the lead. The adrenaline that fueled her through Edgewood was running low. Everything hurt. Her lungs burned with every breath. Her muscles screamed, threatening to cramp. And around her waist, where the ghoul had grabbed her—

Don't think about it.

Keep moving.

The stone angel popped up in front of them so suddenly, Joe almost crashed into it. They veered to the left and scaled a steep hill. A gravel road waited for them at the top. But first, they had to wrestle through a thicket of blackberries and stinging nettle. Ellen gritted her teeth as branches slapped her face, their sharp points digging into her skin.

"I see the way out! We're almost there!" Joe shouted.

Almost there, she reassured her aching body. *Did you hear that? We're almost there.*

She didn't think about the gate until she saw the bars.

The cemetery was closed. Locked up.

Of course it's locked up. The place has been abandoned for years. It's a target for vandals.

Joseph put down Greg and charged the gate, pounding it furiously with his fists.

Ellen watched him for a minute, then fumbled for her cell phone.

Joseph squinted at her. "What are you doing?"

"I'm calling for help," she replied. "Greg doesn't have time for this."

He snatched the phone from her hands. "We can't take him to the hospital."

"If you're worried about getting caught, leave," she snarled. "I'm not risking my friend's life because—"

"They won't know what to do."

"What?"

"The hospital. They won't know what to do."

She started to respond, but a white light blinded them.

"What the *hell* is going on?" a familiar voice shouted.

Relief flooded through Ellen. "Andrew!"

Joseph frowned into the light. "Dr. Carter?" he called out.

The flashlight pivoted, hitting Joe in the face before it flashed back to Ellen.

"What's going on?" Andrew asked again.

"A ghoul attacked Greg. It bit him."

Ghoul.

The word was out.

The reality . . .

Her knees buckled.

"Ellen?" Andrew called out when she crumpled.

When she didn't respond, he turned to Joseph. "Was she bitten?"

"I don't know."

"Was she bitten?" he yelled.

"I don't know!"

The light disappeared.

Ellen wilted. She didn't blame Andrew for leaving. Had she come across this mess, she would have been tempted to flee, too.

Ghouls in Edgewood.

Ghouls in a fucking retirement home.

Joseph put his hand on her shoulder. "We need to move Greg. Dr. Carter's going to pull open the gate."

For a moment, Ellen flashed on an image of Andrew yanking at the bars like King Kong. Then she saw the backup lights of his SUV.

They moved Greg a few feet away. It was only a short distance, but it put them closer to the heart of the graveyard than she liked. Ellen knelt beside her friend and watched for something to jump out and drag him back into the bushes. Her jaw muscles clenched. "Just you fucking try," she threatened the darkness.

The roar of an engine drowned out her words. Her nose filled with the smell of burning rubber. Metal creaked. Then silence. Voices and clanking as chains were repositioned. Trying to control her panic, Ellen kept her eyes fixed on the ground.

If we don't get Greg out soon—

Another roar. The gate shrieked as it tore off its hinges, crashing to the ground with a deafening clatter.

Joseph ran up to her, his face bright with victory, and together, they carried Greg to the car.

Andrew blanched as they approached. "Jesus Christ, Ellen! What happened?"

She barely heard him. The moment they set Greg down, Joseph began to rifle through Greg's pockets.

"What are you doing?" she demanded.

"I need his car keys," Joseph replied. "The van's still at Edgewood, remember? Greg probably left the damn thing wide open. I need to get there before the cops find it."

Andrew Carter stared at her. "Edgewood?" He lowered his voice. "Did you just say Edgewood?"

Joe fished out Greg's keys. "Text me with updates," he ordered her. "Let me know how he's doing, okay?"

As soon as Greg was gone, Andrew snarled, "What. The. *Fuck*. Ellen?"

"Get mad later," she pleaded. "You can get as mad at me as you want. Just . . . later, okay?"

He muttered another curse and slammed the back door.

Chapter Eight

"I suppose you were collecting graveyard dust."

Ellen gawked at the man taking care of Greg.

A twilight doctor.

She had never seen a twilight doctor before. She had only read about them in stories. On-call physicians who operated out of private homes, they handled the cases in Arkham that couldn't go through normal channels. They were like mob doctors. Except they saw much, much worse. And now here she was, in Dr. Caligari's home office (*another fake name,* she thought), watching the man examine Greg.

Her friend's injuries barely made an impression. The doctor hummed as he filled his syringe.

"She doesn't know what you're talking about," Andrew Carter said from his position in the corner of the room.

"You use it in hexes," the doctor explained as he injected Greg. "You mix graveyard dirt with other ingredients to create a powder."

"That's not why we were in Arkham Grove," she insisted. "We—"

Andrew silenced her with a glare.

The man glanced at her. "I'd prefer not to know. And would you please stop fidgeting? You're making me nervous."

Ellen hadn't been aware she was rocking back and forth. Joshua's words taunted her. *Your refills are piling up.*

"Is he going to be okay?" she croaked.

"We'll know in the next twenty-four hours," the doctor replied. "You say it was a ghoul that attacked him?"

"Yes."

"Ghoul attacks are rare. Are you sure?"

"Positive." *And those things are still in Edgewood. With all those helpless people . . .*

Panic shot through Ellen.

"I have to go!" she blurted as she bolted for the front door.

Andrew intercepted her in the hall and grabbed her arm.

"Whoa, whoa, whoa! Where do you think you're going?"

"Edgewood. I have to go back! I need to warn—"

He spun her toward a mirror.

A wild woman stared back at her—speckled with mud; branches and weeds jutted out of her hair. Her face was white, her arms laddered with angry scratches.

"Do you *really* think anyone is going to listen to you?"

Ellen looked at him through the mirror. "Your father," she whispered. "You need to talk to your father."

Andrew scowled. His eyes went dark. Unreadable.

The doctor appeared in the mirror beside them. "I've put your friend in a room to recover. Now it's your turn, Miss Logan."

"Me? No, I'm fine. Really."

Andrew squeezed her shoulders. "Let the doctor look at you. For me, Ellen. Give me one less thing to worry about."

Ellen wanted to keep moving forward, to get to the heart of what was going on at Edgewood Manor. But now that the adrenaline had worn off, she felt woozy. Sick. And how could she be sure she wasn't injured? Everything had happened so fast.

"Go to Edgewood. Talk to your father. Promise me, Andrew, and I'll stay here. I'll get checked out."

His jaw tightened. "All right," he grumbled.

She let the doctor guide her back to the exam room. As she slipped out of her muddy clothes, Ellen felt a crinkle in her jeans. The note Michael Sloane had given her. She pulled it out and looked at it. Even in bright light, it was confusing. A jumble of letters and symbols. She folded it and put it back into her pocket.

When she opened the door, the doctor was waiting—a *twilight* doctor.

How the hell am I going to pay for this? Ellen wondered.

"You don't take student health insurance by any chance, do you?" she joked nervously.

The man's lips curled into a smile. "Dr. Carter has already taken care of the bill."

She lay down on the table and let him examine her. He went through all the basics—blood pressure, pulse, lungs, and reflexes. He checked her body for bites.

Nothing.

But when his eyes fell to her waist, he scowled. A squall line of red welts spread across her skin. He carefully studied the injury. "How did this happen?"

"One of the ghouls grabbed me and squeezed me. Hard."

"That doesn't sound like a ghoul," he replied. "Their attack usually takes the form of a bite."

The doctor moved in for a closer look.

Ellen expected a take-some-Tylenol-and-put-ice-on-it quick diagnosis.

"I think you should get an ultrasound."

"Ultrasound? But I'm not pregnant!"

The doctor looked at her like she was a moron. "I want to check for internal bleeding. Normally, I'd have you drink a lot of water before the procedure, but we don't have the luxury of time."

Internal bleeding.

Those were the only worlds Ellen heard. The words blazed neon-bright in her head. She suddenly wished someone was with her. To hold her hand. Reassure her.

Tom . . .

Ellen looked away, her eyes stinging with tears.

She pushed away thoughts of her ex-boyfriend and the ghouls and settled into the exam. The twilight doctor distracted her by taking her on a grand tour of her body. He paused to point out the world hidden beneath her skin—her stomach, liver, and spleen. She thought about thin places, about the worlds that lurked just on the other side.

"Everything looks fine," Dr. Caligari finally pronounced. "I'd take it easy for the next few days. If there is any change, you go straight to the hospital."

"What about Greg?"

"The next few hours will be rough, but I think he'll make it."

Ellen gasped like a swimmer coming up for air.

The doctor stopped in the doorway. "I almost forgot." His eyes twinkled as he handed her a piece of paper. "A prescription from Dr. Carter."

Ellen examined the terse writing.

1. *Sleep*
2. *Food*
3. *1220 Abermarle Court, 8 p.m.*

She quickly got dressed and shoved the paper in her pocket. She had things to do.

✦✦✦✦✦

There was another to-do item on Ellen's list, sandwiched between food and the mysterious 1220 Abermarle Court.

Mote It Be, 4–8 p.m.

She had the evening shift at the New Age bookstore where she worked. Even worse, it was theme night. Steampunk. Ellen manned the counter, decked out in a leather railroad skirt, billowy shirt, and Victorian boots. She knew she should be grateful; she didn't have to wear revealing clothing or bind herself in a corset. Still, Ellen's battered body protested. Every movement, no matter how slight, hurt.

Norm, the owner of the store, wandered over to where she was stationed.

"Kind of dead tonight," he observed. "And I thought steampunk was hip."

"Steampunk *is* hip," she replied as she fanned herself with a piece of paper. "Just not on a hot summer day in an un-air-conditioned store."

Norm scowled as she launched the latest attack in the battle for climate control. From the moment she started working at Mote It Be, Ellen tried to adjust the thermostat. Every time, Norm chased her away, scolding her about unnecessary luxuries.

"The next thing you'll want in here is an ice cream counter," he grunted.

"No," she sighed. "But I wouldn't mind a bar. I could really go for an ice-cold martini right now."

He shot her a sideways look.

"What's with you, Ellen?"

She tensed. "What do you mean?"

"You seem . . . off."

Well, she thought, *I have massive bruising from a ghoul attack. My best friend is injured and recovering in a twilight doctor's house. And my boyfriend just dumped me . . .*

But Ellen knew the real reason she was "off."

It was Edgewood.

"How long have you lived in Arkham, Norm?" she asked.

"All my life."

Ellen looked at him, surprised. Norm didn't seem like a native. Even though he owned a New Age bookstore, he wasn't the least bit mystical. His interest in the occult was driven exclusively by profit.

"You're an Arkhamite? Really?"

"Born and raised here. My family goes back generations," he insisted, with what sounded suspiciously like pride.

"Then you must know a lot of things."

He gave her a blank stare. "What's this all about?"

Ellen looked at a tarot deck in the display case as she considered what to say. Her eyes lingered on a card. The shadowy form of Nyarlahotep, "the Magician," stared back at her.

"I was ghost hunting last night with friends," she murmured.

"An ordinary night for you so far."

"Okay, so you know I'm not the type who jumps every time a mouse scuttles across the floor. And ghosts . . ." She paused, her cheeks reddening. "I have no problem with ghosts. Lived with them my whole life." *Loved them, even,* she wanted to add but held her tongue. "But the house I was in last night, the house my friends and I were investigating . . . it felt different."

"What do you mean different?" Norm pressed her.

"How do I say this without sounding like a complete lunatic?"

"Don't worry about sounding like a lunatic," he insisted. "I'm not Miskatonic. I'm not here to evaluate you. And by the way, their opinion? It's off. *Way* off."

Ellen let out a ragged breath.

"Jesus! Does everyone around here know about my mental condition?"

"Arkham's a small town. And Miskatonic leaks information like a sinking ship," he replied. "So what exactly did you see on your little ghost hunt?"

"It wasn't what I saw but what I felt." Ellen paused, searching for the right words. "The place I was in last night wasn't haunted. Not in any traditional sort of way. It felt alive. Like a living, breathing thing. When I went in there, it . . . it started to respond to me, to react to the things I did."

It whispered in my ear, told me things about myself I didn't want to know, she thought as the face of Calvin Leonard's victim popped into her head.

The face you smashed with a baseball bat.

Ellen shivered despite the heat.

"You're talking about a sentient house," Norm announced after a long silence.

"Sentient house?" Ellen echoed with a frown.

"There aren't many of them out there. In fact, they're as rare as hen's teeth," he replied as he stared out the window, watching a family stroll by armed with ice cream cones. "People argue endlessly about the definition, so it's more useful to give fictional examples. Poe's House of Usher. Shirley Jackson's Hill House."

"The Overlook Hotel in *The Shining,*" she offered.

He nodded. "All examples of houses that have lives beyond their owners. Or houses that have a life *because* of their owners."

Ellen frowned. "What do you mean?"

"Have you ever read *The Shining?*"

"I saw the film," she offered.

"Apples and oranges," he said, dismissing Kubrick's masterpiece. "In the original story, there was a gangster, Vittorio Gienelli, who saved the Overlook from destruction in the 1940s. He put everything he had into the hotel. Maybe a little too much."

"What do you mean?" Ellen murmured. Her mind returned to the figure who burst through the floor. The strange construct of man and building.

"The guy in *The Shining* put everything he had into the Overlook. His heart and his soul." Norm paused to look at her. "This place you had your experience. It wouldn't happen to be Edgewood Manor, would it?"

Icy tendrils shot through her body.

Ellen rubbed at the goose bumps on her arms.

"Edgewood's a lot like the hotel in *The Shining*," Norm offered.

"No blood pouring out of the elevators, I hope," she joked, but he ignored her.

"There were several hotels that were thought to be the inspiration for the Overlook. The Biltmore in Providence. The Stanley Hotel in Colorado. Timberline Lodge in Oregon. Many people believe Edgewood was the inspiration for the Witch House."

Ellen gasped. She felt like she had been punched in the gut.

"The Witch House? Are you serious? The place in H. P. Lovecraft's *The Dreams in the Witch House*?"

Norm nodded. "The very same."

Absurd, was Ellen's first thought. But was it? All the elements in Lovecraft's story were there. A house built by a witch who was murdered. The strange apparitions that appeared on the property not long after his death. Not to mention the disappearance of Michael Sloane, a boarder who rented a room there.

And the portal.

Don't forget the portal that opened in Lily's room.

"Well, God *damn,*" Ellen breathed.

Norm chuckled. "That's kind of the idea, Logan."

"But that place is a retirement home. People whose bodies and minds . . ." She paused, the anger rising so suddenly she nearly choked. "Who the hell would expose vulnerable people to a place like that?"

"Someone who doesn't believe the stories. And who's looking for a cheap way to house old people."

"That's the most cynical thing I've ever heard."

Norm shrugged. "Not if you reject the stories about the place."

"Do *you* reject 'the stories'?"

He shot her an amused look.

"Are you asking me if I'm cynical?"

"I know the answer to that already," she replied. "Remember how you made me dress up as a psychic elf last Christmas to get more families into the store?"

He flashed her a wicked smile.

"Truthfully, Ellen? I did that just to piss you off."

She smacked the glass display case with an open palm. "I knew it! I freaking knew it!"

They fell into amiable silence, broken only by the summer crowd in the town square. In the distance, Ellen heard music from the gazebo. She had forgotten it was Thursday night on the plaza.

Not that I ever have time to attend.

The thought of stretching out on the grass with a glass of wine and listening to music enticed her.

"Has anything changed recently?" Norm asked.

"What?"

"In Edgewood. Has anything changed? Sentient houses tend to awaken when something irritates them."

"Like sand in an oyster," Ellen murmured.

She thought for a long time before she landed on a potential explanation.

"The place changed ownership a few months ago. Some big corporate health care group took over."

"Who?"

She shrugged. "I have no idea."

"Don't you think that's something you should find out?"

Ellen perked up.

"Does that mean you won't mind if I go back and use the computer for a little sleuthing?"

"Might as well," Norm said as he looked around the empty store. "But if anyone comes through the door . . ."

"I'll be here and ready to serve," Ellen replied, giving Norm a jaunty little salute before she retreated to his office.

Chapter Nine

Under normal circumstances, Ellen would have walked to the address Andrew Carter gave her. But her research into Edgewood's new owner took her down a deep rabbit hole. By the time she looked up, it was five minutes before her scheduled "appointment." Ellen wanted to change back into her street clothes, but there was no time. If she wanted to be even fashionably late, she needed to call for a ride. As Ellen eased into the back seat of the hired car, she tried not to think about the money she was wasting. Money better spent on rent, groceries . . .

My future.

Despite her best efforts, she was twenty minutes late. And at the wrong address—1220 Abermarle Court was a duplex in New Arkham, in the heart of what the Miskatonic students called "Kool-Aid" village. The place radiated domesticity. It was a tidy two-story house, dark blue with white trim. The surrounding houses alternated colors, but the choices were confined to a narrow pallet.

They must have a homeowner's association, Ellen thought as she rang the doorbell. *A strict one.*

No dark rituals allowed here.

When the door opened, she put on her most apologetic face.

"I'm sorry. I think I'm lost."

"You're in the right place."

Andrew Carter stood in front of her. Barefoot, wearing jeans and a Dr. Who T-shirt, he looked like a suburban dad. *A sexy suburban dad,* she thought with a flush. His eyes drifted across her outfit—the railroad skirt, poufy shirt, and Victorian boots—and his mouth curled into a lopsided smirk.

At least it wasn't mermaid night, she consoled herself.

"I see you've drunk the Kool-Aid," Ellen muttered, desperate to get in a jab before he did.

"And I see Norm has a new fetish. What is this? Splatter punk?"

She toyed with the aviator goggles dangling around her neck. "*Steam*punk," she corrected him. "Are you going to let me in? Or do you want the neighbors to think this is your thing?"

He stepped aside, ushering her in with an exaggerated bow.

Ellen stepped into an airy room full of Scandinavian furniture. Not the cheap IKEA stuff; the furniture was imported. A butcher block coffee table; chairs with curved, elegant lines. She didn't realize how dark Joshua's place was until she walked across Andrew's blond hardwood floors. Ellen yearned to kick off her boots and feel the cool surface beneath her feet.

But she couldn't.

Not yet.

She had a question she needed to ask.

"Andrew, what possessed you to put your father in the Witch House?"

She expected him to be shocked, to hem and haw or splutter denials, but he crossed his arms and shot her an amused look.

"Not much for social pleasantries, are you?"

Not much for telling the truth, are you?

Her tongue twitched, but she bit back the words.

"Yeah, okay. Sure." Ellen ventured deeper into the house, letting her hand drift across the buttery cushions of a leather sofa. "This is a nice place. Who does it belong to?"

"Me."

Ellen's head jerked up. "This is your place?"

"Yes. The house that I live in," he added when she continued to stare at him. "What, do you think I sleep in a coffin?"

"No! Of course not! It's just . . ." She sighed and dropped the act. "Do you think it's wise, letting me into your home? I mean, that bureaucrat woman pretty much spelled it out. Everyone thinks I'm crazy."

At the mention of the bureaucrat, he snickered.

"Oh, Cathy. Poor Cathy. You almost gave her a heart attack when you threatened to sue Miskatonic."

She smiled. "I won't lie. That felt good. That felt *really* good."

Andrew fixed her with a steady gaze, one she struggled to hold.

"I don't think you're crazy, Ellen. Not for a second," he said softly.

She looked away, her eyes flooding with tears.

"Thanks." She murmured her gratitude to the floor.

They fell silent, the stillness broken only by a drape flapping in the breeze.

Andrew tossed something onto the coffee table. A plastic bag full of microphones. "My father told me his side. Now you tell me yours."

———— ·•♦♦♦•· ————

The story spilled out of her. It was a mess. Random, bizarre, undigested. Like the one she told him about the Dreamlands and Randolph Carter. Ellen wished she was a better storyteller.

But how do you tell the impossible tale?

When she finished, Andrew leaned forward, resting his arms on his knees.

"You did this for me," he said quietly as he stared at the floor.

"What?"

"You did this for me."

"I was worried about Lily, about everyone at Edgewood," she insisted.

He looked up, his eyes boring into hers. "You did this for me."

This time, it was a fact. A truth she felt. "Yes. I did."

Andrew hissed and jumped to his feet.

Ellen expected him to throw her out like he did when she told him about her adventures with Randolph Carter. She stood and started to gather her things. But when she headed for the door, he stepped in front of her, blocking her exit.

"Your phone. Give me your phone."

"What? Why?"

"Just give me your phone," he insisted, wagging his fingers impatiently.

She unlocked it and handed it to him.

Ellen studied him as he pecked at the screen. Andrew no longer reminded her of his grandfather. There were so many slight differences. His face was less rigid, and his hair a lighter brown. Then there was his mouth. Randolph Carter's rested in a permanent scowl, as if the world offended him. His grandson's mouth was less hostile. It curved up at the corners. A smile always lurked there, waiting to thaw.

Andrew thrust the phone back into her hands.

She glanced down at it and discovered a new name in her contact list.

"Drew Sinclair? Who's Drew Sinclair?"

"I'm Drew Sinclair. Sinclair is my mother's maiden name. Drew—"

She shook her head. "I knew you weren't an Andy. Your father kept calling you Andy."

"I can only imagine what else he called me," he grunted.

"At least you have a name. He kept calling me Andy's girl."

"What did you call him?"

"Oh, I think you can imagine."

The smile that lurked in the corner of his mouth blossomed. He nodded at the phone. "That's my private number," he informed her. "Maybe Tom will stop bugging me in the middle of the night if you have it."

"Tom?"

"Your boyfriend. You remember him, don't you?" he teased her.

Ellen flashed on the van when she and Joseph were preparing to enter Edgewood. Greg's reminder popped into her head. *I'm putting your phone on Do Not Disturb.* "Shit! Shit, shit, shit!" Ellen flicked off the setting, and voice mails flooded her phone, sounding off in a series of frantic pings.

Andrew snorted. "Maybe you should call him back."

"He broke up with me," she replied.

"Excuse me?"

"Tom broke up with me last night."

He nodded at the chirping phone. "That doesn't sound like someone who's an ex-boyfriend."

"He cheated on me. How does that sound?"

Andrew stiffened.

Ellen forced her anger back down. "I'm sorry. These last few weeks . . . they've been a real shit storm." She was about to change the subject when her mind caught on a jagged thought. "Wait a minute. Why does Tom have *your* phone number?"

He looked away, his eyes locking onto a spot just above her shoulder.

"Nothing gets by you, does it?" he grumbled.

"Andrew?"

His eyes returned to her. "Tom was the only way I could keep track of you."

Keep track of me? The words should have bothered her. They made her sound like a child, someone needing constant supervision. But Ellen wasn't mad. Last night's expedition had come close to disaster. If Andrew hadn't been there to tear open the gate, if he hadn't taken Greg to a doctor who knew what to do . . . *If, if, if.*

Ellen held out her hand. "I'm tired of the bullshit, too. Give me your phone."

"Not a good idea," he insisted. "If someone found your name on my—"

"Please. Give me some credit."

"Daphne Blake?" he said when she returned it.

"Everyone else around here has a fake name. I'm tired of being left out," she complained. "You remember Daphne from *Scooby Doo*, don't you? Danger-prone Daphne?"

Anger seeped into his eyes. "You think that's funny? After everything that's happened, you honestly think that's funny?"

Her throat closed. Only three words escaped: "I have to."

Andrew let out another frustrated hiss. "I have no way of repaying you for what you've done, for helping my father and everyone in Edgewood. You know that, right?" he said.

"You took care of me. And Greg. That's more than enough," she insisted. "How is he, by the way?"

"Already bossing people around. Why do you think I have all the microphones? He ordered me to retrieve them. Said it was time I did my part."

Ellen smiled. That sounded like Greg.

"Is he mad at me?" she asked.

Andrew shot her a sideways look. "Why would Greg be mad at you?"

"I'm the one who dragged him into this mess."

"You're also the one who pulled him out of it," he pointed out. "Don't take on any guilt that you don't have to, Ellen."

"What about Lily? The people at Edgewood?"

"They're okay. Freaked out, but okay," he assured her. "Apparently, one of the nurses decided it would be fun to add something special to the nighttime medicines. They're not sure how long it's been going on, but this time, the hallucinations were so strong, the residents called the police."

"Let me guess; they saw dogs running down the halls."

Andrew tilted his head, feigning surprise. "Now, how did you know that?"

Ellen's smile was tinged with sadness. She remembered Joseph's story about his grandmother, how no one believed her when she said something crawled across her face at night.

"He wanted to see again," Andrew said in a quiet voice.

Ellen frowned. "What?"

"My father. You wanted to know the reason he's in Edgewood. In the supposed Witch House," he replied. "When he was young, he went on journeys with my grandfather. He always claimed he hated them, but as he got older . . ."

"He wanted to be close to his father again," she murmured. "And all this time, I thought you put him there to punish him. To get revenge."

He glared at her. "He chose the place. Over *my* objections."

"Do you really think Edgewood is the Witch House?" she asked.

"I don't know. Mystical portals? Monsters? You tell me."

"Jesus," Ellen breathed as her eyes shifted to the curtain flapping in the breeze. She had never been this close to something from Lovecraft's world before.

She moved to the window and closed it.

"I want you to stay with me. At least for tonight," Andrew announced. "You need a place to lie low until we figure out what we're going to do next."

We.

With that single word, a weight lifted off Ellen's shoulders.

She wasn't alone anymore.

Chapter Ten

That night, as she slept under Andrew Carter's roof, Ellen dreamed of art. She drifted down a long hallway, watching while artists labored on their masterpieces. Pablo Picasso capturing the horror of Guernica. Goya working on his Black Paintings. Henry Fuseli bringing his demons to life. In a far corner lurked Cecil Conklin, the Appalachian Hieronymus Bosch. He slapped paint on an old cabinet door, his eyes flicking restlessly from side to side. The room was silent except for the frantic scribbling of pencils and the rasp of horsehair brushes. Ellen was struck by how violent the act of creation was. These men grappled with their visions, struggling to express things that defied the natural world.

Her mind drifted to Vincent van Gogh and *Wheat Field with Crows.* Not so much a landscape as a collapse of reality, a place where land and sky bled into each other.

I wonder if he saw thin places, too. I wonder if it drove him mad. Made him pick up a gun and kill himself.

Ellen shivered as she thought about her own visions, the reality no one believed.

Is this what happens to all dreamers?

A calloused hand grabbed her shoulder. Van Gogh stared at her with steely blue eyes. He pointed to the end of the hall, where a man stood in front of an easel.

"*Kijken*," he commanded her. When she hesitated, he pushed her toward the shadowy figure. "*Kijken!*"

The man at the easel was still. While the others scraped and scrubbed and pounded, his palette hung limply by his side. The artist was as pale as Joseph. Long, greasy hair spilled across his shoulders, brushing against his threadbare suit, the sleeves shiny with wear. He raised his hand and punched the canvas, watching the surface ripple under the force of his blows.

It's moving, she thought, *just like the painting in Edgewood. Right before . . .*

Hypnotized by the movement, Ellen moved closer. The man seized her arm and yanked her toward the blank canvas.

"Go through! Go through already!" he barked at her.

Ellen jerked, fighting his grip. With dead eyes, the artist watched as she tried to twist free. As if she were nothing more than a curiosity, a specimen to observe.

Psychopath, she thought as her heart thundered. *The man is a psychopath.*

The artist arched his eyebrow. "Psychopath? I'm not a psychopath." He leaned closer. "I'm beyond humanity." And he hurled her toward the easel.

Ellen passed through the canvas and into a bright-white world. Darkness appeared at her feet, bubbling out of the ground like oil. She backed away from the pool of muck.

Her eyes swept the empty room, searching for anything to climb onto.

"This is bad. This is really bad," she muttered. The painter reappeared and clucked at her. "How do you know?" he breathed in her ear, his breath as pungent as an open grave. "How do you know what's good and bad?"

Wake up, wake up . . . WAKE UP!

Ellen slammed hard into the waking world—twisting and turning, clutching her waist as she launched herself out of bed. The placid sound of crickets greeted her. Fragrant rosemary wafted in from a nearby garden. She took a long, deep breath and remembered.

Carter's house.

I'm in Andrew Carter's house.

She fumbled for her cell phone on the nightstand—3:46 a.m. Ellen climbed back into bed and tried to sleep. Every time she started to drift off, the painter leaped out of the darkness like a boogeyman.

She checked the time again: 4:05, 5:25, 6:00. Dawn crept into the room.

She gave up on sleep. She jumped out of bed, grabbed her journal, and headed downstairs. As she waited for coffee to brew, Ellen opened the book to a blank page and jotted down the contours of the nightmare: the long hall, the artists and their feverish attempts to bring their creations to life. But she couldn't remember the last painter, the one who threw her into the canvas. None of his features made much of an impression. He was the kind of guy who blended into a crowd. A man you could work with every day and yet be unable to describe.

The kind of guy who keeps bodies in his basement.

Ellen shivered, pushing away thoughts of Calvin Leonard.

She closed her eyes and concentrated. If there was such a thing as spirit writing, maybe there was spirit drawing, too. For a long time, her hand hovered over the blank page, motionless. Then, her hand twitched and leaped across the page. Features appeared. A chin, a mouth, a nose. And eyes, eerie, spectral eyes that seemed to float in place.

"What are you doing?"

Ellen yipped and scrambled to her feet. She stared at the drawing, half expecting the painter to pop out like a genie.

"What's with you, Ellen?" Andrew Carter grumbled as he headed for the coffee.

"I was just writing down a nightmare."

He glanced at the thick notebook.

"You must have a lot of them."

"There's also stuff about the Dreamlands. It's part of my therapy."

"Therapy?"

"If I write it down, I'll get it out of my system. At least that's what they say."

Andrew smirked. "What a great way to gather information."

Information. The thought never occurred to Ellen. She assumed the doctors were there to help her. That everything they did was for her benefit.

"Wait a minute. Don't doctors take a Hippocratic oath or something?"

His smile deepened. "You know, in some ways, you're very naive."

Ellen slammed the notebook shut. She was about to throw it across the room but spotted a piece of paper tucked between the pages. She grabbed the paper and unfolded it, smoothing it out on the kitchen table. The whiff of nicotine and musty books was strong.

Andrew pulled up a chair. "What's that?"

"The note Michael Sloane gave me."

He almost choked on his coffee. "Are you serious? You didn't tell me you had the note! Why didn't you tell me?"

"I don't know. Stress. Fatigue. Blind terror. Take your pick."

Andrew sat down beside her and studied the note. He frowned at the network of dashes and squiggles.

"Does any of it make sense?" she asked.

"I took math in college, but this?" He shook his head. "Out of my league." Andrew folded up the paper and stood. "We need to consult the experts."

Ellen glanced at the kitchen clock: 6:30.

"Isn't it kind of early?"

"You don't understand the people we're dealing with. They probably haven't gone to bed yet."

"Have you ever heard of Kurt Gödel?" Andrew Carter walked ahead of Ellen with a box of donuts.

Ellen's stomach rumbled in protest. She'd grabbed some coffee before they left the house, but nearly twelve hours had passed since she'd eaten. Now, he expected her mind to function.

"We're headed to the math department, so I'm guessing he was a mathematician," she replied, trying to ignore the smell of sugary dough. "Wait a minute. Is Gödel the guy Russell Crowe played in that movie?"

"That was John Nash," he said as he opened the door to one of Miskatonic University's ivy-encrusted buildings. "Gödel was a mathematical genius like Nash. He came up with the incompleteness theorem, which states that 'some truths can't be derived.' That in any logical system, there are some things that can never be proven."

Ellen thought of the New Age "science" they stocked at Mote It Be. She rolled her eyes. "I'm sure *that* idea never gets abused."

"Kurt Gödel's life revolved around math. He rarely thought of anything else. His wife cared for him through it all, even after his breakdowns. Even when he refused to eat anything but her food because he was afraid of being poisoned. When she got sick and was hospitalized for six months . . ."

Ellen saw the ending coming like a freight train. "You're kidding, right? You're making this up."

"He weighed sixty-five pounds when he died."

She fell into a stunned silence. "Wait a minute. I'm confused. What was the point of the story? That mathematicians are crazy?"

Andrew winced. "That was a bad example. Let me try again. Mathematicians live deep inside their heads. So deep, they sometimes forget they have other appetites. It's never a bad idea to bring them food."

"Can you stop for a sec?" Ellen asked when they reached the top of the stairs.

He paused on the landing.

Ellen opened the box and snatched a donut. "That story made me hungry."

He looked at her in disbelief. "Oh, great. Now I'm supposed to offer them a box with a donut missing?"

"There's eleven left. Eleven's a prime number," she pointed out as she took a bite. "That would appeal to them, don't you think?"

A lopsided grin spread across his face.

"I missed you, Ellen. You're a pain in the ass sometimes, but I missed you," Andrew said solemnly, the words a sharp contrast to his crooked smile.

A warm, alcoholic flush shot through her body. Up to this point, her interest in Andrew Carter had been theoretical, as abstract as the equations in Michael Sloane's note. Now, Ellen imagined getting to know him better, envisioned making love to him as something real, something that might happen. Something she *wanted* to happen. Ellen's eyes glanced off his body as questions surged through her mind. *What would he be like in bed? Would he be the man I know, or would he become someone different? Unfamiliar. And the whole psychic thing. How would that work?* Ellen wasn't a romantic. She knew sex with him would be challenging. Turbulent. Like trying to ride a riptide. She could imagine how alive she would feel. *Andrew Carter would bring out things in me I never—*

"Are you having a stroke?"

Ellen tumbled out of her fantasy to find him staring at her. A different kind of smile played on his lips.

He knows. Oh God, he knows what I'm thinking, and he's mocking me. She considered herself—dressed in boyish clothes, her mouth stuffed with a glazed donut.

Of course, he's mocking me! I mean, could someone like him really . . . ?

"I thought I heard your voice, Andrew."

Ellen pivoted, turning her attention to the man down the hall.

The man who approached them wore a generic outfit—khaki dress pants and a sensible button-up shirt. Ellen wondered whether he'd borrowed a page from Albert Einstein. Einstein wore the same outfit every day. He claimed it kept his mind clear, allowing him to devote his attention to more important things like time, space, and relativity.

Better to be like Einstein than the guy who starved to death.

Carter headed off to greet his colleague.

"Bear claws. Your favorite, if I remember correctly," he said, holding out the box.

The man accepted the offering. "Your memory amazes me, Andrew. You know, someone should study you. Peer inside that brain of yours."

The man watched as Ellen approached them. "And you are?"

She juggled her donut and offered him her hand. "Ellen. Ellen Logan."

His stare deepened.

Here it comes, she thought.

"Ellen Logan? The Ellen Logan who traveled to the Dreamlands?"

His response surprised her. Usually, people were only interested in Calvin Leonard. "That would be me."

"I envy you," he said with a sigh. "Tell me, what was it like?"

Ellen blinked. No one ever asked her about the Dreamlands, either. She searched for a way to describe that strange world. To capture its essence. "It was like trying to balance on a beach ball while someone sprays you with a fire hose."

The professor chuckled. "Fascinating. And time?"

"What do you mean?"

"Did time behave differently?"

Andrew interrupted them. "Kyle, there's something you need to look at. Do you have a minute?"

"Of course."

The man ushered them into a room that had once been two offices. Whiteboards densely packed with symbols ringed the wall. In the far corner, a couple of students conferred around one.

Ellen nodded at the murmuring students. "Hard at work deriving equations, I see."

The professor shook his head.

"Actually, they're in the process of agreeing on a formalism. After that comes the equations, and then we'll check whether someone has solved them already," he explained, ushering her to the chair beside his desk.

"What are they working on?" Andrew asked as he grabbed a cheap metal chair and joined them.

"The Keziah Mason formulae."

Keziah Mason. The name was familiar, but Ellen wasn't sure where she heard it.

"You know, you never did introduce yourself," she said to keep the conversation going.

"Oh, I'm sorry. I'm Dr. Kyle Donovan, professor of algebraic topology."

"Sounds deep."

He smiled. "It is deep. You never answered my question about time, Miss Logan."

"To be honest, I didn't understand what you were asking."

"According to the police reports, you were missing for two weeks. How long did it feel like to you?"

"Kyle," Andrew warned him.

"It's okay." Ellen fell silent as she traced her journey through the alternate world. "Months. It felt like months."

"Interesting. That would suggest—"

"Kyle, we're here for a reason."

"Oh, yes. I'm sorry. What did you want to talk about?"

Andrew glanced at her. "It's your story. Tell it."

They had decided earlier how much she should say and agreed on two things—no mention of ghouls or travelers from other dimensions.

"I have a friend who lives in Edgewood Manor. I don't know if you've heard of it. It's a retirement home near Arkham Grove."

"I know Arkham Grove," Dr. Donovan offered.

"My friend's a history nut, and well, Edgewood is packed with it. She was rummaging around in the basement a few days ago and found this." Ellen handed the professor the note. "It looks like math. When I showed it to Andrew, he thought you might know what it was."

Dr. Donovan slipped on his reading glasses, examined the crumpled piece of paper, and peered at her. "What does it look like to you?"

"I know this sounds stupid, but it reminds me of those *Family Circus* cartoons. You know, the ones where Billy wanders around, and you follow his footprints."

"*Family Circus*? Seriously, Ellen?" Andrew scoffed.

"Actually, she's not too far off. It looks like a map."

He frowned. "Really? Of what?"

"I'm not sure. There's no reference point. No cardinal directions. Without those, maps are useless." He took a closer look. "There's also a lot of notational drift."

Dr. Donovan anticipated their question.

"Math is a language," he explained. "Like any language, some words and phrases fix you at a certain place and time. Groovy. Far out. Bitchin'. What you brought me looks old."

"How old?" Andrew blurted.

"Early twentieth century." Dr. Donovan's eyes drifted over the note, following the squiggles and wild curves. When he reached the bottom of the note, he grew pale and slammed the paper on the desk.

The students in the corner stopped what they were doing to look at him.

"No, no. It can't be," Dr. Donovan muttered.

Carter leaned forward. "What is it?"

"If I didn't know better, I'd swear this is the work of Michael Sloane."

Ellen dug her fingers into the arms of her chair, desperate to hold on to something solid. Something to keep her grounded in this world.

One of the students looked up from the whiteboard. "Michael Sloane? Are you kidding me? I thought he was made up."

"Who's Michael Sloane?" Ellen asked.

"He was one of our graduate students back in the 1920s. The best mind this department had. *Ever.*" The professor paused as if to let the statement register. "He was our Ramanujan."

She frowned. "Rama-who?"

"Ramanujan—an Indian mathematician. The man had no formal training, but he created number theory, string theory, a lot of the stuff we use today. When people asked him how he did it, Ramanujan said God gave him the answers. Michael Sloane—"

"His inspiration came from somewhere less . . . divine," one student cracked.

Donovan glared at him.

"Sloane was a brilliant man," Donovan continued. "A natural. He was also deeply disturbed. As his condition grew worse, his math suffered. He . . ."

"He would have scored high on the crackpot index," the second student offered.

"Crackpot index?" Ellen frowned. "What's that?"

Dr. Donovan rummaged in his desk and handed her a laminated sheet of paper.

"John Baez at UC Riverside came up with a list of things that might indicate a person is less than, um, scientific in their claims. I don't know if the crackpot index was meant as a joke, but it's proven very useful here at Miskatonic."

Ellen and Andrew studied the handout.

"Ten points for mailing your theory to someone you don't know and asking them not to tell anyone else about it, for fear your ideas will be stolen," he read.

"Thirty points for claiming your theories were developed by an extraterrestrial civilization," Ellen countered. "Another thirty points if there was a delay in your work while you spent time in an asylum or there are references to the psychiatrist who tried to talk you out of your theory."

Andrew chuckled. "Hell. Some of my colleagues would score high on this."

While they examined the crackpot index, Dr. Donovan continued to eye Michael Sloane's note. He glanced at it in quick bursts, almost as if he was afraid of taking in too much at once. Then his eyes settled on a spot. His body jerked, and he jumped to his feet and rushed to an ancient filing cabinet.

Ellen leaned closer to Andrew.

"What's going on?" she whispered as Donovan yanked out a paper and marched to the whiteboard where his two students were gathered.

"No idea."

Math poured out of Dr. Donovan. He didn't use chalk; the equations squeaked out of a dry-erase pen. Still, Michael

Sloane's rhythm was there—the tapping, the frantic Morse code. She thought about her earlier encounter with Michael Sloane—how when he grabbed her, jagged shapes pierced her skull.

Was I seeing his math in my head? Could I . . . ?

Her eyes locked on Dr. Donovan's back. A cluster of lines swam in her head. At first, they appeared to be random. Then, as Ellen "watched," Donovan twisted them. The lines came together to form a passage.

"Thin place," Ellen murmured as she rose to her feet. "Those equations. They're about creating a thin place."

Dr. Donovan paused mid-equation, his pen hovering in the air. "Now, how would you know that?"

Watch out, she thought. *You're giving away too much.*

"Aren't thin places the Holy Grail?" she chirped, trying to make the question sound as light as she could. "What everyone at Miskatonic seeks?"

"Not *everyone* at Miskatonic," he sniffed. "And we don't call them thin places. That's a New Age term."

"What do you call them?" Andrew asked.

"Eldritch tensors," one of the students offered. "You see, the idea is—"

Professor Donovan silenced the man with a lethal gaze.

The mood in the room darkened. Only a moment ago, they were fellow academics in search of answers. Now, the professor and his students huddled close together, their bodies blocking the scribbled notes on the whiteboard.

Like we would know what it meant without their help, Ellen thought.

Andrew Carter felt the change in the atmosphere. His expression became less collegial, and he advanced on Dr. Donovan. "I need that note back," he said softly, as if speaking to a child.

"You can't have it," Dr. Donovan snapped.

Ellen's phone hummed, and she glanced at the screen.

She shot Andrew an apologetic look. "I need to take this. Are you going to be okay?"

"I'll be fine," he assured her, his eyes never leaving the mathematicians.

"You sure?"

"Go."

She drifted into the hall.

"Hey, Greg. How are you? Are you feeling better? When does the doctor say you can come home?"

Her friend chuckled. "Jesus, Logan, so many questions!"

"Sorry." Ellen paused before she settled on the one that mattered. "How do you feel?"

"Like shit," he admitted. "The doctor wants to keep me here a little longer, just in case . . . well, he won't tell me why. Dr. Caligari is pretty tight-lipped."

"Most twilight doctors are."

"Twilight doctor?" he echoed. "You mean . . . you found me a twilight doctor?"

"I didn't. Andrew did."

"Andrew?"

"Andrew Carter. You know, the Big Guy?"

Stunned silence greeted her.

"Still think he's an asshole?" Ellen teased her friend.

"Okaaay. I may have to reconsider my opinion." Greg admitted. "Anyway, forget that. That's not why I called. Joe brought me the recordings we made at Edgewood so that I could go through them."

"Wait a minute. You're working from your sickbed?"

"The doc said it was okay as long as I got some rest."

Ellen smiled. Her friend was on the mend.

"I picked up a conversation. Between some guy and the man who helped you plant the devices. What was his name?"

Ice water trickled down Ellen's spine. "Robert," she breathed.

"You need to hear it."

Andrew stormed out of the mathematician's office, phone plastered to his ear.

"I'll be over as soon as I'm done here," she told Greg.

"Here? Where's here?"

Ellen hung up and chased Andrew Carter down the hall.

"Andrew? Andrew?" she called out.

He spun around and pressed his finger to his lips. "Yes. Yes. Of course. I will."

"Was that the cops?" she asked when he finished. "Did you call the cops?"

Andrew frowned. "The cops? Why would I call the cops?"

"They were trying to steal the note!"

"Let me get this straight. You thought I was calling the cops because some mathematicians took a note?"

"It's dangerous. Leaving the note with them," she insisted. "Didn't you see the gleam in Dr. Donovan's eyes? I'm sure that scores high on the crackpot index."

He stopped and glared at her.

"What was I supposed to do? Leave it with *you*?"

Ellen bit her lip, stung by the slight.

Joshua's voice taunted her.

Your refills are piling up.

Andrew nodded at his cell phone. "That was Miss Strauss. I've been summoned to a meeting. Apparently, my car was caught on a security camera tearing down the gates of Arkham Grove."

"Shit!" Ellen cursed. "You want me to come with you?"

"And do what? Threaten to sue again?"

Ellen's mouth curved into a smile. "Okay, okay. Maybe going another round with Miss Strauss isn't such a great idea," she admitted. "It's just as well. Greg called. He has something he wants me to listen to."

"Keep me informed."

"Okay."

Andrew reached out and squeezed her arm. "I mean it, Ellen. Don't shut me out of this." The physical contact made her tingle. Desperate to hide her reaction, Ellen jerked free from his grip.

"Don't worry. I'll keep you in the loop," she promised. "Good luck with Miss Strauss."

Chapter Eleven

"You know, we're not a hospital. We don't *do* visiting hours."

A middle-aged woman blocked the entrance to the twilight doctor's house. At first, Ellen thought she was a nurse, but her attitude went way beyond professional inconvenience. Resentment oozed out of every pore—that and a fine layer of sweat. Ellen glanced at the woman's outfit. Expensive yoga pants, sneakers, a complicated sports bra. She had clearly interrupted the woman's workout.

This is the doctor's wife.

Ellen felt a pang of sympathy. She couldn't imagine what it would be like to be a twilight doctor's wife. To see such horribly injured people dragged into your home. Into the one place a person should feel safe.

God, the cleanup alone . . .

As the woman drummed her fingers on the door, jewels glinted off the rings on her fingers. Ellen frowned. *She doesn't clean things up,* she thought. *She pays people to do the dirty work.*

"The doctor said I could drop by."

"I don't care what—"

"For God's sake, Rose, let her in!" a voice boomed.

The woman sneered but opened the door a little wider.

Ellen still had to push her way into the house.

Dr. Caligari came striding down the hall, coffee mug in hand. "Finally! Maybe you can explain the idea of bed rest to your friend."

"Maybe you can get him out of here," Rose suggested.

The doctor shot her a cool look. "Why don't you go back to your Pilates?"

The woman stormed off, disappearing into the depths of the house.

Dr. Caligari studied Ellen as he took a sip of coffee. "You're looking better."

"I'm feeling better."

"I don't suppose you'd let me take a look at you, just to make sure?"

Ellen agreed to a quick exam. She felt sorry for the guy. The man had his hands full between his Pilates-loving wife and Greg. Giving him peace of mind cost her nothing.

Once they were in his office, she perched herself on his table, but he made no move to examine her.

"Why is your friend so interested in Edgewood?" Before she could reply, Dr. Caligari cut her off. "Don't bother denying it. He's been hard at work all day."

Ellen cursed. She could imagine Greg banging away on his laptop, oblivious to the doctor's presence. She gazed at the floor, considering her words. *Well, Doctor, there's this thin place and a missing mathematician.* It sounded like a bad joke. A dangerous joke. The last thing she needed was another doctor questioning her sanity.

"Miss Logan?"

"I'm not sure," Ellen answered.

"What?"

"I have no idea what Greg is doing."

"Would it surprise you that the state is investigating Edgewood Manor?"

Ellen looked up. "For what?"

"Medical irregularities."

"What does that mean?"

"You tell me."

Ellen thought about the Alzheimer's patients and the locked doors, and the other doors held open by cinder blocks. A surge of relief coursed through her. *Whistleblower. He's looking for a whistleblower.* That wasn't her part to play. Joe planned to do it. *He may have done it already.*

"I don't know anything about medical irregularities, Dr. Caligari."

The man clicked his tongue. "You Miskatonic people. Liars. Every single one of you." He drained the last of his coffee and thumped the mug on the desk. "Come on. Let's get this over with."

Ellen cocked her head. "No examination, then?"

"No," Dr. Caligari shot back as he headed for the door, his curiosity extinguished.

He led her through a warren of small bedrooms upstairs. In one of them, she found Greg, propped up on a mountain of pillows, his bandaged foot elevated. He had headphones on, his head bobbing to a noiseless beat as he tapped on his laptop.

Ellen shook her head. *Oblivious.* She should have been mad, but seeing him there, being so Greg . . . She ran to the bed and threw her arms around him. All the stress of the past few days melted, swept away by a torrent of tears.

"Whoa! Jesus!" her friend shouted.

"Don't reinjure my patient, Miss Logan," the doctor said dryly.

As if she could cram the emotions back inside, she clapped her hand over her mouth and pulled away.

"Sorry. Sorry, sorry," she apologized to the blurry blob that was Dr. Caligari.

"Ten minutes," he said as he left the room.

Ten minutes, she told herself. Ellen tried to pull herself together, but the tears started again every time her eyes settled on Greg. Along with all the what-ifs. *What if the bite had been deeper? What if Joe hadn't come when he did? What if the doctor hadn't been home?*

"Logan."

What if, what if, what if. The questions swirled, making her dizzy.

Greg reached out and took her hand. "Ellen."

She looked up. He never called her Ellen.

"It's okay. *I'm* okay. You got it?" He squeezed her hand.

More tears threatened to spill. Ellen pushed them back. "You scared the hell out of me, you bastard."

He tossed her a box of Kleenex and watched her mop her face.

"You know, you're an ugly crier."

"Shut up," she sniffed.

"You almost showered me in snot."

"Shut. Up." This time, the words came out as a titter.

"And have you gained weight? God, it felt like a football player hit me."

"I said *shut up*, Greg."

They looked at each other and dissolved into laughter. Ellen savored the sweetness of the moment. She needed it.

"So, what are you so eager to share with me?" she asked once she recovered.

Before he could reply, she leaned over and typed into his computer.

Don't say anything. The doctor might be listening.

Greg handed her his headphones.

His fingers darted across the keyboard.

Recorded in Robert's room the morning after our stakeout.

As the recording started, Ellen leaned forward unconsciously. She expected she would have to eavesdrop on the conversation. But the voices blasted into her ears. They were clear. Distinct. The men sounded like they were right next to her.

"I'm putting an end to this," Robert Carter snarled. "Innocent lives are in danger."

"Innocent people are *always* in danger," another man replied. "That's the nature of the business. You, of all people, should know that."

A moment of silence. Then a question from the stranger. "Do you really think they're coming through to—"

"No. They're coming to book a room at Edgewood! To make the most of their golden years."

Ellen shifted on the bed.

The stranger's voice sounded familiar.

"You need to move that thing," Robert Carter insisted. "They're getting bolder. If your girl hadn't been there with her friends—"

The stranger cut in. "Ellen's involved in this?"

The skin on the back of her neck prickled. *Joshua.*

The man with Robert Carter was her uncle.

"Bastard!" she hissed.

"What? What is it?" Greg demanded.

Ellen waved him off.

"—dare back out of this now," Joshua threatened Andrew's father. "I warned you about the dangers. I took you through everything that was involved. Soup to nuts."

Her stomach dropped. *Soup to nuts.* That was one of her uncle's favorite sayings. Plucked from the Patrick O'Brien books he loved so much.

It's Joshua.

"I don't care what you *took* me through," Robert growled. "I want that thing out of Edgewood. Now!"

Another moment of silence.

"Okay! Okay! I'll make some calls!" Joshua relented. "But it might take a while."

"Just get it out of here."

Ellen ripped off her headphones and stared at what Greg typed before playing the clip.

Recorded in Robert's room the morning after our stakeout.

She tried to calculate how much time had passed since the conversation. Ellen bit her lip. *Twelve hours at least,* she thought. "I have to go," she murmured as she hopped off the bed.

"Be careful."

"Always."

Her friend grabbed her wrist. "No. Look at me, Logan. Be careful. That man Robert's talking to. He sounds like a serious criminal."

"Criminal?"

Joshua?

"'I warned you about the dangers. Let me make some calls,'" her friend quoted the conversation. "Whatever they're doing, this isn't that man's first time."

Joshua, a . . . . Ellen pushed away the thought. She had to get to Edgewood Manor. She hoped she wasn't too late.

Chapter Twelve

Ellen texted Andrew Carter as she speed-walked across Arkham. She smiled at the sight of their fake identities.

Daphne Blake: I'm onto something. Going back to Edgewood.

Drew Standish: Wait for me.

Daphne: Can't. Time is essential. You still in bureaucratic hell?

Drew: How'd you guess? Hope this won't take another twelve hours.

Daphne: I know a lawyer if you need one, Drew.

Drew: Oh, so I'm Drew now?

Daphne: That IS the name on your account.

"Miss Logan?"

Ellen glanced up from her screen.

Nurse Worden stood by Edgewood's mailbox.

She tapped off a quick farewell and pocketed her phone.

"What are you doing here?" the woman asked as she approached.

"I heard something strange happened the other night," Ellen offered, using the explanation she'd rehearsed on the way over. "I wanted to make sure Lily was okay. You know how easily she gets scared."

The woman's eyes narrowed. "What did you hear?"

"Something about monsters and party drugs. It didn't make a lot of sense."

Nurse Worden chuckled, but her amusement didn't last long. Her eyes locked on a van headed toward them. It had a cartoon of a stooped old man on the side. The logo reminded her of Father Time. *Geras Enterprises*, the name above it read.

Nurse Worden's face tightened.

"I was wondering when they'd show up," she muttered.

"Who are they?"

"Corporate. About to pay a surprise visit to the problem child." The woman grabbed Ellen's arm and pulled her toward Edgewood. "Look, I don't know what you're up to with Robert, and I don't care," Nurse Worden declared. "You need to get your stuff out of the basement."

"My stuff?" Ellen echoed.

"Robert said it would only be a week or two, until you got your living situation straightened out."

Stuff? Living situation?

The woman scowled as they walked into the house. "You don't know what I'm talking about, do you?"

A voice screamed in Ellen's head. *Say something, you idiot!*

She smacked her forehead.

"Oh my God, is this where I left my stuff? I was wondering where it went!"

"Wondering?"

"I just broke up with a guy. It was sudden," she explained. "I didn't have much time to plan anything, so I left some things with friends and family. I completely forgot I left some here. With Robert."

"Well, I need you to get your stuff out of here before those corporate drones start buzzing around."

"Of course. How much is there?"

"You don't remember?"

Ellen shrugged, shooting her an apologetic look. "Like I said, it was a real sudden breakup. I've been kind of spaced."

Nurse Worden paused at the door to the basement. The potted plant still stood sentry. Ellen tried not to look at the microphone poking out of the dry soil.

You missed one, Andrew, she thought, her mouth curling into a smile.

Miss Worden stared at her for a long time, then fished out her key ring.

"Move that plant, will you?" she asked Ellen as she sorted through her collection.

Ellen glanced at the potted plant that blocked the door. A wave of nausea rose in her throat.

The basement. She wants me to go into the basement.

Her mind swam with visions of bodies. Chunks of people in various stages of assembly. Calvin Leonard's "projects."

"Miss Logan?"

Outside, car doors slammed. Ellen gnawed on her lip. Took a deep breath.

Miss Worden pushed the potted plant aside.

"The inside knob is unlocked, but once you leave, you won't be able to get back in. The light switch is just inside. On the right," Nurse Worden instructed as she opened the door to darkness. "Got it?"

Ellen nodded.

The woman's expression softened. "I know what happened to you, Miss Logan. But you're okay. This isn't the same place."

No, Ellen thought. *This is a brand-new nightmare.*

"Go," Nurse Worden urged her.

Ellen took a deep breath and crossed the threshold. Before she could think twice, the door shut behind her. She heard a rustling sound as Miss Worden slid the plant back in place. Ellen made a mental note not to fall over it when she left.

For a long time, she didn't move. Her back pressed to the door, Ellen lingered at the top of the stairs and waited for her eyes to adjust. She took a few more deep breaths to calm her thundering heart. In the distance, she heard the front door open and a muffled, intense conversation. The floors creaked as Nurse Worden led the visitors down the hall.

Did the woman have anyone to help her?

Was she facing this all alone?

All alone, she thought as the smell of concrete filled her nose. *Just like I was when . . .*

Ellen's heart raced. "Not the same place," she whispered, echoing Miss Worden's words. "This isn't the same place."

At least I know where the mystery item is, she told herself. *I won't have to spend time searching every square inch of Edgewood.*

But what am I looking for? How will I know if I find it?

Ellen punched the light switch.

The place had been cleaned up since the night they chased the ghoul. Industrial-size boxes had been rearranged in neat piles, grouped according to need. Food, cleaning supplies, medical supplies, office supplies . . .

The boxes changed as she moved deeper into the basement. The "problem" section started—adult diapers, enemas, creams for warts and hemorrhoids. Ellen saw the portable toilets, and her nose wrinkled.

When she turned away, she spotted it. A thin object wedged between boxes of laxatives and mineral oil. She maneuvered carefully around the bathroom equipment and wiggled the thing out of its hiding place. It was a crate. A tall, thin crate.

The label on it read:

Ellen Logan
c/o Edgewood Manor
Arkham, MA

Ellen shuddered. It felt like she'd walked into a stranger's house and discovered a shrine devoted to her.

THUNK.

A sound came from deep in the basement. And underneath that, skittering. *Mice? Or . . .*

Ellen crouched beside the package, her eyes sweeping the gloom. A message chimed on her cell phone. She yelped, almost falling on her butt.

Ellen silenced her phone as she glanced at the message.

Drew Standish: Updates?

Her fingers flew across the screen.

Daphne: I found something in the basement. A package addressed to me. Apparently,
some of "my stuff" has been stored here for a
while. And I don't remember putting it there.
Imagine that . . .
Drew: I don't like this.
Daphne: Me either.

The sound of scraping. Louder this time. Ellen ducked between some cardboard boxes, taking the mysterious package with her. Just as she nestled into her hiding place, a shadowy figure emerged.

The tunnel, she thought. *Someone or something is coming out of the tunnel from Arkham Grove.*

A clamor of voices rose outside the basement door.

"Nothing to see down there," she heard Miss Worden announce loudly. "Just a bunch of—"

"Open the door," a man commanded.

Ellen heard the jingle of keys, followed by the thunder of feet on the stairs. She opened her mouth to warn Miss Worden about the intruder, but before she could say anything, Miss Worden's nursing shoes squeaked to a sudden stop. A startled sound escaped from the woman's lips.

"Oh, you," she exclaimed. "What are you doing here?"

Ellen peered from her hiding place as the mysterious figure stepped into the light. Tall. Pale skin . . .

Joseph Turner.

Ellen scowled. *What the hell is he doing here?*

"I'm looking for some documents. For my thesis," Greg's friend explained. "Lily told me they might be down here. This is where you keep the historical records, right?"

"Umm . . ." was all Miss Worden could manage.

The official shot Joseph a sharp look.

"Are you an employee here?" he demanded.

"No, but I'm working on—"

"I don't care what you're *working* on. If you're not an employee, you're trespassing." The man consulted someone Ellen couldn't see. "Escort this gentleman off the property."

As Joseph was led away, the official turned to Nurse Worden.

"Nothing to see down here, huh?"

"I'm as surprised as you are."

"Which is exactly why I'm here," he insisted, his voice dripping with smugness. "Is there anyone else hiding down here?"

Ellen held her breath and waited to be discovered. She wouldn't blame Nurse Worden for giving her up. After all, her job was on the line.

"There is nothing else down here, sir."

"Good," the man replied, oblivious to the contempt in Nurse Worden's voice. "Let's see if there are other surprises upstairs, shall we?"

Ellen waited a few minutes before she crawled out of her hiding place. As she stretched her aching muscles, she weighed her options. Leaving through the front door was out. The Edgewood officials had already discovered an "intruder." Their guard was up. For all she knew, they posted someone to keep watch during the rest of their visit.

And if they saw her walking out with a package . . .

Ellen sighed, her eyes drifting to the tunnel's gaping mouth.

Joseph Turner just came out of there. That means the passage is open, doesn't it?

"No way," she whispered. "No fucking way."

Yes way, a voice responded. *The only way.*

A vibration jolted Ellen out of her reflection.

Drew: What's going on?

A wobbly laugh escaped from her lips.

She ignored the question and pecked out one of her own.

Daphne: Where are you?

Drew: Arkham Grove. Discussing how the university will replace the gate. At my expense, of course . . .

Arkham Grove.

Yes way, she thought again. *The only way.*

Daphne: Did you drive there? Is your car in the graveyard?

The pause seemed like a lifetime.

Drew: Yes. Why?

Daphne: Can you unlock it? I'm trapped in the basement. My way out is through the tunnel. Tell me where your car is parked. I'm going to sneak into the back seat.

More time passed.

Ellen shifted back and forth, rubbing at the stiffness in her legs.

Drew: Unlocked it. Just heard it chirp. It's on the lane near the stone angel. You know where that is?

She sighed in relief. She and Joseph had carried Greg past the statue the night he was injured.

Daphne: Yes. See you on the other side . . .

Drew: Be careful. Strauss is here.

Ellen let out a long sigh. Going through the tunnel was bad enough.

Ms. Strauss at the end of it?

Ellen stared at the opening and took a deep breath.

Positive thinking, she told herself.

Of all the things her psychiatrist taught her, it was the last thing she expected to work. Positive thinking had no place in Ellen's world. The worst-case scenarios were what you planned for at Miskatonic University. What you trained for.

"'Let the eye of vigilance never be closed,'" Ellen murmured.

Miskatonic words of wisdom borrowed from a founding father.

Ellen closed her eyes and imagined the next steps—plotting her journey in the warm glow of positive thinking. *No complications. Through the opening, down the passage. Down a* dark *passage,* she corrected herself, *but the cell phone will throw enough light. And there will be no ghouls. Joseph came through, and he had no problems.*

And if the passage out of the tomb is closed?

You just turn around, she told herself. *You turn around and come back and wait until the inspectors leave.*

"I can do this. No problem," she whispered. She picked up her package and headed into the tunnel. *Through the opening, down the passage.*

An earworm stirred.

Over the river and through the woods
To Grandmother's house we go.
Hopefully, there are no wolves in Grandmother's house.
"You're mixing up your stories," she scolded her brain.

The muddy ground had been churned since the last time she was there. Everywhere she looked, she saw footprints—a frantic crossroads of activity. Ellen studied the tracks. She wondered whether there had been more commotion since their night in Edgewood.

Did the ghouls visit regularly? What were they doing? What did they want?

In the darkness behind her, she heard a splash.

Something falling from the ceiling or . . . ?

"Keep moving," she ordered herself.

Ellen picked up the pace. The package she carried wasn't heavy, but it was bulky and hard to handle. She had to stop several times to shift the load in her arms. Every time she did, her fear ratcheted up another notch. The tunnel wasn't like the basement where she was held captive, but it smelled like it. The air was thick with a wet, earthy stench.

Her heart batted against her ribs like a frightened bird.

THUNK.

This time, the sound came from her head—a baseball bat connecting with human flesh. *You swung the bat,* a voice whispered, *at one of Leonard's victims. You killed . . .*

The spray-painted accusation flashed before her eyes.

WHERE IS SOLOMON REYE?

Ellen clutched the package tighter and ran. The passage seemed to be changing, stretching and contorting like a funhouse mirror. She'd counted the steps the first time she entered. The tunnel was only a hundred feet long. She knew she should be reaching the end soon.

All she saw was darkness, bathed in the bluish glare of her cell phone light. Ellen glanced at the walls. Not just blue. Purple streaks trickled down the muddy surface.

Thin place, she thought. *A thin place is opening.*

A startled bark escaped her throat. "No. Please, *please . . .*"

Visions of being kidnapped, pulled unwillingly into the Dreamlands, filled her head.

A rectangle of light appeared ahead—the exit to the tomb.

Ellen dove for the passage, tossed the package through the narrow gap, and scrambled after it. As she crossed the threshold, her foot caught on something, and she fell.

Pain shot through her knee. Ellen looked down at her leg, half expecting to see a ghoul leering at her. It was a brick holding open the hidden door.

Joseph? Again? Ellen wondered.

She kicked the brick free.

The door ground shut, separating her from the thin place.

I hope . . .

"Positive thinking. Positive thinking," Ellen panted.

She crawled over to retrieve the package. One side was dented, but it was otherwise intact. She curled up on the floor of the tomb and waited. Waited to catch her breath. Waited for her panic to subside. Waited . . .

To hear something from the thin place clawing on the door.

There was only silence. The calm of the dead, long since buried.

Adrenaline slowly leeched from her body.

Ellen's focus drifted in the gloom. In the far corner, she spotted a sleeping bag. Beside it sat a backpack and some cans of food. She scrambled to her feet and hobbled over to the makeshift camp. The name on the backpack didn't surprise her.

Joseph P. Turner.

Her phone buzzed.

Drew: Where are you? Meeting wrapping up.

Can't stay much longer.

The midafternoon sun blinded Ellen as she emerged from the tomb. Getting to Carter's car without being seen was easy. The grass and weeds were high enough to conceal her. She didn't need to crouch, which was a good thing. Ellen could feel her knee swelling, straining against her cargo pants. She hobbled over to Andrew's Range Rover. She could see Andrew and Miss Strauss a few rows away in the cemetery. Their backs were turned, and Ellen could tell by their gestures they were having an intense conversation.

Good. Keep that woman occupied, she thought as she quietly popped open the back door of the SUV.

A wave of heat rushed out to greet her.

No air-conditioning, she thought as she slid the package into the Range Rover. *Terrific.*

"Beggars can't be choosers," she murmured as she climbed into Andrew's SUV, shut the door, and tossed a blanket over herself and the package.

She instantly regretted it. The inside was oven-hot.

As she broiled in the car, she heard the crunch of gravel and Miss Strauss's strident voice.

"—need to stop acting like a new faculty member. You're a tenured professor. You have nothing to prove."

"It's not about proving things," Andrew Carter insisted. "I have to be there when the students need me."

"No. You have to be there when *she* needs you."

She. Ellen knew Miss Strauss was talking about her.

"It was too dark to see any figures clearly, but I know she's a part of this," the woman continued. "Tell me, is it worth it? Is she worth all this trouble?"

"Look, Cathy. I'm hot. And I'm tired of getting the bureaucratic first degree."

"All right, all right," Miss Strauss relented. "You've been lectured. You've been warned. The next time won't be as pleasant."

"Pleasant? This was pleasant?"

"Even you can be replaced, Andrew." The words dripped with venom.

Carter said nothing as he threw himself into the driver's seat and turned on the car.

Bong, bong, bong.

"You left the door open," he announced.

"I didn't want to slam it," she replied from her hiding place. "You could have at least cracked a window."

"I suppose you wanted me to leave a bowl of water, too."

Water. She smacked her parched lips. "I would kill for some water."

The car rocked as Andrew got back out. He tossed her his bottle before he slammed the door.

Ellen downed half of it, the coldness cramping her throat. "Thanks," she croaked when he got back into the car.

"You're a pain in the ass, you know that?"

"You've told me that a few times," she replied.

He let out a long hiss. "Where am I taking you?"

"*Us.* Where are you taking *us,*" she corrected him. "We're going to my place. To see what's in the box."

Chapter Thirteen

The creature raised its sword above its head, its jackal-like face twisted in triumph. A crowd gathered at the base of the altar. They leaned forward in anticipation, ears pricked, teeth bared. They waited for the blow to land, the deed to be done.

Ellen studied the painting as she wandered in from the bathroom down the hall.

"Opening a package that isn't addressed to you? That's against the law, you know," Ellen announced as she toweled off her hair.

Andrew Carter gave her a crooked smile. "You going to turn me in?"

"I'll let you off with a warning this time," she replied. She didn't mind. After Arkham Grove, she desperately needed a shower. To wash away the sweat and grime, to change into fresh shorts and a shirt . . . it was worth it to let Andrew open her "present."

Ellen stared at the picture propped on the bed.

"You're hurt," he said in a quiet voice.

She glanced at her battered knee. "It wasn't easy dragging *that* out of Edgewood. And I sort of had a panic attack when I was in the tunnels."

Andrew pulled up a chair and guided her into it. "Wait here. I'll be right back."

Ellen squirmed. She didn't want to be left alone with the painting. It wasn't a new experience. Her uncle Joshua dealt in strange art. Some works were so intense, they drove her from the house. This was different. There wasn't anything actively evil about the painting. The mob of monsters, the lead figure (*a priest?* she wondered) wielding a sword over a fiery altar adorned with skulls—the canvas dripped with violence. But Ellen felt no threat. Even the creature in the corner of the painting, turning toward the viewer with its teeth bared, seemed more startled than menacing. It was as if the artist had stumbled onto a secret ritual and had captured the image.

No, it wasn't threatening.

Not yet.

It's the moment before, she thought. *The moment before the creature grabs the artist. Before they toss him into the fire.*

Ellen leaned forward, drawn to the altar's red glare. The light flickered, casting shadows on the wall. She yelped and hopped to her feet.

"Ellen?"

Andrew Carter stood beside her with a bag of ice.

She rubbed her eyes.

"Wow! That painting packs quite a punch. For a second, I thought the flames were crackling in the fire," she said, trying to pass it off as a joke.

He stared at her, stone-faced.

She nodded at the ice. "Is that for me?"

"Uh-huh," he grunted as he passed the bag to her.

Andrew sat down on the floor, planting himself between piles of her dirty laundry.

At first, she had no idea what he was doing, but then she realized. *He's trying to see things through my eyes.* A rush of affection rose inside her, sudden and sweet. Ellen stepped toward him.

"It's an illusion," he blurted.

She froze in her tracks. "What?"

"The fire moving. It's a visual illusion. A pretty good one." He pointed at the canvas. "The artist lined up the holes in the cave so that your eyes focus on the ghoul at the altar. And the flames are painted at an angle, suggesting a gust of air. Your brain fills in the rest."

Her brain latched on to a single word. "Ghoul?"

He nodded at the figures in the painting. "Those are ghouls."

Ellen frowned at the creatures. "They don't look like ghouls," she insisted. "Not like the ones I saw in Edgewood. Not like—"

Andrew looked at her. "Don't censor yourself, Ellen," he said quietly. "Not with me."

"They're not like the ones I saw in the Dreamlands."

"Ghouls aren't a distinct group," he replied. "Some of them aren't even the same species. They have a lot of evolutionary branches. Just like us."

Like us. The words crawled up Ellen's skull like a poisonous spider.

A map of human evolution popped into her head. Things had been straightforward only a few years ago—everything mapped out in clear, easy-to-follow steps. *Australopithecus* to *Homo erectus* to *Homo sapiens.* Now, the family tree spread like a web of broken glass—*Paranthropus aethiopicus, Paranthropus robustus, Paranthropus boisei. Homo habilis, Homo ergaster, Homo heidelbergensis, Homo longi.*

Ellen spotted two figures standing to the right of the crowd. "Why are there humans in the painting?" she asked.

Andrew glanced up from the canvas. "Huh?"

Ellen pointed at the robed women. "There are two humans. Off to the side."

He rose from the floor to get a better look and stumbled over a pile of dirty clothes.

"Jesus, Ellen! Do you *ever* do laundry?"

Ellen looked away, cheeks burning. "It depends."

"On what?"

"On whether I have the money. If it's between food and clean clothes . . ." She let the sentence trail off.

"Why don't you just do it at home?" Andrew asked.

Home. Ellen pursed her lips. "I no longer live with Joshua. I moved out."

He gawked at her. "Moved out? Why?"

Her mind flashed on all the reasons: Joshua's secrecy, his withdrawal from the world, his unreasonable demands. But one scene played in her mind repeatedly: her uncle ramming her with his wheelchair—the blind, animal fury in his eyes when she confronted him.

Ellen's eyes drifted to the painting. "I didn't feel safe there anymore," she admitted. The words felt like a betrayal. She looked down at the floor and waited for the awkward moment to pass. For Andrew to talk about the painting again.

"I had no idea things were so bad."

She kept her eyes focused on the floor.

"You've had your own problems to deal with. Miss Strauss, for a start."

"That's no excuse," he snapped. "I should have known something was wrong when you showed up at my office. I should have followed up." He let out a frustrated hiss. "Let's face it, Ellen. I've been a shitty friend."

Her head jerked up. *Friend.*

Andrew Carter had called her that once, but it was so long ago. Before she was kidnapped. Before she returned with the whole bizarre Dreamlands story. Before she was diagnosed as mentally unstable. Ellen assumed that whatever connection they had was dead. Crushed under the weight of . . . *well, everything.*

"I'm your friend?" Ellen chirped, hating the neediness in her voice.

He grimaced. "My point exactly. You shouldn't *wonder* if you're my friend. You are," he insisted, his eyes lingering on her. "Grab your stuff."

"What?"

"You can do laundry at my house. In fact, it might be good if you stay with me for a while."

"Stay with you?" she echoed. "But what about . . . what about Miss Strauss?"

"Fuck Miss Strauss," Andrew snapped. "If Miskatonic is out to get me, they'll find a way, no matter what I do."

"I don't want to be the reason for—"

He flashed her a hard stare. "You're not the reason. You're an opportunity. Understand?"

Ellen nodded, even though she didn't believe him.

He grabbed the painting.

She jumped, half expecting it to respond. To resist him.

"We'll take this with us. I have some things at home I can use on it."

✦✦✦✦✦✦✦

I have some things at home.

That was a major understatement. Andrew's basement reminded Ellen of a mad scientist's lab. Everywhere she looked, she saw machines: microscopes, UV lights, a portable X-ray machine. And books. Shelves and shelves overflowing with books. Most were too esoteric for her, but a few caught her interest. Between loads of laundry, she curled up on the couch near his desk and flipped through them. She was deep into a book on Egyptology when Andrew glanced up from the canvas.

"I need your eyes."

"You don't mean that literally, I hope," she joked as she put down the book. Ellen was only half kidding. The picture still gave her the creeps. Even now, in the brightness of his lab, she advanced on it carefully, her eyes fixed on the ghoul at the edge of the painting. The one turning toward the viewer with its arm raised. It returned her glare, its red eye flared in disgust.

Was the look in the ghoul's eye disgust, or was it surprise? Ellen wondered. *And the raised arm. Was it meant to be threatening? Or was the creature beckoning her? Inviting her into its world?*

She thought of the first time she saw Solomon Reye, and just like that, the demon's voice was in her head.

There you are. I've been looking for you. Solomon Reye said the words like they were friends, playing a little game of hide-and-seek.

Andrew stepped in front of her.

"Ellen?"

"I'm sorry. I . . ." She hesitated before she remembered his words. *Don't censor yourself. Not with me.* "I just had a flashback. To Solomon Reye. I was staring at that lead ghoul, and . . ." She offered him a smile she didn't feel. "They said it might happen."

"They?"

"My psychiatrists. God, what do they call themselves? *My wellness team.* They said I might have flashbacks."

Andrew shifted in place.

"Um, I don't know how to ask this, but are you on medication?"

"They want me to be," she admitted. "I fill the prescriptions. Play the part."

His eyes returned to her. "But you don't take them."

"No."

"Why not?"

Ellen stared into the murky blue of Andrew Carter's eyes. There was no fuzziness, no doubt in her mind. Even with a beard, she knew the man in front of her was Andrew Carter, *not* Randolph Carter. Her feet were firmly planted in the waking world. Sure, there were ghouls and secret passages and mysterious paintings, but . . .

"I know which world I'm in, Andrew."

She waited for the questioning to continue the way it did during therapy. The doubts expressed in soft, mellifluous voices. *How can you be sure? How do you know what* really *happened?*

Andrew motioned her to sit in the chair beside him at his desk. "Good. Because I need you. Here. With me."

The painting waited for her, magnified on a large computer monitor. Somehow, looking at it indirectly was less intense.

He leaned over and fiddled with the mouse.

"Do you know what a palimpsest is?" he asked.

"No idea."

"It's when a piece of paper or a document has been reused. The original writing might be erased, but traces of the older work are still there. Artists do the same thing with canvas. They'll start something, decide they don't like it, and paint over it. But that doesn't erase the image. It's still there. With the right tools, you can examine what's underneath."

He clicked on the image. "This is what the painting looks like under an infrared filter."

Ellen looked at the gray world on the screen. The ghouls were still there, but they were faint. Ghostly. The cave behind them, or what looked like a cave, took center stage. The more she studied it, the more the features seemed artificial. Everywhere she looked, black lines intersected, forming jagged shapes.

"What you're seeing is the artist's charcoal sketches, the initial framing of the picture," Andrew explained. "Many artists use geometry to establish dimensions, to make their paintings look deep and realistic. This artist didn't. He wanted to make the picture look as *un*real as possible."

He fiddled with the images. As more of the hidden structure emerged, the shapes grew larger. They loomed over the painting like a mountain range. A crawling sensation scratched at Ellen's eyes. It was how she felt when Michael Sloane grabbed her arm and begged for help. How she felt when she peered into the mathematician's mind.

All those sharp, pointy edges, she thought. A bolt of recognition struck her. "Oh my God! That stuff behind the painting! That's Michael Sloane! That's what Michael Sloane drew in his note."

Andrew reached over and clicked the mouse. Another picture appeared on the screen. Michael Sloane's note with its strange topography. He merged the image with the painting. An exact match.

Ellen looked up at him. "But . . . what? How did you get—?"

He flashed her a wolfish grin. "You didn't think I'd just give those crazy mathematicians the note without taking a picture of it, did you?"

She clapped her hands in delight. "Andrew, you're brilliant!"

He blushed and looked away. "I wouldn't go that far," he grumbled into the keyboard.

Joshua's voice popped into her head.

Shy. Underneath all that bluster and bravado, Andrew Carter is a shy boy.

He snapped his fingers at her. "Earth to Ellen."

"Sorry. I was thinking."

"Yeah. I could tell."

She ignored the snipe and focused her attention on the screen.

"We have two men. Michael Sloane and this artist. An artist who put some of Sloane's . . . visions . . . into the background of his paintings." Ellen paused, her mind churning as she digested the new information. "The artist had to be familiar with Sloane's work."

"I'd go a step further," Andrew offered. "I'd say Michael Sloane *knew* the artist. I did some analysis on the varnish and pigment. Both materials date to the 1920s. When Michael Sloane was around."

"So, Sloane collaborated with some artist?"

Andrew Carter fixed her with a long, level look. "Not just some artist." He moved the image on the computer screen, centering it on the bottom corner of the painting. Flowery writing glowed beneath the frame.

Ellen leaned closer to examine the script: *Al-Uqdah.*

"It's Arabic," he informed her. "Roughly translated, it means 'the knot.' It's also the name of a star system. Alpha Piscium."

She frowned. "*The Knot*? That's the name of the painting? Never would have guessed."

Andrew said nothing. He peered into the canvas like it was a crystal ball.

Ellen felt a strange excitement brewing inside him—turbulence mixed with equal parts wonder and fear. "What is it?"

When he didn't respond, she nudged him. "Andrew, talk to me. Tell me what you see."

He looked at her, tears sparkling in his eyes. "You *ran* with this. You dropped this *in the mud*."

She nodded at her bruised knee. "I fell."

The reminder snapped him out of his haze.

"This is a Pickman," Andrew announced.

The blood rushed from Ellen's head, and for a moment, she thought she would pass out.

Richard Pickman.

The master. The Goya of ghouls. No other name was as famous. No other artist was as elusive or mysterious as Richard Upton Pickman. Finding a Pickman was like stumbling across a lost Picasso. Or a Rembrandt. *No,* Ellen corrected herself. *It's more than that. It's like discovering the lost continent of Atlantis. A place where myth and legend are born.*

"What makes you think it's a Pickman?" she asked.

"Because of what it *isn't*."

"Okay. You're going to have to explain that."

"What do you think when someone says Pickman?"

The name spilled from her lips before she could stop it. "Martha."

Her friend.

Another victim of Calvin Leonard.

She was missing and presumed dead, just like her famous relative.

Andrew paled. "Oh, God, I forgot. You knew Martha Pickman."

"*Know*. I *know* Martha Pickman," she corrected him. "They haven't found a body."

Not yet.

The unspoken words hung in the silence between them.

"Did she ever talk about her family?" he asked.

"Not with me."

"But you were friends, right?"

She shot him a pointed look. "Do you ever ask me about Randolph Carter?"

Ellen expected him to back off, to dodge the subject.

"No, but I want to. Very much."

His confession surprised her. "What's stopping you?" she asked.

"They said . . ." The sentence died in his throat.

They. Ellen felt a wave of fatigue. *More advice from Miskatonic.* "What did *they* say? That questions would upset me?"

"'Destabilize' is the word they used."

"I'm tougher than they think," she insisted. "You can ask me whatever you want. And if I can answer the question, I will."

"*If* you can answer the question?"

"I don't claim to be an expert on Randolph Carter."

"You just slept with him."

Ellen stiffened, stunned by the remark.

"Sorry, I'm sorry," he blurted.

His hand shot up to his beard, rubbing it. "Later," he finally decided. "Maybe later, okay? We've got enough to deal with right now."

"Sure," she replied, eager to return to the painting. "What makes you think this is a Pickman?"

"When people think Pickman, they imagine works steeped in blood and gore. And while there are some gruesome, violent paintings, that wasn't what the man was about. That's just the popular image."

"The tale that Lovecraft told."

Andrew shook his head. "Actually, he didn't. I've been rereading 'Pickman's Model.' The paintings that horrified him weren't about blood and guts." He handed her his iPad.

Ellen read from a highlighted section.

"There was one thing called 'The Lesson.' You know, the old myth about how the weird people leave their spawn in cradles in exchange for the human babes they steal? Pickman showed what happened to those stolen babies—how they grew up—and then I began to see a hideous relationship in the faces of the human and nonhuman figures."

Andrew winced. "Another example of Lovecraft's racism, but that doesn't take away from the theme. The central message in Pickman's work."

"Message?"

"Look at the painting again," he urged her.

Nothing had changed, but Ellen found herself looking at a different world. The ghouls clustered at the altar no longer seemed menacing. Their excitement was driven not by the leader's raised sword but by the fire blazing on the altar that brought them together as a group. This wasn't a sacrifice. It was a gathering of the tribe. And the human women in the background? They were dressed for the occasion in their most sumptuous robes. They stared at the creature by the altar with excitement. Eagerness.

Not prisoners. Or victims. Willing participants.
Members of the tribe.

"Al-Uqhad. The Knot," Andrew murmured. "A moment in our ancient past when ghouls and humans bound themselves together."

"Bound themselves?" she echoed, even though the realization was already there, spreading through her like venom.

"Interbred," he replied. "You're looking at a communion. A welcoming ceremony for the newest addition to the tribe."

San loss.

Ellen had heard the words many times. It was a trope. A worn-out cliché. But sanity loss was also very real. Her vision blurred as if her eyes were retreating, refusing to see what was there.

A voice lectured her. *Is it so hard to believe? We did the same thing with the Neanderthals. And the Denisovans. Our ancestors had sex with other species. Offspring.*

That led to another revelation. One that took her further away from the world she understood. "They're still with us, aren't they? The children of this tribe."

"What do you think Joseph Turner is?"

This time, Ellen swayed on her feet. Joseph's face surfaced from memory. *White skin. Light eyes . . .* A bark of laughter escaped her throat. "Albino. He said he was an albino."

Andrew shook his head.

"That man is *not* an albino."

"Is that why you reacted so strangely when you saw him?"

"Yes."

"What is he? Is there a name for his kind?"

"We don't have a word for him."

"Why not?" she shot back.

"Because his kind doesn't exist. At least not officially."

Ellen's attention returned to the painting. She stared at the ghoul giving her the stink eye. A grim smile twisted her lips. "And I thought we were just *mouqabillat* to them."

"What?"

"A ghoul called us that in the Dreamlands. When I asked Randolph what it meant . . ."

Andrew Carter raised an eyebrow. "Randolph? He wouldn't let you call him Randy?"

Ellen couldn't tell whether he was joking.

She decided to play it straight. "I don't think he lets anyone call him Randy. Except maybe his wife, Olivia."

Carter gave her a measured stare, one Ellen recognized. It was the same guarded look her therapist gave her when Ellen slipped too deep into her "dreams."

"*Mouqabbilat* is Arabic for 'appetizer,'" she offered. "The ghouls were calling us snacks. Tasty little morsels."

"'For a ghoul is a ghoul and, at best, an unpleasant companion for man,'" Andrew muttered.

She brightened. "That's what Randolph said!"

He glared at her and stabbed his finger into his iPad.

"That's what Lovecraft wrote. *The Dream-Quest of Unknown Kaddath.* I could keep quoting if you like. You're using the standard text, right? The Del Rey version?" Andrew asked.

Ellen looked away. She knew what he was implying. Her psychiatrists suggested the same thing—that she had made up the story of her trip to the Dreamlands, cobbling it together from bits and pieces of Lovecraft. That she used her tale as a security blanket, a way to escape the horrors of Calvin Leonard's basement. A tattered cloth she clung to, even now.

Her diagnosis leaped out at her.

Schizotypal personality.

She pressed her fingers into her eyes. *Sharp edges. All those sharp, pointy edges.*

"Hey." Andrew Carter's voice was soft.

Ellen gasped, startled by the wetness trickling down her cheeks. She swiped angrily at her tears. "I'm sorry. I'm a fucking mess."

"It's a lot to absorb. Seeing art like this . . . it changes you." Carter paused to glance at her. "And I'm not helping."

She stared at the painting, finally letting herself believe. "Have you ever seen a Pickman before?"

"I thought I did once, but now that I see this . . ." The words drifted off, and he shook his head.

"Miskatonic doesn't have any Pickmans?" Ellen asked.

"Nothing that's listed in the archives. Even if they had one of his works, it wouldn't be in the official records," Andrew replied.

She glanced at him. "Why not?"

"The university doesn't want to draw attention to the more sensitive materials. People would use the records like a shopping list. Cultists, religious fanatics—"

"Thieves," Ellen offered. Her mind returned to the conversation between Joshua and Robert Carter. And Greg's warning. *That man Robert's talking to. He sounds like a serious criminal.*

Her phone buzzed.

Ellen looked down, expecting to see her ex-boyfriend's face, but it was an unknown number. An unknown local number.

She answered the call.

"Ellen Logan?" a voice called out.

"Yes?" she responded.

"This is Miss Worden. From Edgewood Manor."

"Yes?" she said again.

"I think it's time you and I talked."

"Okay, okay." Ellen nodded in agreement as Miss Worden gave her a time and place.

When she hung up, she looked forlornly at the book lying open on the couch and thought about all the homework she had to finish. The grade-point average she needed to stay in the special program at Miskatonic.

Further behind, she thought. *Every step in this journey puts me further behind.*

Andrew stirred beside her. "Ellen? Who was it?"

"Miss Worden. She wants to have a little chat."

"Good," he said as he turned away from the painting. "Let's see what she has to say, shall we?"

Chapter Fourteen

Miss Worden's probably anxious to get home.

Ellen suspected that wasn't the only reason she insisted on meeting them at a Starbucks in New Arkham. People unaffiliated with Miskatonic University rarely ventured into the old part of town. Even in the summer, when the daylight hours lingered, shadows still stained the ancient streets.

It had been years since Ellen had been in a "normal" coffeehouse. As she and Andrew walked through the front door, she immediately felt a difference in the atmosphere. This place was less intense than Unhallowed Grounds. Customers weren't hunched over books or talking in fierce whispers, fearful their conversations might be overheard. Here, there was an openness, an efficient, businesslike hum that seemed strange to her. As they placed their order and the barista asked them for their names (something that was never done at Unhallowed Grounds), Ellen nudged Andrew.

"I thought you said you should never share secret knowledge at a Starbucks."

"What?" he said as his eyes wandered across the menu and its bewildering coffee and tea combinations.

"When we first met, you told me never to share secret knowledge at a Starbucks."

He shrugged. "More a guideline than a requirement. You go wherever someone feels comfortable to talk."

"Where they're more willing to share their secrets," Ellen offered.

"Precisely," he replied, wincing as the barista bellowed his name.

A moment later, her order was ready.

"Daphne!" the man shouted.

Ellen winked at Andrew as she plucked her order from the counter.

"No real names. Especially out here, in the real world," she chirped.

He chuckled. "I could learn a thing or two from you."

Miss Worden occupied a table in the back. She didn't see them at first. She was deeply engrossed in a book. Ellen ducked a little so she could catch the title.

Killers of the Flower Moon by David Grann.

"I've been dying to read that. Is it good?" Ellen asked as they approached.

"It's gre—" the woman started to answer, but when she looked up and saw Ellen with Andrew Carter, her mouth twisted into a smile. "Well, I'll be damned. It is true! You really are Robert's daughter-in-law!"

Andrew stiffened and spat out a single, ominous word. "What?"

"It's your father's idea of a joke," Ellen explained as they took the seats opposite Miss Worden. "He introduced me to Miss Worden as your wife."

"So the two of you two aren't . . ."

"No," they replied in unison.

"I'm old enough to be her father," he objected.

Ellen rolled her eyes. "Oh, Andrew, please. You are not. Unless you got lucky when you were twelve. And I doubt that ever happened."

He glared at her. "I could have been a Don Juan in my youth, for all you know. A preteen stud."

"And they think *I'm* the one who's delusional?" Ellen shot back.

Miss Worden shook her head as she marked her place in the book. Ellen noticed she had a fancy, tasseled bookmark. No scraps of paper or old receipts for her.

"You're just like Robert and Lily," she observed.

Andrew frowned. "Lily?"

"Lily Graham," Ellen replied. "You talked to your father, and he never mentioned Lily?"

He looked at her blankly. "No. Why would he?"

She turned to Miss Worden and shook her head.

"Men," Ellen sighed as she took a sip of her green tea.

"Can we get on with it, *ladies*?" he grumbled, spearing them both with a sharp look.

"Actually, I'm glad you came, Dr. Carter, because I have a few questions for you, too."

Andrew gave her a flat stare. "I'll do my best."

"Is Miskatonic University doing something at Edgewood?" she blurted. "A secret project or experiment or something?"

He sat back and folded his arms.

"Miskatonic doesn't do secret projects, especially when it involves the general public," he replied. "Any research we conduct goes through our modified human subjects committee."

"*Modified* human subjects?" Ellen exclaimed, unable to contain her curiosity.

He fixed her with a cool gaze. "We're not a typical school. We don't go through a typical review process. But that doesn't make us thanatologists."

Ellen frowned. "Thanato-what?"

"I find it hard to believe that Miskatonic isn't behind all the recent . . . mayhem," Miss Worden interrupted. "Especially since our troubles started after two of your students gave us a little house tour," she said, nodding at Ellen.

Oh, your troubles have been going on for a long time, Ellen thought.

The nurse scowled at her, almost as if she picked up on the thought. "Look, I don't know what you think you're doing, but I don't appreciate you endangering the lives of our residents. Security doors being left open. With cement blocks, no less! It's bad enough you got people stirred up with all your stories, but for you to physically endanger the residents—"

"Wait a minute," Ellen interrupted her mid-tirade. "Cement blocks? You saw them, too? Holding open the doors?"

Miss Worden's face clouded with confusion. "You mean you didn't . . ."

"No. I would never do that. Ever. For the reason you just mentioned."

"Well, then, who did?"

Ellen sighed. She didn't want to reveal what she'd found. Her research was far from complete, but they needed Miss Worden on their side.

"I looked up the corporation that just bought Edgewood. Geras Enterprises," Ellen started.

Andrew snorted. "Geras Enterprises? A retirement company named itself after Geras, the god of old age? The guy's a demon! The son of Hades!"

Ellen ignored him. She knew Miss Worden wouldn't be swayed by mythology.

She fed the woman another name.

"Have you ever heard of Charles Cullen?" she asked.

"No," Miss Worden replied—a little too quickly.

"I'm surprised. Everyone in Miskatonic Medical School knows who Charlie Cullen is," she continued. "He was a nurse who was a serial killer. Police aren't sure how many people he murdered, but some estimates place it as high as four hundred. He managed to keep his murder spree going by switching hospitals whenever people started to suspect something was wrong. No one ever connected the dots."

Miss Worden's face darkened. "Wait a minute. Are you accusing me of . . ."

"Geras Enterprises is being investigated in four different states for what the authorities termed 'medical irregularities,'" Ellen announced.

"Medical irregularities? Like what?" Andrew demanded.

"I don't know. The records are still sealed, but I'm going to bet that cement blocks holding open doors is the least of their violations." Ellen paused to look at the woman. "Have you noticed anything different? Anything strange since the new company acquired Edgewood?"

Miss Worden fiddled with the book she had just been reading.

"It's them," she breathed as she stared at the cover. "Jesus Christ, it's not you. It's them!"

Andrew leaned forward, blue eyes blazing. "What the *hell* is going on?"

The nurse hesitated, unnerved by Andrew Carter's anger.

Like father, like son, Ellen thought.

Like grandfather, like grandson.

A shiver scuttled down her spine.

"Please, Miss Worden," she urged the woman. "We might be able to help."

Miss Worden sat back and took a deep drink of her coffee.

"After your friend told us about the history of Edgewood, I decided to do some investigating of my own," she admitted. "I heard rumors about a secret passage when I was first hired. People even told me where it might be. But I wasn't interested in finding out."

"Why not?" Ellen asked. If it were her, she would have gone into full Sherlock mode.

"I'm originally from New Orleans. My mother was a voudon priestess." Miss Worden's lips tightened at the mention of her past. "There's a reason I came north."

"You wanted to get away from all that," Andrew offered.

"I didn't even want to come to Arkham. I mean, it's just as witchy as New Orleans, but the job offer was too good to pass up." She shook her head. "That's neither here nor there. Like I said, after your guided tour, I went into the basement to see what I could find. And I found this."

Miss Worden stabbed her cell phone and passed it across the table.

Ellen and Andrew leaned in for a closer look.

The image was dim, but Ellen could see a series of concentric circles. Each one had an opening that led to a path to the center. She shivered. The design reminded her of a labyrinth, a place where people got lost.

Andrew pinched the image and enlarged it.

"What are the materials they're using?" he asked as he squinted at the phone. "I can't quite make it out."

Miss Worden plunked a stone on the table. "This."

Ellen picked it up and rolled it in her hands. It was a green pear-shaped stone flecked with what looked like black spiderwebs.

"Prehnite," Ellen breathed. "The stone of dreaming. People believe it allows you to communicate with other planes of existence."

Miss Worden narrowed her eyes. "How do you know that off the top of your head?"

"I work in a New Age store, and the owner is obsessed with stones. He makes me pass a test every few months."

Andrew shook his head. "It's not enough that Norm dresses you up like his own personal Barbie doll. He expects you to pass regular exams?"

Ellen shrugged. "I don't mind. It's interesting." She looked down at the stone. "Miss Worden, did you take this from the . . . um, design?" she asked.

The woman rolled her eyes. "Give me some credit. I told you I'm the daughter of a voudon priestess. I know better than to break what's obviously a ritual circle. The stone was from a pile of surplus material on the side."

"You're sure about that?" Andrew demanded.

Miss Worden fixed him with a withering glare.

"Positive," she hissed. "Not that it really matters. The circle was disrupted before I got there."

Did we do that? Ellen wondered.

"When did you find this?" she asked, half fearing that in their rush to pursue the ghoul, she or Joseph or Greg had plowed through a magic circle.

"Like I said, right after you finished your little tour. That afternoon."

Ellen breathed a sigh of relief.

Not us, then.

"You think the new corporation is behind all this?" Carter asked.

"Look, I know there are stories about Edgewood. That people think it may be the source of a famous story. And I'll admit, there is something strange about the place, something that goes beyond a garden-variety haunting." Miss Worden paused to look at the people waiting for their coffees. "But whatever was there was quiet. At least until Geras Enterprises took over. After that, people started seeing things. The staff started seeing things."

Ellen's breath caught in her throat. It had never occurred to her to interview the staff.

"Now that place"—the nurse shuddered—"feels like it's alive. It's full of energy and getting stronger even as we speak."

Miss Worden's phone buzzed on the table, making them jump. At the same time, Ellen's phone burst into song, blasting the opening tones of Metallica's "Enter Sandman."

"Ellen. Help me," a voice begged when she answered.

It took a moment for Ellen to recognize Lily Graham's voice. Her friend sounded muffled. Like she was trying hard not to be heard.

In the background, she heard pounding.

Bam, bam bam bam, bam bam, ba-bam.

She looked over at Miss Worden, whose eyes were wide with terror.

"Edgewood," they both said simultaneously.

Chapter Fifteen

Ellen didn't need Greg's equipment to know something was happening at Edgewood Manor. As they approached the house, a van with a Geras Enterprises logo sped past them, nearly running Carter's car off the road. And the moment Ellen stepped out of the Range Rover, a wall of pressure hit her. The air was heavy with the same oily reek she smelled just before the ghouls broke through.

"Jesus Christ, what's happening?" Miss Worden blurted, scanning the residents clustered outside in anxious pods.

Ellen barely heard her. Her gaze was drawn to the windows on the upper floor. Imprinted on one of the thick panes of wavy glass, the distorted face of a man stared back at her.

"Thijmen," she breathed.

Inside the house, the lights dimmed, then flickered in a familiar rhythm.

Bam, bam bam bam, bam bam, ba-bam.

Miss Worden latched on to her arm.

"The witch? Is it the witch?" she demanded.

When Ellen didn't respond, Miss Worden followed her gaze. The woman's expression froze. Her eyes locked on the lights that pulsed like a heartbeat.

"Miss Worden?" Ellen called out.

The woman didn't respond.

"Miss Worden? Miss Worden, I . . ." She shook her head. "I can't keep calling you that. What's your name?"

The woman blinked. "Huh?"

"Your name."

"Susan," she replied vaguely.

"Susan, you need to take care of the residents. There are a lot of people out here in the heat." She paused, scanning the crowd for Robert and Lily. There was no sign of them.

"You need to take care of them. Find a place for them to stay. At least until . . ."

Her words trailed off as she remembered the "protected" wing.

All those people. Held prisoner by a keypad.

"Is everyone out of the house?" she demanded. "Is everyone safely out of the house?"

"I don't know."

Ellen squeezed the woman's shoulders. "You *need* to know. Take a head count. What's the code to the Alzheimer's wing?"

Susan Worden rattled off a string of numbers.

"I'll check if there are people still inside. And I'll bring them out here, okay?"

The woman stared at the strobing lights coming from the house. "Uh-huh," she agreed in a faint voice.

"*Susan, do your job,*" Ellen ordered her.

The nurse jumped. A cool look crept into her eyes as her professional training kicked in. She pulled out her cell phone and marched toward the people on the lawn. Ellen waited until the woman issued orders. As soon as she spoke, Ellen headed toward the house.

A hand latched on to her shoulder.

Ellen screamed, half expecting Thijmen to be standing beside her.

"Hey, hey, it's me," Andrew reassured her. "I'll go into the basement and see if the circle's active. I'm going to guess that's why that van was hauling ass out of here."

Anger rose in her, a bitter bile that tickled the back of her throat.

"Those bastards! Those cowardly bastards!"

He tightened his grip on her shoulder. "Forget about them, Ellen. People are depending on us right now."

She took a deep breath and nodded.

They headed up the stairs and to the front door, which had been left open, as if inviting them to enter.

Inviting us or daring us? Ellen wondered as they crossed the threshold.

Edgewood Manor was alive. There was no other way to describe it. Ellen had been in haunted houses before. She'd even lived in a haunted house. This wasn't a residual haunting, an endless replaying of a dead person's routine. The floors hummed under her feet, vibrating with intent. Bristling with intelligence. And those lights. Those goddamn lights.

Bam, bam bam bam, bam bam, ba-bam.

This time, the lights were accompanied by a sound that thundered around them, shaking the walls.

Andrew's hand landed on her shoulder again.

"I'm going to the basement. You help the others."

"Yes," Ellen agreed through gritted teeth. She didn't even notice she had spaced out until he broke the spell.

She waited until Andrew plunged into the basement before she moved.

The house didn't make her mission easy. The floor surged beneath her feet as she made her way to the locked ward. Ellen felt like she was walking on a ship in the middle of a fierce storm.

She punched in the numbers: 1-2-0-8-0.

The code to the Alzheimer's ward was the average blood pressure of an adult. She would have found it funny if her heart wasn't about to explode. The keypad glared red when she entered the code and buzzed a warning. Panic shot through Ellen. *How? How could it be wrong? How, how?*

She closed her eyes, silencing the jittery voice. She listened to the house. Waited for a pause, the space between beats.

Ba—

Her fingers flew across the buttons: 1-2-0-8-0.

Bam.

The keypad chirped its approval.

Ellen tugged on the handle, and the door hissed open like she had broken an airtight seal. The sound made her stomach drop. *What if I'm letting something in? What if things were better with the door locked?*

The pale-faced nurse on the other side of the door quelled her fears.

"Oh, God! Thank God! I've been trying to open this forever, but it was stuck. Who are you?"

"Susan sent me," Ellen offered. "Something's going on with the house. The electrical system's gone nuts."

"Fucking budget cuts," the male nurse muttered.

Budget cuts. Good. Let him think it's something normal.

"We're moving the residents," Ellen said. "Susan's arranging transportation so that we can get people out of here. At least until we can figure out what's going on."

The man nodded, but when she turned to leave, he howled, "No! You have to stay here. I need you!"

"What do you want me to do?"

"You can start by keeping that door open."

Ellen looked around wildly.

A cinder block would be nice right about now, she thought.

Manic laughter escaped her throat, an outburst the nurse mistook for panic. He grabbed an office chair and shoved it at her.

Ellen wedged it against the door.

"Good! Now help me with the patients," he commanded.

"Help you with the . . . ?"

"Please," he pleaded. "There's no one else here to help me."

"Fucking budget cuts," Ellen swore.

Handling the patients terrified her. Ellen felt how fragile they were as she helped people out of their beds and into wheelchairs. Delicate, birdlike bones creaked, threatening to break under the slightest pressure. She forced herself to slow down, to handle the residents as gently as she could. Ellen couldn't imagine what it was like to be them, what they thought was going on. Fortunately, no one struggled. No one became combative.

The nurse lined up the patients, clustering them around the door. "Take them through one at a time," he ordered as he lowered a resident into the wheelchair. "I'll stay here and keep an eye on the others."

Take them through. She looked down the hall at the strobing lights. *All that humming, that vibration. Going through was hard enough for me. What will it do to a mind already ravaged by disease?*

She imagined the residents' brains cracking under pressure. Shattering like glass.

The nurse slugged Ellen in the shoulder. "Get moving!"

Ellen took a wheelchair and raced the resident down the hall. Despite the smooth wooden floors, the wheelchair rattled, its metal frame jittering ominously. She worried about her passenger (*those bones, those brittle bones*), but slowing down wasn't an option. The building flexed and contracted, bulging under an invisible force. Pictures fell off walls. Bookshelves crashed to the floor, spilling their guts.

As Ellen ran through the frightening fun house, a wave of pain forced her to stop. The energy of the house hit her like a malevolent wall. An image popped into her head of the workers who had "cleaned" Chernobyl after the nuclear meltdown. She pictured them racing through the ruins, digging up shovelfuls of radioactive dust and tossing the debris into the reactor core.

Minutes, she thought. *They only had minutes before becoming fatally contaminated. Before their bodies were damaged beyond repair. How long do I have?*

Ellen looked at the woman huddled helplessly in the wheelchair.

More time than she does.

"Move your ass," she growled to herself.

In the short time Ellen had been away, Miss Worden had mobilized the troops. A pair of attendants rushed to meet them, lifting the patient out of the wheelchair and onto the patio furniture. Ellen didn't stop to help. As soon as the chair was empty, she spun around and headed back into Edgewood. She repeated the process, chanting her Chernobyl mantra. *Shovel, run, shovel, run . . .*

She was on one of her final trips when someone stepped in front of her. Ellen swerved to avoid a crash.

Andrew Carter stood before her, looking pale and disheveled.

"Are you okay?" Ellen called out.

"Air. I need air," he gasped. His eyes fell to the man curled in the wheelchair. "I'll take him outside."

Ellen nodded, and he sped away with his passenger.

As she headed back, the nurse intercepted her halfway down the hall. He yanked her along with him. Just as they reached the front door, it flew open. Andrew came rushing through with the wheelchair.

Ellen leaped to the side and threw up her hands. "We're good! We're good!"

He blinked at the nurse scurrying out the door. "What?"

"The house is clear. Everyone is outside."

"Not everyone. My father, your friend—"

EEEE-OOO-EEEE-OOO. A long, ear-splitting sound drowned out his words. The alarm alternated, high-low, and seemed to come from everywhere. Ellen's first thought was that all the vibration had tripped Edgewood's security system.

One look at Andrew changed her mind.

"Fuck, fuck, fuck. *Fuck!*" he chanted.

"What is it?" she demanded over the blare of the alarm.

"It's the doomsday siren."

"Doomsday siren?"

"It hasn't sounded since 1928. Since cultists stormed the library and tried to steal *The Necronomicon*."

The Necronomicon. Another legend of Miskatonic.

Like ghouls.

And Richard Pickman.

Dear God, what's next? she wondered.

Their cell phones buzzed. Two very different messages popped up on their screens.

Ellen's read:

> Toxic gas leak on campus.
>
> Students must evacuate NOW.

His was shorter:

> Shadow Zone.
> Julia Floor.
> Mandelbrot Hall.

Andrew looked at her, his eyes sick with panic and fear. "Those bastards. They did it," he muttered.

"What are you talking about?"

"Dr. Donovan." He spat out the words like a curse. "You were right. I should have taken that note from him. I should have known he was up to something when he started muttering about the Keziah Mason formulae."

"The Keziah what?"

"Keziah Mason. The witch from the Witch House."

Ellen's insides twisted. "Thin place," she croaked. "That's what he did. He just opened a thin place, didn't he?"

The lights pulsed in agreement. Thick tendrils of terror shot through Ellen, making it hard to think.

Andrew handed her his things.

Wallet.

Keys.

Gun.

He had done this once before, when he was sure he was going to certain death in an abandoned mine.

She looked at the objects in her hands in disbelief.

"Andrew—"

His jaw tightened. He spoke to her in a quiet voice. "My father and Lily are still in her room. Get them out. Take them to my house. You'll be safer there."

"Wait! What about you? Where are you going?"

"I'm being summoned. Called to duty."

He's going to close the thin place.

She grabbed his arm. "No. You can't!" she spluttered.

He jerked free from her grip, anger flaring in his eyes. "I *have* to go. It's what I've trained for. It's what I promised to do the day I joined . . ."

"I can't do this alone," she insisted. "I need you here. With me."

His eyes settled on her. She expected to see more anger, but they shone with a tenderness that made her vision blur.

He nodded out the window at the patients gathered on the lawn. "You don't need me. Look at everything you've already done."

"But, but—"

"Ellen. Take care of my father. *Please.*"

She wanted to say no. She wanted to beg and threaten, to grab hold of him and refuse to let go. "Okay," she whispered as she stuffed his belongings into her pockets.

He cupped her face in his hands, pressing his forehead to hers. "That's my girl."

Girl.

The word would have rankled if it hadn't been delivered with such affection. If Andrew's mask hadn't slipped, revealing what everyone had been telling her all along. The voices rose like a Greek chorus: *You two have a strong connection. I could feel it across the room. Friend of the family, my ass. What's the deal with you and the professor? They say he's in love and runs after you like a puppy.*

Andrew's face darkened as he realized his mistake.

Ellen kissed him before he could get away. She expected him to resist, to wrestle out of the embrace, sputtering indignation. But Andrew was there for her like he always was. He pulled her into his arms, his mouth open, his warm tongue seeking hers. His touch consumed her. Ellen pressed against him, absorbing his strength, savoring the feel of his body. For a few breathless moments, the house was gone; the strobing lights were gone. The embrace lifted her above the madness. Nothing existed in the universe except Andrew Carter.

Then he pulled away, leaving her gasping for more.

"Be careful," he warned her.

For a second, Ellen thought he was talking about himself. It took a moment for gravity to return, for the doomsday siren to creep back into her head. She touched the side of his face. "You better come back, or I'll be so fucking pissed," she said in a choked whisper.

Andrew swept her into another kiss, one she felt sizzle to her toes.

Then he was gone.

Ellen slumped against the front door, her fingers drifting to her mouth. *That was enough,* she told herself. *More than you ever expected to get.* But it wasn't enough. She wanted more. So much more.

Edgewood Manor lurched under her feet, reminding her of the urgency of the situation.

You don't have time for this. Get back to work.

As Ellen headed to Lily's room, the energy around her intensified. She wondered if Thijmen was jealous of her moment with Andrew, of the time she spent not thinking about what was happening in Edgewood.

Don't be ridiculous, she thought.

And yet . . .

Ellen felt like she was inside an angry creature—as if she were passing through the belly of a beast. *A thing that could kill me in a heartbeat. Not just me. Everyone here.*

"Stop thinking," she whispered through clenched teeth.

Even though things were quieter in the corridor where Lily's room was, her friend waited outside, pacing the hall and worrying the cord of her velour hoodie.

"Oh, thank God!" she exclaimed when she spotted Ellen. "Robert has completely lost it. I tried to get him to leave, but he won't move. He keeps staring at the wall."

Ellen shivered. She remembered her own experience in Lily's room, how Robert Carter pulled her away before the thin place engulfed her. She put her hand on Lily's shoulder. "You go ahead. I'll take care of him."

Her friend scowled. In her former life, Lily Graham had taught elementary school. Ellen knew she was used to being the leader, the one responsible for keeping her tribe together. The thought of leaving Robert behind went against every fiber of her being.

"They're gathering people on the lawn. Wait for us there," Ellen suggested. "And if Miss Worden asks, tell her you and Robert are coming with me."

"But my daughter . . ."

"You can call her when we're safe."

"She not going to like that."

"Do you hear the siren? This is no ordinary emergency."

Yeah, a voice quipped. *Things are so bad, Andrew Carter kissed you.*

Ellen ignored the thought.

"Trust me on this one, Lil."

Lily hesitated another moment. "Okay," she agreed. She flipped up the hood of her sweatshirt and ran down the hall as if she were dashing through a sudden burst of rain.

When Lily rounded the corner, Ellen headed deeper into the storm.

Robert Carter stood motionless in the middle of the room, staring at the wall. Late-afternoon sun glared through the windows. Ellen shielded her eyes as she approached him. She followed his gaze to see if he was looking at the same spot where her thin place had appeared.

My thin place, she thought. *Like it belongs to me. Like it's something I want.*

There were no purple streaks on the sun-washed wall, no alternate planes bleeding into each other. All she saw was dust particles drifting in the air. When she turned to ask Andrew's father what he was looking at, a spiky shape punched through the wall. She yelped and jumped to the side.

"You see it," Robert Carter announced in a flat voice.

Her eyes darted to the wall.

Nothing.

"What—?" The question died in Ellen's mouth. She remembered a recent field trip she took with Dr. Kaku, when her astronomy class ventured into the Arkham hills to look for a comet. Even though they were miles away from the city and surrounded by a pitch-dark sky, they still couldn't see it. As the crowd grew restless, Dr. Kaku said they needed to look away to see it. Only when they averted their eyes did it appear, its long tail dancing on the edge of their vision.

She looked down at the floor and moved her eyes from side to side like she was dreaming.

Out of the corner of her eye, she saw the wall in front of her come to life, its surface seething with energy. "Bad," she whispered. "Oh my God, this is bad."

Robert Carter's gaze settled on her. "He wants you," he said, continuing to speak in a flat, alien voice. "Can't you feel him reaching out? He wants you back. No. It's more than that. He *needs* you."

Solomon.

The name slithered across her body. *He's the one behind all this. The one trying to open a thin place.*

"No. No, no, no," she chanted, as if the word had power. As if it could push everything back into place, to the way things were.

"He needs you," Robert Carter repeated.

A surge of anger, raw and fierce, ripped through Ellen. "*No!*" She grabbed Robert Carter by the arm and yanked him out of the room. The old man meekly went along, as if he were one of the Alzheimer's patients. Now that Ellen knew how to see, everything in Edgewood moved. As she led him out of the house, Ellen wondered if a thin place in one spot caused problems elsewhere.

If there's a breach at Miskatonic, does that mean other places are opening?

She imagined the town of Arkham riddled with holes, like a slice of Swiss cheese.

"Stop thinking," she whispered.

Lily had resumed her pacing on the front lawn. When she saw them, she ran to Robert, wrapping him in a tight hug. At first, he did nothing. Then the strange spell of the house broke, and he melted into Lily's arms.

"Stupid man," Lily scolded, the words thick with affection. "Stupid, crazy old man."

To give them privacy, Ellen looked away—to the house. Edgewood's front door hung open—a gaping mouth ready to devour. She ran up the porch stairs and slammed the door shut. It was a pointless thing to do. She knew that. Whatever was punching through the walls would have no trouble with an ordinary door. But she had to do something, anything, to stop what was coming.

What is coming? Ellen wondered. *Is it more ghouls or . . . ?*

Nurse Worden waved to her from across the lawn, and Ellen gladly abandoned her thoughts.

"Mr. Carter said you're going to take them to his house," she announced when Ellen joined her.

It took her a moment to realize "Mr. Carter" referred to Andrew.

"Yes, I'll take care of them," Ellen volunteered. "What's going to happen to the rest of the residents?"

"They'll be transferred to our other facilities, at least until things settle down." Miss Worden paused. "Things *are* going to settle down, aren't they?"

Nightmare images of Chernobyl and its Exclusion Zone flashed through her mind. A thousand square miles of blight and nothingness.

Nothingness if we're lucky. "To be honest, I don't know," she admitted. "This is all new to me."

Miss Worden nodded at Lily and Robert. "At least they're not fighting anymore."

"It only took the end of the world."

The nurse stiffened, her face tightening with panic.

"Kidding. Just kidding," she reassured the woman.

Ellen gathered Lily and Robert before Miss Worden had second thoughts and decided they would be safer with her than Ellen. Now that he was out of Edgewood, Robert looked better. Still, he was weak. He had to lean against Lily for support.

Ellen stepped in to take her friend's place, but Lily shooed her away with a wrist flick. "You go ahead. Get things ready."

The inside of the car smelled like Andrew Carter. Ellen took a deep breath, savoring the rich, musky scent. Everywhere she looked, she saw the debris of his everyday life. Cheap sunglasses were tossed onto the dashboard. A thermal coffee mug was wedged in a cupholder next to a tin of mints.

Mints, she thought with a pang.

Did he taste like mint when we . . . "Stop it," she croaked. She busied herself with clearing space and preparing for her passengers.

When Lily arrived at Andrew's Range Rover, she was eager to hand off Robert. Ellen maneuvered Andrew's father into the front seat. He gazed at her with unfocused eyes as she bent over to fasten his seat belt.

"Where's my boy?" he asked in a soft voice.

Ellen wondered why Robert couldn't hear the doomsday siren blasting across Arkham. Only then did she realize it had fallen silent. She looked toward Miskatonic University.

Did that mean things had started?

"He had to leave. Official business," she muttered, turning her attention back to the seat belt.

"You know, I've never seen the two of you in the same room together."

Ellen stopped what she was doing and looked at him.

A weak grin spread across his face.

Joking, she thought. *The old man's joking.*

Trying to make me feel better.

She returned his lopsided smile.

"What can I say? We're kind of like Bruce Wayne and Batman that way."

"Superheroes?" Lily snorted as she climbed into the back seat. "You're talking about superheroes in the middle of *this*?"

Robert shrugged. "Seems like the perfect time for them to show up, don't you think?"

Yeah, if they existed, Ellen almost said.

"So, where are we headed?" Robert asked when she started the car.

The GPS sprung to life, and the answer popped on the screen.

She pressed the "Home" button.

Chapter Sixteen

The floodlights of Miskatonic University scoured the night sky. Ellen stood in Andrew's house, gazing out the window at the river's far side. Under normal circumstances, seeing the campus lit up like Times Square would have delighted her. It would have been a sign of celebration. The first day of a new academic year. The homecoming football game against arch-rival Salem State.

Not these lights. They were being used as weapons to push back the darkness. To expose the inky corners that hid the approach of unwanted things.

"Shadow zone," she whispered.

Ellen had never heard the phrase before. She knew it by other names. Thin place. Cascading reality. Transdimensional gateway. Epistemological breach. Or her favorite, abyssal oculus. Different words that described the same situation. Someone (or something) had punched a hole in reality, exposing humanity to other worlds and the hostile gaze of the unknown.

And Andrew Carter's out there. In the thick of it.

All alone.

Ellen batted away the thought.

He's not alone, she told herself. *He's with an army of people who have much more experience with this kind of thing.*

The nagging voice persisted.

Do they? The last time the doomsday alarm sounded was in 1928. No one who fought the last shadow zone is still alive.

She shook her head. "Goddamn it," she muttered.

Robert Carter joined her at the window. "Sucks to be on the other side, doesn't it?" he asked, his face clouded with memory. "My mother and I did a lot of this. Waiting. Hoping my father would remember us and come back. Sometimes my mother sent me in after him. To fetch him like he was down at the neighborhood bar." His voice dropped to a whisper. "I saw things. Things a child should never see."

I'm sorry. The apology almost tumbled out of her mouth, but Ellen swallowed the words. They seemed so inadequate, insulting in the face of Robert's pain. She silently shook her head as they stared at the floodlights in silence.

"I was the product of one of his return visits; did you know that?" he said. "Lovecraft wrote about it. My father's return visit, not the . . . homecoming he had with my mother. "Through the Gates of the Silver Key." Have you read it?"

"I probably have. In Lovecraft 101," she ventured. "Refresh my memory."

"After my father was missing for several years, my mother decided to have him declared legally dead. This was in the depths of the Great Depression, so she needed the money. Fortunately, she found a lawyer willing to do it for free. Ernest

Aspinwall was his name. Unfortunately, he had to notify the public of the legal hearing. That's how *he* found out."

He. Ellen noticed that Robert Carter never referred to his father by name.

"He crashed the hearing, disguised in a ridiculous outfit. Claimed he was a mystic. Swami Chandaputra. He wore a mask, but my mother must have recognized him because"—his mouth twisted into a bitter smile—"she dropped the claim. All the careful work the lawyer had done, the months and months of building a case, was ruined. Mr. Aspinwall was furious. Almost had a heart attack right there. And later that night, after everyone left—"

"She dropped more than her claim," Ellen murmured.

The bitter smile deepened. "Nine months later? *Moi!*"

"Wait a minute. That story was written in the 1930s. That would make you—"

"Be very careful with your math, Ellen," he purred.

"You're older than you look."

This time, Robert Carter's smile was more genuine. "Well played," he replied. "The Dreamlands does strange things to people. Slowing down the aging process is one of them."

Ellen thought about the Randolph Carter she met. According to Lovecraft, he was fifty-four when he disappeared from the waking world. But the Carter she knew (*the Carter you slept with,* a voice whispered) didn't look middle-aged. He was in his late thirties—a year, two years older than Andrew Carter, tops.

And William Kuranes, the creator of the Dreamland city of Celephaïs, vanished in 1912. That made him more than a century old. *Definitely older than he looks,* she thought.

Ellen tensed, her eyes settling on Robert Carter. "Why are you telling me all this?"

He returned her gaze, his face as rigid as a mask. "You left a book on the kitchen table."

A book?

It took Ellen a moment to realize she'd left her journal that described her Dreamland journey, step by excruciating step, in the kitchen. She raced to the kitchen, where Lily was cleaning up after a meal Ellen had eaten but barely noticed. The book lay open on the table. A half-finished drawing of a man stared back at her. The sketch she'd started that morning before she and Andrew paid their fateful visit to the math department.

The man from my nightmare—the artist who threw me through his canvas.

Ellen whipped out her cell phone and logged onto Miskapedia, the university's database. There were two known pictures of Richard Upton Pickman. She only needed one to identify him as the painter from her nightmare.

"Who's that?" Lily chirped beside her.

Ellen slammed the book shut, shielding her friend from Richard Pickman's evil gaze. His venomous hiss bubbled up from memory. *Go through! Go through already!*

Lily frowned. "Ellen, what's wrong? You look sick."

"No. No, no, no," she whispered.

"Ellen?" This time, Robert Carter called to her.

She held up a hand. "Quiet! Just, just . . . quiet. Please!" she begged him. An idea was forming—a ghostly shape skirting the border of conscious thought. *Shapes. Forms. Numbers.* Her eyes widened. "Holy. Shit."

She darted past Robert and Lily and ran to the basement. Andrew had locked the door before they'd left, but Ellen had the keys. She galloped downstairs, past her folded laundry and the couch she had curled up on only a few hours before. The Pickman sat on the easel, uncovered. Ellen woke up Andrew's computer, hoping she didn't have to feed it a password.

The infrared image of the painting popped up on the screen, revealing the world lurking beneath the canvas.

Ellen looked back and forth between the two images. "Not erased," she murmured. "Hidden."

A figure stirred at the foot of the stairs.

Andrew's father said nothing as he approached the painting, moving toward the Pickman like it was a snake coiled to strike. As he got closer, his expression wavered.

"Is it real?" he demanded in a gruff voice.

Ellen laughed. "What do *you* think?"

He appraised her with his eyes. "I think Joshua underestimated you."

"How long have the two of you been working together?" she asked, unable to contain her curiosity.

When he objected, Ellen cut him off. "Microphones in Edgewood. Remember?"

He exhaled a curse. "Ffffucck."

"How long?" Ellen pressed him.

"A couple of years. Since you arrived in Arkham." He shrugged and crossed his arms. "But I suspect Joshua's been dabbling in the Eldritch Market much longer."

"Eldritch Market?" The words felt slimy on her tongue. Unclean.

"You've heard of murderabilia, right? Those places on the internet where people buy serial killer stuff? Letters from Ted Bundy. Clown paintings from John Wayne Gacy. The Eldritch Market makes all that look like child's play."

A shudder shot through Ellen. The locked study. The spur-of-the-moment business trips. His refusal to let her see specific works of art. And the man Joshua was arguing with when she'd gotten back from Edgewood.

A thief, she thought, *just like my uncle.* "Black market," she murmured. "Joshua is dealing in stolen art."

"Not everything he deals with is stolen," Robert Carter objected.

"Just enough to cause him trouble," Ellen shot back. She stared at the Pickman. *Years . . . this has been going on for years.*

Robert shook his head. "Crazy bastard. I knew it was only a matter of time before the mighty Joshua Logan got his hands on a piece of art so hot that even *he* couldn't handle it."

"If only it were that simple," Ellen said with a sigh.

"What do you mean?"

A siren wailed in the distance just as Ellen's cell phone buzzed.

Toxic gas cloud spreading.

Residents must evacuate Old Arkham NOW.

The thin place.

Spreading.

"I have to go."

"Where?"

"Back to Edgewood," she said. "And I need to take the Pickman with me."

"What? Why?"

"I think it's the only way I can help stop what's happening. Or at least slow it down."

He studied the painting as if gauging the risk. Running the numbers.

"Robert, your son is out there! Risking his life!"

At the mention of Andrew, the calculating look vanished.

"You're right. Of course you're right," he grumbled. "I'll let Lily know where we're going. You wrap that damned thing up."

"We? I don't need—"

He silenced her with a glare. "Yes, you do. You *do* need me there."

Ellen gulped back a knot of fear and nodded. She fetched a drop cloth from a nearby shelf and draped it over the painting, keeping her eyes focused on the floor.

How? she wondered. *How did I not realize what the painting really did?*

The answer came sharp and swift.

Because they made you doubt yourself. Your doctors. Your wellness team.

Ellen cackled, the bitter laughter rising like bile in her throat.

Out of the corner of her eye, she spotted a glint of red. A ring sat on Andrew's desk, sparkling as if beckoning her. Ellen picked it up and turned it over in her trembling hands. It was the ring Martha Pickman gave her right before she disappeared. A ring that transported its wearer to the Dreamlands. She gave it to Andrew after she returned from the Pine Barrens. Now it was here, waiting for her.

"Coincidence," she whispered. "This can't be a coincidence."

"What's taking you so long?" Robert bellowed from above.

Ellen snatched the ring, dropping it into her pocket. Then she grabbed the painting and headed upstairs.

Chapter Seventeen

Ellen drove against the surge of humanity. The police diverted traffic, turning all the roads out of Old Arkham into one-way streets. It made little difference. Fifteen thousand people were trying to leave, all at once. The ancient arteries of the city were clogged. A necklace of headlights stretched from campus to the bridge that spanned the Miskatonic River.

Ellen's cell phone chirped, pleading for attention. She kept her eyes on the road as she drove on sidewalks, over front lawns, through narrow alleys, inching toward the street that would take them to Edgewood. Robert read her the alerts on her phone. Shelters and rendezvous points for families separated by the emergency were being set up. Hospitals prepared triage tents to handle potential casualties. A call went out to Herbert West Memorial personnel to report to the sites and offer their "special skills."

Special skills.

The words chilled Ellen to the bone.

Dear God, this is real. This is happening.

A car horn blasted, and she slammed on the brakes. The painting in the back wobbled ominously, but it didn't fall.

Ellen breathed a sigh of relief.

A man rolled down his window. "You're going the wrong way, you stupid bitch!" he bellowed as they passed, his wife sitting stone-faced beside him.

Ellen ignored him and kept going. Her eyes darted between the road and the GPS. *A quarter of a mile before the turn.* She groaned and rubbed her face. *It might as well be a thousand.*

Robert Carter nodded at an approaching street sign.

"Take Selby Lane. There's a shortcut this car doesn't know about."

She turned off the main road, slipping into a tributary untouched by traffic. Robert Carter navigated her through narrow neighborhood alleys, passing rows of garbage cans lined up for collection. Ellen glanced at the houses, their windows blue-lit by the glow of televisions. The crisis at Miskatonic had yet to reach them, but the residents were anxiously watching the horizon. A few were already in their garages, packing their cars. Ellen thought about the terrorist attack on the World Trade Center, 9/11. How, after the first plane hit, the people who survived didn't wait for the order to evacuate. They abandoned their offices, reaching safety as the second plane appeared in the sky.

"Park here." Robert Carter pointed at a vacant spot a block away from Edgewood. "We'll walk the rest of the way. Just in case someone's watching."

Ellen shot him a confused look.

"In case someone's watching?" she echoed. "*Who* would be watching? If you mean the police, I think they have other things to worry about."

"It's not the police."

"Miss Worden left with the other res—"

"It's not her, either."

Ellen frowned. "Then what is it?" She paused. "Edgewood. You're talking about Edgewood, aren't you? You want to sneak up on it."

His face crumpled. "You must think I'm a crazy old man," he muttered.

"Not at all. Edgewood . . . well, it's not just made of wood and stone, is it?"

Robert Carter said nothing, but his hands twisted nervously in his lap.

"That's why you insisted on living there, isn't it? You knew about the house's reputation as a thin place. You hoped all the stories were true."

"Yes," he replied in a small, childlike voice. "I wanted my father back. I wanted to see him one more time . . ."

"Before you died," Ellen said, finishing the thought when he faltered.

The old man nodded, his chest heaving as he tried to hold back his tears.

Ellen reached down and squeezed his restless hands.

"You're never too old to want your father," she said softly. "Andrew said that to me once."

A sob escaped from his lips.

"I don't know why he would say such a thing. I was a shitty father."

"You had a shitty father, too, but that didn't stop you from needing him," she pointed out.

Robert stared out the window, looking at nothing.

"I wasn't good to Andrew when he was growing up," he admitted, his eyes filling with tears. "He looked so much like my father that I took things out on him."

Took things out on him.

The words made Ellen shiver.

She shifted in the driver's seat, feeling the ring move in her pocket.

Ellen watched as shadows pooled on the sidewalk.

Was that just a trick of the light? she wondered. *Or . . .*

"Come on. Let's get this done," she murmured.

Edgewood waited for them in the darkness. The ominous building shimmered in the still summer air. It was no longer pretending it was an ordinary house. When Ellen climbed the stairs with the painting, she felt a tug. A strong, almost tidal force pulled on the painting.

Only one thing stood in its way.

She set the painting down and stared at the keypad on the front door.

"Is there a problem?" Robert Carter asked.

"Not if I know human nature," Ellen replied. She punched the code Nurse Worden had given her for the Alzheimer's unit: 1-2-0-8-0.

The door flashed green and unlocked.

"Unbelievable," she snorted as she opened the door, groping for a light switch.

The entryway flooded with harsh, institutional light.

They ventured silently into the thing that was Edgewood.

Lily's room was as she'd left it. Ellen studied the half-finished glass of tea and a paperback propped open on the armrest of a chair. It was hard to believe her friend had started today like any other day. Normal was so far from Ellen's life that she couldn't even see it in the rearview mirror.

She took out her phone and brought up the picture she had taken of Andrew's computer screen. She compared the infrared image in the painting with the dimensions of the room. The walls, the doors, the windows. Everything lined up. Ellen's heart hammered in her chest. She felt like a pirate about to dig up buried treasure.

"*X* marks the spot," she murmured. She dug into her backpack and brought out a hammer and some nails. Two more things she'd "borrowed" from Andrew.

Robert Carter watched from the doorway. "What are you doing?"

"I think Thijmen did something to this place," she explained as she tapped a nail into the wall. "Something that Richard Pickman and Michael Sloane knew about. Something they explored. Amplified."

"The painting—"

"Is a map. To a hidden passage."

The old man stiffened. "A way into the Dreamlands?"

Ellen stepped back to compare the photo to the painting on the wall. "That's the theory, at least."

"And if you're wrong?"

"If I'm wrong, I bounce off the wall, and we go back to Andrew's house."

Robert gave her a long, searching look. "You must love my son very much to consider doing this."

Love.

She tried to push the word out of her head, but there was no denying it. Andrew mattered to her so much, she was willing to face the darkness, to return to a place where a demon waited for her.

You're heading to your own private shadow zone, she thought, *all for a man who couldn't possibly love you.* Ellen shook her head. *I'm not doing it for him. I'm doing it for everyone, for the good of . . .*

Liar, her rational mind sniped. *You're doing it for him, and you know it.*

"Ellen?" Andrew's father called out.

She looked up at Robert, her eyes brimming with tears.

"Oh, my girl. My poor, sweet girl," he whispered.

Ellen hated the pity she heard in his voice. She swiped at her tears, forcing her attention back to the task at hand.

"I need you to stay here and take the painting down," she instructed him. "Because if I can go in . . ."

"Something can come out."

"Right." She folded her hands together and tapped her chin. "When I'm ready to return, I'll signal you to put the painting back up. Let's keep it simple. The code for SOS, okay?"

Robert tapped out the rhythm, but she grabbed his wrist.

"The house listens. Don't give away our secret," she hissed, cringing at her own paranoia.

Uncle Joshua's voice echoed in her head. *Your prescriptions are piling up.*

Yeah, she thought back. *I don't want to hear it, Mr. Art Thief.*

A stab of concern shot through her at the thought of her uncle. Earlier, as she drove Robert and Lily to Andrew's house, she stopped by to pick up Joshua. She was prepared to drag him out of his study kicking and screaming to get him to safety. But he wasn't there. Ellen did a quick search of the house and discovered that his suitcase (and the travel documents he kept in his desk) were missing.

He was gone.

What happened? she wondered. *Where the hell did he . . .*

Ellen closed her eyes, fighting back another wave of tears. "You don't have time for this," she scolded herself.

She moved to the doorway and focused her attention on the task at hand. If things worked the way she expected, she would run for the wall, and the painting would "open" it for her. Send her through to . . .

Where exactly?

Hopefully, where I'm needed. Where I can make a difference.

"Wish me luck?" she said to Robert, her voice trembling.

Andrew's father shook his head. "There's no such thing as luck," he insisted. "I wish you safe travels. There *and* back."

The blessing wasn't enough. Ellen rocked from side to side, trying to loosen feet that seemed glued to the floor. She didn't want to leave the waking world. Every cell in her body resisted the pull. She wondered whether this was how skydivers felt before they leaped out of the plane. Before they hurled themselves into a hostile, alien world.

And they don't have a demon waiting for them on the other side.

"What are you waiting for? *Move your ass!*" Robert Carter bellowed.

Ellen raced across Lily's room toward the white wall, approaching with alarming speed. When she reached it, she turned her head and threw her hands in front of her so that if she hit the hard surface, she wouldn't break her nose. One more step . . . and the painting came to life. The eyes of the ghoul flared. Its long, spindly fingers twitched, flicking the welcome frozen in place for decades.

A hot sensation spread through Ellen's body as the thin place opened. Oily warmth oozed down her scalp, pouring across her arms and back, covering every inch of her skin. An intense light flashed, and then the world plunged into dark nothingness. A square shape popped up in front of her. She bounced off it, and pain exploded through her hip.

Ellen crumpled on the ground.

"Ow! Son of a . . ."

The curse died in her throat as a figure stirred in the gloom.

Solomon, her mind shrieked.

"About time you showed up."

Chapter Eighteen

It took Ellen a moment to recognize the voice, the clipped British accent of the man who'd left the waking world long ago. The creator of the Dreamland city of Celephaïs.

"King Kuranes? Is that you?" she called out.

His grim chuckle chilled the air. "I'm no longer royalty, my dear. I've been overthrown. Deposed."

Her eyes drifted over a small square place. The smell of moldy dirt filled her nose, making it itch. A distant water drip echoed in her ears. And in the center of it all was the object she crashed into when she crossed over.

Ellen recognized the altar from the Pickman painting. It sat in the middle of the room, like the monolith from the movie *2001*.

What on earth is it doing here? she wondered as she approached it.

She was so distracted by the altar that she didn't see Kuranes until he shifted on a small cot anchored into the stone wall. Dressed formally in a suit and a tie, he sat ramrod straight. Ellen couldn't remember whether he was royalty or whether he bestowed the title of king on himself. All she knew was that William Kuranes was a prominent character in the Dreamlands, one of the only humans to permanently reside in this monster-haunted world.

King Kuranes . . . overthrown.

It took a moment for his words to register, for her to recognize her surroundings as a prison cell.

"Wait a minute. Did you just say you're no longer king?"

Kuranes offered her a weak smile.

"It happened so fast," he said as he fiddled with the tattered bedsheets on his cot. "I thought I had him under control, that I'd taken care of the problem. I guess I was wrong. I was never any good at strategic thinking. Probably why I flunked out of military school."

He flashed her a sheepish look that made her want to scream.

You lost control of Solomon Reye?

"He wasted no time. Gathered an army of ghouls. Stormed my city." His face clouded over. "We tried to fight, but there were too many of them. My forces were overwhelmed."

"Celephaïs fell?"

He stiffened. "Celephaïs was *taken* from me."

"But not destroyed? No burning? Looting?"

"Not the last time I saw it."

Relief coursed through her. "How long ago was that?"

"I don't know. Time crawls rather slowly when you're in a dungeon."

She fell silent, letting her eyes drift across the cavern walls.

"There's more," he announced. "I'm about to be executed."

Ellen's body jerked. "What?"

"I'm so glad you weren't here to see the trial. What a sordid little affair that was," he said with a sniff. "One of those old-fashioned kangaroo courts."

"What were you accused of?"

"It hardly matters. He saw an opportunity to settle a score and took it." Kuranes's eyes settled on her. "If this were just about me, I wouldn't have bothered you. But this affects everyone. He's gathered an army of ghouls, and he's . . . he's . . ." King Kuranes sighed. "He's gone mad. Declared war on every human who lives in the Dreamlands. He thinks we're vermin—a corrupting influence. And I don't think he'll stop here. He might set his sights on your world, too."

Ellen thought about the last time Solomon Reye visited the waking world. He appeared at Miskatonic University, masquerading as an expert on "the veil" that separated the natural and supernatural worlds. She remembered how he strutted across the stage dressed as Baron Samedi and delighted in the crowd's outrage when they saw a white man dressed as the voudon god. Ellen was under no illusions. Solomon Reye was a demon. A dangerous, demented demon. But he was fond of humans. His twisted affection influenced everything he did. That this soft spot had hardened, turned into genocidal hatred, frightened Ellen. It made him even more dangerous than he already was.

"What can I do to help?" she asked quietly.

"I'm not the dreamer I once was, and being separated from my city has diminished me," he said, his body sagging with the words. "Forces are gathering nearby—young warriors who want to take up the fight to reclaim Celephaïs. I need to reach them. Everything they need to know is here."

He tapped his head.

That's why Solomon wants him dead, she thought. *He wants to destroy everything and remake the world in his own image.* Ellen shivered.

"You're the key," Kuranes continued. "He's warded this place against anything I might do, but you? I don't think he expects you. You're his blind spot."

"His Achilles heel," she murmured.

"Randolph Carter told me you play a game that helps you dream. That lets you manipulate this world."

"Dungeons and Dragons," she offered.

For the first time since she arrived, King Kuranes brightened. "That's it! Seems perfect for the spot I'm in, no?"

Ellen only half heard him. A question blazed in her brain.

Where the hell is Randolph Carter? She was about to ask when Kuranes tilted his head, listening to sounds she strained to hear.

"We must hurry, my dear. They'll be coming for me soon."

Ellen wasn't sure what she was supposed to do. Even if she had an idea, how could she be sure it would work? She had spent *so* much time in therapy, being told this dream world didn't exist. All the whispers and strategically placed doubts were bound to affect her, chipping away at her abilities, bit by bit.

At least I didn't take my meds, she thought as Kuranes led her to the door of the cell.

It was straight out of D&D: solid metal with a small window the guard could slide open to check on a prisoner.

Ellen closed her eyes and imagined the lock. Pictured the pins and tumblers, the latch that held the door in place. The image of a twenty-sided D&D die used to decide her character's fate popped into her mind.

She reached out and touched the cold steel. "Come on. Good roll. Roll twenty, roll twenty, roll twenty," she chanted.

The door clicked and swung open on rusty hinges. King Kuranes clapped his hands in delight. Ellen was less enthusiastic. She peered into the hall, waiting for guards to come running, alerted by the shriek of metal.

No one came.

Typical.

The last time Ellen visited the Dreamlands, Solomon Reye's security had been lax. She had slipped away from him several times. After that experience, she thought he would have tightened things up a little.

"Guess he still doesn't think much of humans."

Kuranes frowned. "What?"

"Nothing, nothing," she muttered and looked over at him. "I hope you know the way out."

Her companion smiled. "Follow me, my dear."

King Kuranes guided her up a flight of uneven steps out of the dungeon. The rough stone soon gave way to sleek, polished black marble. A network of dark veins crisscrossed the smooth surface. Ellen moved carefully across the floor. Like Edgewood, this place thrummed with energy.

The onyx walls pulsed with a hot, orange light. Periodic flares streaked through the stone like lightning. Ellen shielded her eyes from the sudden orange bursts of light. They reminded her of something she had experienced in the waking world. She groped for the memory, but it slipped away from her.

"What is this place?" she breathed as they made their way down the glowing halls.

Kuranes glanced at her over his shoulder. "You don't know?"

She shrugged.

"This is Ilek-Vlad, the last major city in the human Dreamlands. The new capital of his kingdom."

Ellen's eyes wandered across the castle. Solomon's last headquarters had been a grim, time-tattered monastery. This place felt clean. Modern. History had yet to lay its moldering hands on it.

"Impressive," she said before she could stop herself.

Outside the walls, a roar filled the air.

"We must hurry," Kuranes urged her. "Their little rally is almost over. Can you create some robes for us to pass through the crowd?"

Ellen tensed. "Crowd?"

He raised his eyebrows. "You don't think he would have an execution without a crowd, do you? Someone of my status *deserves* an audience."

The outrage in King Kuranes's voice barely registered. Ellen's mind traveled back to another crowd—a pack of girls who'd jumped her in school. Her vision blurred as she remembered how they'd held her down—grinding her face into the dirt as they beat her unconscious.

She spent a week in the hospital, half of it in a medically induced coma.

And those were just schoolgirls, she thought. *What were Solomon Reye's ghouls capable of?*

She looked toward the dungeon.

SOS, she thought. *That's all I need to do to get back.*

Her hand twitched, eager to tap out the signal.

I've already done enough. Springing him from the dungeon was all I needed to do.

King Kuranes picked up on her thoughts and gave her a sad smile. "I wish it were that simple, my dear, but I need you to take me to Hazuth-Kleg. That's where the army is gathering. Where I can make a difference."

"I'm scared," she croaked.

King Kuranes laid a hand on her arm. "Don't be. You're more powerful than you think. *A kore memagmeni.*"

"Core what?"

He paused and made a clicking sound with his tongue. "You're like a yeti."

"A yeti?" She frowned. "I'm like the abominable snowman?"

"No, no, no. That story you told me about. The moving picture about the desert boy and his mechanical creatures."

Ellen smiled as she remembered the first time she met King Kuranes. He demanded she tell him everything about the waking world. The *Star Wars* universe was part of his history lesson.

"A Jedi," she corrected him. "I'm like a Jedi."

The moment she thought of *Star Wars*, clothing appeared in her hands. Two rust-colored robes, the kind Obi-Wan Kenobi wore.

Kuranes looked past her, at the crowd gathered outside.

"Very good, but can you make them dark gray?"

The robes turned a charcoal color.

Ellen giggled. "A Jedi. I'm a fucking Jedi."

He shot her a stern look.

"Don't go around *announcing* yourself. And for God's sake, keep your head down!" Kuranes hissed at her.

Jedi, she thought again. The weight of her ability settled on her. This wasn't something she could play with, swing around like a toy lightsaber.

"With great power comes great responsibility," she murmured as she slipped on her disguise, yanking the hood over her head.

She smelled the crowd even before she stepped outside. They were packed together, their robed bodies filling the courtyard with a fetid stench that made her eyes water. No one noticed the short "ghouls" that skirted the crowd's edge. Their attention was riveted to the figure on the stage.

Not a stage, she corrected herself. *A gallows.*

A sideways glance revealed the method of execution—a chopping block.

The back of Ellen's neck tingled. Solomon tried to kill her with an ax the last time she was in the Dreamlands. King Kuranes stopped him. She grabbed onto King Kuranes, determined not to be separated.

Although her Jedi robe kept her from being recognized, it did nothing to shield her from the hate spewed from the platform. Ellen didn't understand what Solomon was saying. He rallied the ghouls in their native language, a mix of ancient Arabic and another, older tongue. He barked and spat, the words peppering her like buckshot. She kept her head down, burrowing deeper into her disguise, willing herself not to react. But her body betrayed her. That voice made her tremble, made her sweat and shake.

And yet . . .

Despite the darkness and the madness, it called to her like a siren song.

I'm a sitting duck, she thought.

The air stilled around her.

It was only then Ellen realized she had made a mistake. She'd just imagined herself as a target. She glanced over her shoulder at the figure up on the stage to see if Solomon noticed her.

Randolph Carter stood on the platform, his head tilted back, howling at the sky. He was bare-chested, his exposed skin smeared with gray mud. His dark hair was pulled back in a top knot, his face painted with tattoos. Ellen recognized the patterns. They belonged to the ghouls who'd helped her escape Solomon Reye, who had risen against the demon that had dominated them for so long.

Randolph Carter.

All this time, I thought it was Solomon Reye, but it's . . .

Dear God, Randolph Carter is the problem.

Kuranes's voice whispered in her head: *He's gone mad—declared war on mankind.*

A strangled cry escaped from Ellen's throat.

Randolph Carter jerked, his head swiveling wildly as he tried to locate the human sound. His nostrils flared like an angry bull, and he threw back his head, bellowing the only ghoulish word she understood. "*Mouqabbilat!*"

Ellen's insides turned cold.

Appetizer, she thought. *That's what he's calling me. A tasty little morsel.*

The crowd stirred, eager to find the intruder in their midst.

"We have to get out of here," King Kuranes urged her.

One of the creatures near them turned, drawn to the sound of Kuranes's voice. Its red eyes blazed at them from under its cowl. Except for the fact that this ghoul wore a robe, the scene was an exact reproduction of the Pickman painting.

The creature bared its teeth and took a deep breath to sound the alarm. Another robed figure stepped forward and smashed the ghoul in the head. It dropped with a sickening thud.

The stranger pulled back its hood, giving them a quick glimpse of its face.

"About time you showed up," Kuranes complained again.

Joseph Turner gawked at Ellen. "How many people did you summon, old man?" he whispered.

There was no time to talk.

The other creatures noticed their fallen comrade. A ripple of confusion shot through the crowd. It would only be a matter of time before the disturbance reached the stage.

Before Randolph Carter noticed the commotion and zeroed in on them.

Joseph Turner grabbed their arms and spirited them away from the courtyard.

Ellen's mind spun as Joseph guided them through unfamiliar territory. She tried to make sense of her surroundings, but between her whirling brain and the robe, she only caught glimpses of the strange city. Like the castle they'd escaped, Ilek-Vlad was made of smooth black stone. She recognized it from her time at Mote It Be. Onyx. The stone of protection, a mineral meant to absorb bad energies. As her eyes drifted across the alien city, she was struck by how much Ilek-Vlad looked like a fortress. Broad, sterile boulevards stretched before them. There were no medieval mazes or dense market squares, no places that gave a city its pulsing heart.

The cold, dead city of a dictator, she thought.

Randolph Carter.

Dictator.

Ellen's stomach clenched.

Behind them, the sounds of an unruly mob filled the air. It didn't take long for them to organize. To pick up their trail.

King Kuranes stiffened.

"They're onto us," he murmured, glancing at Joseph Turner. "I hope you know where you're going."

"This was our city long before *he* took over," Turner replied, offended.

Our city. Joseph Turner. Part ghoul.

Ellen doubled over, suddenly overwhelmed by the world.

"Too much," she whispered. "This is all too much."

Joseph squeezed her arm. "I know, but we need to keep moving. We'll slow down when we have a chance, okay? I promise."

He guided them between two buildings—grim, looming edifices that looked like the governmental buildings of the waking world. As they slipped into a narrow alley, Ellen looked up. A black cloud loomed ominously above the city's pointed spires. Her flesh crawled at the sight of the viscous sky. The churning cloud made her feel exposed. Her hand fluttered to the back of her neck, to the phantom ax poised there.

Randolph Carter.

Ellen found it hard to believe. The Randolph Carter she knew was rough. A man riddled by trauma and despair. But the figure she saw on the stage, the fierce leader covered in war paint, whipping the ghouls into a murderous frenzy . . .

What happened? she wondered. *What's changed since the last time I saw him?*

A grating sound interrupted her thoughts.

Joseph Turner wiggled a manhole cover loose. He looked at her eagerly, like a child showing off a new toy. "No matter what city you're in, you'll always find a sewer to crawl into," he declared.

King Kuranes wrinkled his nose. "I'm not going down there."

Turner scowled at the old man. "You'd rather lose your head?" he shot back. "Because if you stay here, that's what will happen. It's only a matter of time before they find you."

Turner made a series of barking sounds, and a ladder appeared out of the gloom.

Ellen didn't hesitate. "Hell, I'll roll in shit to get away from that man," she muttered as she climbed into the darkness.

Joseph Turner beamed. "That's the spirit!"

A ghoul waited for her at the end of the ladder, steadying her as she descended. Its skin was cool and dry, like the firm hide of a reptile. The hands that held her had long Nosferatu nails, talons ideal for digging and scavenging. The ghoul kept its grip light so that the talons didn't break her skin. The creature's tenderness surprised her. When Ellen stepped off the ladder, she bowed to offer her thanks.

The creature cocked its head, studying her with curious eyes. Its facial features were more human than those of the ghouls gathered in the courtyard. Its forehead was flatter, its snout less pronounced. Ellen thought about the evolutionary tree again. Less a tree than a bush. A dense thicket of connection.

She looked at the creature and felt a rush of kinship.

"This is Salima," Joseph offered.

Ellen nodded at the creature. "Hello, Salima."

There was no more time for social pleasantries. Above her, the sounds of the mob grew louder.

Ellen helped King Kuranes make his way down the ladder. Guilt shot through her as she watched him struggle on the rungs. The dash across the city had left him flushed and out of breath.

How long? she wondered. *How long has he been wasting away in Randolph Carter's dungeon?*

As soon as Kuranes reached the bottom, Joseph jumped in, dragging the manhole cover over them.

A moment later, the crowd arrived in a thunder of stomping feet and shouting voices. Ellen held her breath, waiting for the manhole cover to collapse under the mob's weight, for the ghouls to discover their hiding place.

"Come on," Joseph Turner said gently, tugging at her sleeve.

Ellen jumped, startled.

She wasn't aware she was clutching the ladder until she looked down at her hands, at the knuckles that were death-grip white.

She sighed, looking up at the entrance that led to the surface world.

The last thing she wanted to do was go farther underground, but she knew she had no other choice.

Not if she wanted to get out alive.

With a sigh, she let go of the ladder and followed Joseph Turner into the darkness.

Chapter Nineteen

"So, what's the plan?" Ellen asked once they were a safe distance from the entrance.

A lantern flared in response. Salima, the ghoul who helped her down the ladder, shrieked, throwing up her claws to shield her eyes.

"Sorry," Joseph muttered to the creature as he hooded the light. "Salima will show us the way. She knows all the paths under the city. One of them will take us outside, near the harbor. I have a ship ready to take us to Hazuth-Kleg."

King Kuranes bristled at the suggestion. "A *woman's* going to lead us?"

Ellen crossed her arms.

"You didn't seem to mind when a woman sprang you out of prison," she grumbled.

"Yes, but that was different," he protested.

She speared him with her eyes. "How?"

Kuranes turned to Joseph for support.

"Hey! Don't look at me!" Joseph muttered.

The old man sighed, deflating like a balloon. "I'm sorry. You're right. Of course you're right. I . . . I just feel so . . ." He burst into tears.

The outburst stunned Ellen. King Kuranes was an eminence, half-human, half-other. His displays of emotion tended to be strategic, a mask he donned to get what he wanted. This went beyond manipulation. The imprisonment and his scheduled execution at the hands of the man he once considered his friend had clearly taken a toll on him.

She reached out and squeezed his shoulder.

His face twisted, and he recoiled. "Don't touch me, you . . . you Flatlander!" he spat, using the epithet they called people who came from the waking world.

Randolph Carter had called her that.

Many, many times.

Ellen withdrew, stung. The party fell into an uneasy silence as they hiked deeper into the sewers. They walked single file along a narrow stone walkway, trying to avoid the river of filth that oozed down the center. The stench made Ellen's eyes water, making it hard for her to see the path ahead. The farther they moved beneath Ilek-Vlad, the rougher the passage got. The carved rock narrowed. Soon, they parted ways with the human-made tunnels. The smell of sewage faded as they turned onto an uneven dirt path. Painted figures appeared on the walls, hovering over them like ghosts.

Cave art, she thought as she stared at what looked like dancing jackals. Ellen reached for her cell phone before she remembered she had left it behind in the waking world. Not that it mattered. She was sure anything electronic would have fried when she passed through the thin place.

Salima paused in an archway buttressed by two stone columns and conferred with Joseph.

"We're about to enter Nuzarus," he informed the group.

A look of wonder spread across King Kuranes's face. "Nuzarus? Are you serious, my boy? This is the lost city of Nuzarus?"

Joseph glared at him. "It was never lost. We've always known where it is."

Ellen looked at the two men, felt the heat of what was obviously an ancient feud.

"What's Nuzarus?" she asked.

"The ancient city of the ghouls," Joseph offered. "Where humans and ghouls forged their first alliance."

Ellen looked at Joseph's pale features and the gray eyes meant for the shadows. "You mean where they interbred?"

Joseph said nothing. He turned away, motioning the party to follow.

The tunnel opened into a vast cavern. Across a wide, glassy plain, the ghoul city waited for them. Unlike Ilek-Vlad, Nuzarus was carved out of rich blue stone that glowed in the darkness. Ellen couldn't identify the rock. All she knew was that it suffused the ghoul city with warmth. It was a much less dictated place than Randolph Carter's cold capital. Dwellings blended seamlessly into the side of a sheer cliff. The homes were connected by a network of ladders that crisscrossed the rock face. Ellen thought about the ancient cities she had learned about in her civilization class. Çatalhöyük in Turkey.

Mesa Verde in Arizona. Angkor Wat in Cambodia. The ghoul city combined elements of all of them. Ellen's eyes swept over the structures, searching for signs of life. There was nothing: No voices. No children scurrying between buildings, alerting the adults to the arrival of strangers.

A wall of houses stared blankly at them.

King Kuranes frowned.

"Where is everyone?" he wondered aloud. "This place is dead."

"They probably fled when the instability started," Joseph Turner offered.

Randolph Carter. Dictator. Ellen shook her head. She still couldn't believe it. *What happened to him? What happened that made him so—*

Her thoughts were cut short by the sound of weapons being drawn.

A band of ghouls materialized out of the darkness, surrounding her party in a tight ring. Ellen stared at the point of a drawn arrow. An arrow aimed directly at her heart.

"Don't anyone move," Joseph advised.

"I hadn't planned on it, my boy," Kuranes quipped.

An uneasy ripple passed through the ghouls, as if language alone was a threat. A potential weapon.

Joseph advanced with his hands raised, trying to defuse the situation. He only uttered a few words before one of the ghouls lashed out, punching him in the stomach.

"*No!*" Kuranes yelled and rushed to help.

Another ghoul from the pack stepped forward, felling him with a powerful blow.

They targeted Salima as well, shoving their guide to the ground. One of the ghouls lashed out with a word that was obviously an insult.

Seeing a mob attack her comrades enraged Ellen. Anger seeped into her body, thick as syrup, burning away her fear. She stepped forward, in front of her comrades, so that they lay protected at her feet. The ghoul's weapons pivoted, centering on her. For what seemed like an eternity, the only sound was the creak of drawn bowstrings. Ellen turned in a slow circle, looking each ghoul in the eye.

"Go on. You try it," she snarled at the mob. "You just *fucking* try it."

A deep-throated growl pierced the deadly silence, and a shadowy figure passed through the dense crowd. The ghouls swirled to admit the creature, whose head loomed high above the hunched members of his tribe. He held himself in a way that reminded Ellen of the figure she had seen in the Pickman painting—the ghoul who stood, sword raised, over the altar.

The alpha male, she thought.

He turned and shouted, gesturing frantically at a hole in the ground.

"That. Bastard!" Joseph Turner gasped. "Randolph Carter stole the altar where the Great Unification took place. It's sacred to their tribe."

The altar. Ellen had crashed into it when she crossed into the Dreamlands. It had been in the dungeon with King Kuranes. Imprisoned like him.

Ellen frowned. "Why would he do that? That thing must weigh at least a ton. It must have been a nightmare to move."

"Why did the British steal Egyptian statues and stash them in a museum?" Joseph Turner countered. "Why did white men carve the faces of American presidents into the Black Hills?"

"He wants to rewrite history. To . . . erase things," Ellen said, a cold hand gripping her heart. "He wants power."

A wave of sadness washed over her. She knew then that Randolph Carter wouldn't stop at a single altar. Nuzarus would be next on his hit list. Terrible visions filled her head of his mob attacking the city—hammers smashing rock, the mighty buildings crumbling into pieces on the cave floor.

As if it sensed her thoughts, the ground lurched beneath her feet. The ghouls turned, chattering frantically as they pointed their weapons at a new threat.

"What the hell—" She turned to Joseph Turner, who looked like he was about to get sick.

"Oh, no. The altar, it"—he took a deep breath—"it's not just important because of its history. It shields our community. Protects us."

"From what?" King Kuranes demanded.

The ground shook again. This time, the movement was accompanied by the same orange light she saw in Randolph Carter's castle. It streaked across the glassy plain that separated them from Nuzarus, coursing through stone. As Ellen watched the display of light, a thought gnawed at her brain.

Familiar. Why does this all seem so familiar?

"We need to move quickly," Joseph Turner urged them. "Before that thing can gather strength."

"Thing?" Ellen frowned. "What thing?"

The question was barely out of Ellen's mouth when she made the connection.

The orange light. The earthquakes. The thing in an underground cavern.

"Chthonian," she breathed. "They're holding a chthonian captive."

"They use it to fuel their city. His, too," Joseph informed them, eyes nervously flicking to the cave ceiling as if he feared Randolph Carter might hear them.

The leader stepped in front of her, blocking her view of the dancing lights. The closeness forced her to raise her head, to assume the submissive role. Ellen studied the figure standing before her. Except for a loincloth and mace strapped to its side, the lead ghoul was naked. Tattoos covered every inch of his exposed skin. The intricate designs glowed in the darkness.

The ghoul exploded in another flurry of words.

Salima stepped forward, staring at Ellen in wide-eyed wonder.

"He says he knows you. That you've met before."

A jolt of recognition shot through Ellen. She and the ghoul had crossed paths the last time she was in the Dreamlands. She had been with Randolph Carter, and this ghoul had helped them escape Solomon Reye's clutches. When she'd returned to the waking world, she sketched the patterns she had seen on his body to remember and pay tribute to him.

Ellen nodded at the creature, remembering the way Randolph Carter greeted him. "*Masaa el Kheer, Assayed Jinn.*"

The ghoul showed her its teeth. More grunts escaped from its curled lips.

"He says flattery will get you nowhere. That you are nothing but Randolph Carter's bitch," Salima translated, wincing as she spoke the last word.

Ellen shot the leader a fierce glare. "I am *not* Randolph Carter's bitch!"

"What are you, then?" the creature countered, switching to English.

"She's a Persephone. A *kore memagmeni*," Kuranes offered as he rose to his feet, rubbing at his battered head. "The one who stands over the two worlds, guards the borderlands, and maintains balance."

The lead ghoul glared at them. "Prove it!"

"How?" Ellen replied.

The ghoul said nothing.

He tilted his head and stared across the glowing expanse that separated them from the abandoned city of Nuzarus.

Chapter Twenty

The smooth stone spread like a carpet in front of Ellen. Fierce orange light flared across its glassy onyx surface, surging from the depths like an aurora borealis. She peered into the glare, searching for the source of the illumination, the power that fueled Randolph Carter's city as well as the ghoul city of Nuzarus. Just then, a glowing tubular shape passed beneath the surface. She felt heat bleed into the soles of her shoes.

If ever there was a moment when she wondered if her psychiatrists were right, if the Dreamlands was just the product of her delusions, this was it. Ellen couldn't believe what she was seeing.

This is all way too convenient, she thought.

A darker voice chimed in: *That's because it's a trap.*

Ellen recognized the form.

A chthonian. A huge subterranean worm that bored through the earth. The grand creatures that bioengineered the depths of the waking world.

She had encountered a creature like this before, on her first case with Andrew Carter. A Miskatonic professor had imprisoned a chthonian in an abandoned mine outside of Arkham. To liberate it, Ellen allowed it to possess her while Carter worked to free it of the magical bonds that held it in place.

And now, here's another one.

Trapped just like the one in the mine.

Way too convenient, her mind whispered again.

Ellen looked down at her hands, flexing them. Testing their reality.

Is this real? Is history really repeating itself? Or am I passed out in Edgewood, dreaming about my old adventures?

King Kuranes and the lead ghoul stirred beside her. The ghoul chieftain had led them down a narrow, arduous path to the shores of the stony lake. It was a harrowing passage, one meant to test their mettle. Fortunately, Ellen, Joseph, and Kuranes passed the test. So did the other members of the tribe. She could see them spread out across the lake, forming the points of a magic circle.

"We need to get to Nuzarus," the lead ghoul announced, nodding at the abandoned city on the other side of the glassy plain. "The way out is through the old city."

"Only one problem," Ellen murmured.

"Slave labor," the ghoul leader looked at the creature circling restlessly in the stone. He shook his head. "Randolph Carter showed my tribe how to do this, how to imprison these creatures and harness their power. We thought he was different. We wanted to believe he had our best interests in mind because he opposed Nephren-Ka."

Nephren-Ka? The name was unfamiliar, but Ellen assumed he was talking about Solomon Reye.

The ghoul shook its head.

"The moment we defeated the demon, Carter built his own kingdom. He convinced some of my pack to join him. To betray their roots." The ghoul closed its eyes as if holding back a wave of pain. "He promises them a return to a golden age when our tribe ruled the Dreamlands. His world is a lie, built on nothing but—"

"Slave labor," she murmured, her eyes following the flickering trail of the chthonian.

"We need to set it free," King Kuranes announced. "To rob Randolph Carter of his power."

The ghoul stiffened. "That would endanger our city."

Kuranes's eyes swept the barren landscape of Nuzarus. "I'm afraid your city is already doomed, my friend," he said quietly.

Ellen shifted. She didn't like the idea of liberating the creature.

Like holding a tiger by the tail, Andrew warned her when they faced the one in the waking world.

"What about the residents? The civilians who still live in Ilek-Vlad?" she asked, hoping to find a reason to avoid confronting the creature. "We can't endanger innocent lives."

"There are no more innocents up there. Not anymore," King Kuranes offered. "Those who resisted Randolph Carter were exiled. Forced out of Ilek-Vlad. He flushed them out into the wilderness where they—"

Kuranes' face darkened.

Where they died, she thought. *Where some of them died.*

"His city is an armed camp now," the ghoul added. "Enemy territory."

Randolph Carter. The enemy. Ellen didn't want to believe it. Deep down, she hoped the time she spent with Randolph Carter had healed him and made him a better person.

King Kuranes laid a hand on her shoulder.

"He isn't the man you knew, my dear. Not anymore."

She nodded through her tears.

"Tell us what to do. Tell us how we can free this creature," the ghoul leader urged.

What, so you can twist it to your own needs? Make it do your bidding? She bit down on the words before they could escape her mouth. Even so, a voice rose inside her. *You are the mixed daughter who stands over the two worlds. Maintains balance.*

"There is nothing you can do. *I'm* the one who must do this," she insisted, gazing at the glassy plain that imprisoned the creature. "Give me your weapon."

The lead ghoul hesitated, glancing down at the mace on his hip.

"Please, *Assayed Jinn*," she said as she held out her hand. "We must free it. It's the right thing to do."

The creature grunted and slapped the weapon into her grip.

Ellen balanced it in her hand, testing its weight. "Have your tribe hold their positions while I go in. The magic circle must stay intact. No matter what happens."

"You're going in? With that?" Joseph squeaked, nodding at the restless creature.

Ellen looked at him. He hadn't said much since the ghouls of Nuzarus ambushed them. She offered him a weary smile. "And coming back, I hope."

She marched out across the glassy black surface. This was Bentham Corners all over again—an abandoned city, a cave housing an otherworldly creature, a creature held prisoner by human greed. The only thing missing was Andrew.

As she approached the center of the stone lake, Ellen wondered what was happening in the waking world.

Did Andrew and the others succeed in closing the thin place? Or is it still growing, spreading toward the suburbs of New Arkham?

Her mind replayed Kuranes's warning: *He's gone mad— declared war on mankind . . . He might set his sights on your world, too.*

Ellen froze in her tracks.

Were the ghouls in Edgewood Randolph Carter's shock troops? Did they use Edgewood to practice their assault on the waking world?

She bowed her head and let out a deep sigh. Her desire to get out, to return to the waking world as soon as possible, evaporated.

I need to stay.

I need to stay and do whatever I can to stop this.

She gripped the mace with both hands and swung it at the stone floor. A chant from deep memory spilled from her lips.

Amayo De A Coasaga

Zorge

Torsi

Consiata Ol Alonusahi

She struck the surface three times, repeating the words. The last time the mace hit the floor, a low hum shook the cavern. The vibration sped up the weapon and coursed through her. Orange light burst against her closed eyelids. Embers rained down on her, landing on her head. She heard a sizzling pop as the chthonian entered her body. A familiar heat surged through her. She had been possessed by a creature like this before. The last time had been agonizing, but now . . .

It's easy.

"Hello, friend," she said softly.

An angry buzz filled her head as it tried to express its rage. The sound reminded her of the fury of a trapped insect.

The physical creature shot past her and raced toward the city, intent on destroying Nuzarus.

Ellen grabbed the creature's glowing tail and held it back. A tingling sensation spread through her fingertips when she touched it. The chthonian bucked against her grip, furious at being denied its revenge.

"*Not them!*" she roared before remembering chthonians communicated through images. She closed her eyes and imagined the halls of Randolph Carter's castle, showing the creature how Carter used them to power his kingdom.

"Let me guide you," she whispered. "Let me channel your rage."

"Ellen, are you *mad?*" King Kuranes yelled.

She ignored the old man and focused all her attention on the creature. "As above, so below. *Consiata Ol Alonusahi.*

Make me your power. Show me the way, and I will guide you to your true enemy."

The creature thrashed in another paroxysm of rage, and then it settled. Ellen felt it relax into her body, slip into her brain. Almost immediately, a stream of information coursed through her. Ellen found herself looking down at a labyrinth, experiencing it through the senses of the chthonian. It showed her a way out of the maze, a way to escape Randolph Carter's city.

When she came out of her trance, Ellen stared down at a piece of black stone that lay on the ground beside her, knocked loose when she hit the floor with the ghoul's weapon.

Orange light pulsed through it like a heartbeat.

Onyx, she thought. *The stone of protection and strength.*

And a safe spot to hide from your foes.

She picked up the chip of warm stone and put it in her pocket.

"I will carry you with me, my friend. I will take you where you need to go," she promised it.

When she returned from the magical circle, King Kuranes fell to his knees, pressing her hands to his mouth. "Persephone, Persephone Epopteia," he whispered as he kissed them. "Persephone Epopteia."

Ellen jerked free from his grip.

She didn't like people groveling, even when she carried an otherworldly creature . . . *especially* when she carried an otherworldly creature.

She turned and directed her next words to the party.

"I know the way out. It showed me the way."

Gazing intently at Ellen, the lead ghoul said nothing. Ellen sensed the direction of his thoughts, could almost hear him wondering how he could use this strange girl for his own purposes.

Ellen moved closer, her hand tightening on the weapon at her side.

The mighty warrior stepped back, retreating from the heat that burned in her eyes.

"Don't, *Assayed Jinn*. Do *not* make the same mistake twice," she warned him.

The ghoul grunted and led the party across the vast stone plain and to the city's edge, where a series of ladders took them into the heart of the ghoul city. As they scurried across the roofs that spanned Nuzarus, their world narrowed, reduced to a band of light cast by Joseph Turner's lantern. Ellen was relieved to have the creature in her head. It helped her orient. The ghouls may have built Nuzarus, but the chthonians carved out the caves that housed their city. Whenever the ghoul leader hesitated, the creature inside Ellen guided them, taking them down older, more obscure paths.

After an eternity of worming their way through ancient passages, she caught a whiff of salt air. The briny hint of a seashore. Ellen dismissed it as a hallucination. She'd experienced phantom sensations with this creature before. Phantom smells. Phantom sights. Phantom sounds. Even phantom touch.

Then one of the ghouls in front of her stirred, shielding itself from a light her human eyes were too weak to detect.

A hollow, flutelike whistling filled the cave, the unmistakable sound of wind passing through rock. One by one, the party squeezed through the narrow aperture that led to the outside world.

A vast inland sea greeted them on the other side, its black waters stretching to the far horizon. Ellen shielded her eyes as she stepped onto the rock ledge where the rest of the group gathered. After the claustrophobic tightness of the cave, the panorama overwhelmed her.

"The Twilight Sea. Sister to the Cerenarian Sea," Joseph Turner announced.

"The Cerenarian Sea?" Ellen glanced at Kuranes. "Isn't that near your city?"

"My city is *on* the Cerenarian Sea."

"Do the two waters connect?"

The old man nodded. "That's why I need to get to Hazuth-Kleg. A canal runs between them. If I can get there—"

"You can get to Celephaïs."

"I can get to Celephaïs," he repeated her words softly, like a prayer.

"We just need to get down those first." Joseph pointed to the spot below their feet.

Ellen had been so absorbed in the view, she didn't notice the narrow staircase etched into the rock. It zigzagged down the cliff face in a series of switchbacks. Most of the path was hidden, but there were a few places where someone could ambush them from above. Then there were the stairs. They were worn out, crumbling. To say they were hazardous was an understatement.

One slip, and you're not coming back from the Dreamlands.

The ghoul leader shifted in the shadows of the cave. "This is as far as we go. To the edge of our world. No farther." His eyes drifted to Ellen. "You saved our city. I will not forget this."

Before Ellen had a chance to respond, the ghoul leader and his tribe melted back into the darkness.

King Kuranes looked at their escape route, his face tight with fear. "I don't think I can do this," he stammered. "I'm not the man I once was. Even when I was young, I wasn't sure-footed."

Salima, their guide, exchanged a few quick words with Joseph Turner.

"Salima knows the way. She will show you where to step," he suggested. "Ellen, you get in front of Kuranes so he can grab onto you if he needs to. I'll follow behind you."

They took their places and started their long descent. Ellen kept her eyes on Salima, mirroring the ghoul guide's every move, no matter how slight. Kuranes followed behind them. He triggered mini-avalanches of rock that skittered down the trail. Ellen stopped and dug in every time he faltered, preparing to break his fall. But Kuranes proved resilient. He caught himself and kept moving. Still, their progress was slow. Not all of it was his fault. Midway down the stairs, a strong wind blasted the cliff, threatening to blow them into the dark waters below.

Salima barked at Joseph Turner. "Not good," he murmured.

"What is it?" Ellen demanded.

"The Abbott's Howl. The wind that blows off the Plateau of Leng. It's starting. After that, the fog will come."

"The Plateau of Leng?" Ellen echoed.

Joseph Turner pointed to a distant curve on the horizon. A gray mist was drifting across the Twilight Sea, approaching them with catlike stealth.

Ellen shivered and pulled her robe tighter.

H. P. Lovecraft had written about the Plateau of Leng. None of it was good. Her mind filled with images of semihuman creatures and the faceless priests who lorded over them. She also remembered what Randolph Carter had said when she told him what Lovecraft had written about his travels through the Dreamlands. How he had been one of the few humans to see this dreaded land.

Leng? Randolph Carter had exclaimed, his mouth curling in revulsion. *Why on earth would I go there?*

If there was a dark spot on a map, a place where monsters dwelled, the Plateau of Leng was it.

"We don't have to go there, do we?" Ellen asked, dread creeping into her voice.

"No. Thank God. But the wind might slow us down." Joseph Turner turned to Kuranes. "You really need to pick up the pace, old man."

King Kuranes puffed up like an angry bird. A low animal growl started in his throat, another reminder he was half-human.

Half-human on a good day, Ellen thought. She put her hand on his shoulder. This time, he didn't resist.

"Just do your best, okay?"

His body relaxed a little. "Okay," he echoed.

They continued down the cliff. Kuranes picked up his pace, but the strong wind and an even more treacherous set of stairs slowed the party's progress. Ellen kept her eyes on the ground, trying to think only as far as the next step. All while the creature thrummed in her head, circling like a fish in a bowl.

"Soon," she whispered to it. "Soon."

A bloodcurdling cry erupted from the city above. An outburst she could hear even over the roar of the wind. Her neck tingled. *Randolph Carter is up there,* she thought. *He's up there, and he's spotted us.*

Ellen refused to look back, lest she freeze, turn into a pillar of salt.

Arrows whizzed by them, bouncing off the surrounding rocks.

Plink. Plink, plink, plink.

Ellen dropped to the ground but kept moving, scooting down the stairs on her butt. The others followed her lead. Crawling turned out not only to be safer but faster. They covered the next series of switchbacks in half the time. All while arrows rained down on them. Fortunately, the volleys were blown off course by the same fierce wind that assaulted the group.

As Ellen approached one of the last turns, she spotted Joseph Turner's ship. Anchored in a narrow cove, it bobbed in the water, waiting for them.

Ellen scanned the beach below, trying to gauge distance.

A twenty-foot drop, maybe thirty. Too risky to jump.

An arrow thumped into the ground, narrowly missing her. "Fucking lunatic!" she spat.

Their ghoul guide chittered at Joseph Turner.

"Salima has taken us as far as she can go. She needs to return to her people," he translated. "We must protect her."

Ellen's hand closed on the stone in her pocket. She looked up, spotting Randolph Carter gathered with his troops on the city's walls.

An oily, dark cloud hung over him. Thin tendrils extended down the mist's mass and swirled around Randolph Carter's head like a snaky crown.

Ellen stared at the roiling form in disbelief. "What the—"

Her question was cut short by the thrumming of the stone in her pocket. The creature she carried was restless, eager to escape its confinement.

Ellen reached out and pulled the stone from her pocket.

"Run!" she roared at Salima.

Out of the corner of her eye, she saw the ghoul dash for an opening in the cliff wall.

A split second later, a flash of orange light exploded around Ellen.

The creature blasted out of the rock in her hand, streaking toward the ramparts of Ilek-Vlad. She thought it would attack the city, destroy the source of its enslavement, but it targeted the black mass that clung to Randolph Carter. Like a magnified lightning strike, massive energy pierced the cloud, severing the strings that held Randolph Carter hostage. Carter staggered backward, clutching his head and howling in agony.

A low vibration shook the foundations of the city. The onyx towers of Ilek-Vlad flared. The murky cloud withdrew, scuttling away from the sudden illumination. The retreat didn't last long. It churned in the sky and quickly regrouped, settling back on Randolph Carter and the troops surrounding him.

Kuranes grabbed her by the arm and chanted in her ear. "*Run!* Run, run, run!"

The ghoul army on the city wall unleashed another volley of arrows. Ellen vaulted down the stairs, half running, half stumbling. As she hit the beach, her feet sunk deep into the sand.

An arrow ripped through her robe. Sharp, searing pain erupted in her calf.

Ellen gasped and groped for the stone in her pocket before she remembered.

You just set it free.

Her fingers closed on the ring instead—the ring she'd "borrowed" from Andrew Carter.

On the ramparts of the city, she saw Randolph Carter stiffen and turn. He looked down at her, eyes wide with confusion and wonder.

You, his voice whispered in her head. *Dear God, it's you.*

For a moment, the storm clouds cleared in Randolph Carter's head. He broadcast his memories of the night he had taken refuge in the warmth of her body. The night they had surrendered to each other.

There was no time for memories. The members of his ghoul army were reloading their weapons.

"Stop!" she snarled. "You stop them, Randolph Carter!"

Randolph Carter spun to face his ghouls. As he did, the city around him swayed. Orange tendrils, thick as weeds, climbed the walls, cracking open the stone like an egg. Ellen watched in horror as Carter's city crumbled, raining massive stones on the cliffs below.

Joseph Turner grabbed her from behind. Her legs bounced painfully on the gangplank as he dragged her aboard. He deposited her roughly on the deck. All around her, the vessel crawled with activity. Joseph Turner's crew boiled around her, running in all directions. Bringing up the gangplank. Lifting anchor.

She heard the flutter of canvas being unfurled. Wood groaned as the ship moved beneath her. In the distance, she heard thunder's fury as the creature destroyed the city.

Ellen searched the ramparts for Randolph Carter, but everything, and everyone, was lost in a cloud of rising dust.

Dead, she thought. *He must be dead. No one could have possibly survived.*

"Randy, oh God, Randy," she groaned, her eyes brimming with tears.

King Kuranes glared at her. "He got what he deserved," he insisted.

Ellen's anger flared. "No, he didn't," she shot back. "That wasn't him."

Kuranes frowned. "What do you mean?"

"He's possessed," she gasped. "Something else is responsible for this."

Kuranes looked at Joseph Turner. "Help me get her below deck, will you?" Kuranes asked before he turned his attention back to her. "You had a bad injury, my dear. We'll talk later when your head has cleared. Okay?"

She wanted to resist. King Kuranes was dismissing her, like everyone else in her life. But when she tried to get up, her head spun. Blood seeped out of her leg. Lots of it. She let the two men help her into the belly of the ship, away from Randolph Carter and the ruins of his kingdom.

The sight of the feather bed in the cabin brought fresh tears to her eyes. She surrendered to it with a cry of relief. Ellen was dimly aware of her pant leg being cut, of gentle hands probing her wound.

The rest dissolved into the mist.

Chapter Twenty-One

As the ship glided across the Twilight Sea, Ellen Logan dreamed.

"Where are you? Where are you, child?" a man's voice asked.

Ellen's eyes flickered open, but all she saw was darkness. Her body was crammed into a tight, humid space. All around her were strange sounds—ticks, bells, and whistles—a riot of noise that made her body quake. As she emerged from her stupor, a fierce cramp shot through her leg. She tried to reach down, to rub away the pain, but there wasn't enough room. Her surroundings rocked as she shifted, creaking ominously under her weight.

She couldn't see the man who called out to her, but she felt his eyes dart to her hiding place, to her refuge from . . .

What? What happened?

"Are you in there? My God, are you actually *in there*?" the stranger gasped.

Ellen shrunk from the voice. A hard metal object dug into her back. When she pressed against it, she heard a sharp click.

Something behind her yielded. A whisper of cold air chilled her skin.

"You listen to me, young lady. Don't move. Do. Not. Move," the man commanded. "And close your eyes. It's better if you don't see."

Ellen obeyed. A door opened. White light flared against her eyelids.

"There you are," the man said, trying to keep his voice level, but she could hear the tremor beneath it—his fight to stay calm.

If a grown-up is scared, she thought. It was only then that she realized she was a child hiding from something terrible.

"Good. Your eyes are closed. Keep them closed," he advised her. "I'm holding out my hand. Take it."

"Don't hurt me!" she squealed.

The voice softened. "I'm not going to hurt you."

A hand closed on her shoulder.

Ellen cringed, waiting for the man to yank her out of her safe place.

"Take my hand and move slowly," he urged her. "Very slowly."

Ellen did as she was told. Her hand felt strange against the stranger's warm palm. Clammy.

As soon as she emerged from the hiding spot, the man's demeanor changed. He cursed and shouted. "Ambulance! I need an ambulance! Now!"

She opened her eyes. The world exploded in a universe of red. Red hands. Red dress. Everything was red—even her teddy bear, Winston. He lay on the floor a few feet away, his head stomped flat by unknown feet.

That's when the scream lodged in her throat escaped, and her ears rang with the sound of her terror. The world joined her in a high-pitched chorus.

"Ellen?"

She twitched.

"Ellen!"

Her body lurched, bucking her free of the nightmare.

Joseph Turner looked down at her.

The shrieking continued. She sat up, her gaze drifting across the room.

"What—?"

"It's the Abbot's Howl. The wind that blows off Leng," Joseph explained. "When you sail into its teeth, it bites. Gives you bad dreams."

Ellen rubbed her eyes, hoping to clear her vision. It took her a moment to realize she was on a ship. She felt the vessel groan and sway around her, battling what was obviously a strong wind.

"Why are we sailing *into* the wind?" she grumbled. "Don't we want to get away from it?"

"When we reach the right spot, we're going to turn. Use the Howl to take us where we need to go. Where Kuranes needs to go."

She gazed at the lantern swinging from a post, her mouth twisting into a bitter smile.

Joseph Turner arched his eyebrow. "What's so funny?"

"Transfer student," she snorted, remembering how he had introduced himself at the coffee shop. "I can't believe I thought you were a transfer student."

"In a way, I am. I came to the waking world to learn some things."

"Like what?"

"Like how far Randolph Carter's madness has spread."

Ellen flashed on an image. A fire blazing, its embers lifting into the sky, touching down in other places. Carrying the inferno to other worlds.

"Andrew. Oh my God, Andrew!"

Turner scowled. "Andrew?"

"Dr. Carter! You don't think *he's* a part of this, do you?"

"I had my suspicions, but when I saw him in the coffee shop and how he responded to the threat in the graveyard . . ." He shook his head. "Dr. Carter is not the problem."

"Am I?"

The question spilled out of Ellen's mouth before she could stop it. It was an old fear, rooted in the bedrock of her childhood. She was an orphan. Her parents had given her away. Her parents and an entire family had abandoned her: grandparents, uncles, brothers, sisters, aunts, and cousins. No one stepped forward to claim her except for a stranger masquerading as her uncle. And a demon intent on making her his wife.

I'm bad. That's why.

I'm a bad person.

They can all see it.

Joseph Turner cocked his head, almost as if he sensed her thoughts. "Do you know who I am?" Before she could reply, he answered the question. "Joseph Turner's not my real name. I'm Simon Pickman. Martha's cousin. Well, distant cousin," he added, gesturing at his pale features.

All Ellen could do was stare. Her friend never talked about having a family, but that didn't surprise her. Martha Pickman avoided the subject. Her life was devoted to rejecting her legacy, the infamy passed down to her by her great-grandfather.

Richard Upton Pickman. Martha's great-grandfather. Seeing a living relative lifted her hopes.

"Martha! Is she here?" she asked. "Is she with us in the Dreamlands?"

Simon Pickman's face darkened. "No. She's not," he muttered. "She's dead."

"Dead?"

He nodded.

Ellen closed her eyes, her heart curling shut like a flower. *Dead,* her mind tolled. *Dead, dead, dead.* Her thoughts retreated to the painting, to the creature with eyes like the man standing before her.

"You," she breathed. "You were the one who brought his painting into the waking world. You knew what it could do."

Confusion clouded Joseph Turner's face.

Not Joseph Turner. Pickman, she reminded herself. *Simon Pickman.*

"His painting?" He frowned before he understood what she was saying. "Wait a minute. You have one of my great-grandfather's paintings?"

"It's what brought me here," she replied. "You didn't send it?"

"No one sent it. You can't control things like that," King Kuranes said from the doorway. "It shows up when it's needed. Or when it needs something."

"One ring to rule them all," Simon Pickman murmured.

Ellen looked at the two men. "Wait a minute. What are you saying? That the painting is alive?"

Kuranes fixed her with a level stare. "You tell me."

Edgewood.

Ellen remembered how the house had stirred, animated by a force strong enough to resurrect the resident ghost. Her stomach churned as she remembered Michael Sloane's touch. The jagged shapes that punched through her skull.

The painting was there the whole time. Tucked away in the basement. Calling for help.

"My great-grandfather did that," Simon Pickman said, his voice glowing with pride. "He was so much more than an artist. He was a visionary. The master of dreams."

"Your great-grandfather was a lunatic!" Kuranes snapped before the young man could say anything more. "A man who experimented with—" Kuranes eyed Ellen. "Where's the painting now?"

Dread swept through Ellen like a sudden storm. "Oh my God! Robert Carter has it!"

Kuranes stiffened. "What?"

"Robert Carter has it. Andrew's father."

Simon Pickman chuckled. "That thing really does have a mind of its own."

Kuranes ignored him. His eyes bored into Ellen. "Can he be trusted?"

"Well, he hates his father, so if you're worried about him being on Randolph Carter's side, I'd say it's unlikely," Ellen offered.

"Unlikely but not impossible," Kuranes replied.

She held the old man's gaze. "Impossible is no longer a word in my vocabulary," she insisted.

King Kuranes's eyes lingered on her. "You've changed," he announced after a long, appraising silence.

"How?" she pressed him.

"This is the first time I've heard you say Randolph Carter's name," Kuranes pointed out.

In her mind, her psychiatrist cheered. *That's the way you do it. That's how you rob him of his power.*

"So, what now?" Ellen demanded, if only to silence the clinical voice.

Before Kuranes could respond, one of the crew entered the room. The ghoul pulled Simon Pickman aside, and the two had an urgent conversation.

"He's following us," Simon announced after the ghoul left.

"Who?" Ellen asked.

"Who?" he echoed, mocking her. "Randolph Carter. His ship has been spotted. It's still a fair distance away, but it's approaching. Fast."

"I guess he doesn't like it when people destroy his city," Simon Pickman observed.

"Randolph Carter? He's, he's—"

"Alive. Somehow," Kuranes said, shooting Simon Pickman a sharp look. "*And* in a better ship."

"I'm not a sailor! I had no idea what to pick!" Simon protested. "The plan was to get you out of Ilek-Vlad before he even noticed you were gone. I didn't expect him to find us so quickly. Much less chase us across the sea like a demented pirate."

The old man held up his hand. "I'm sorry, my boy. I don't mean to sound ungrateful," Kuranes replied. "I do appreciate everything you've done for us."

Us. The world closed in on Ellen.

She moved to her feet and headed for the door.

"Where are you going?" Simon Pickman called after her.

"On deck. There's something I need to see."

Chapter Twenty-Two

The Twilight Sea pounded the ship with watery fists. Whitecaps salted the surface. Everywhere Ellen looked, she saw nature's rage. Even the brief trip above deck required protection. They donned rain gear to shield themselves from the relentless spray and goggles to protect their eyes from the biting wind. As they inched their way past the ghoul crew huddled on deck, the trio looked like polar explorers—strangers in a harsh and hostile land.

Ellen looked south toward Randolph Carter's ship. If it was there, it was hidden, cloaked in the fog that poured off the Plateau of Leng. There was no chance to get a closer look. To see whether the dark presence was still with Randolph Carter. Driving him. *Possessing him,* Ellen thought with a shiver.

"This is bad," Kuranes muttered as he shifted beside her. "I haven't seen fog this thick in ages."

Ellen shouted to Simon Pickman over the din. "Where are we headed?"

"Drunken Cow," was what she heard.

"What?"

Simon pulled the group into a tight huddle. "The Sunken Crown," he yelled over the wind. "It's a series of islands off the coast of Leng. When we get to the Crown, we're going to make a quick turn. With any luck, we'll get there before he reaches us."

"If the rocks don't sink us first," Kuranes mumbled. "Don't forget there are jewels in the Crown, my boy. Big, ship-eating jewels."

Simon Pickman ignored him and turned to Ellen. "The Sunken Crown is the last human outpost in the Dreamlands," he explained. "Monks run the Tiara, a string of lighthouses. They watch the borderlands and keep wayward travelers from crossing over into—"

"The Abyss," King Kuranes sighed. "Let's be honest. You're going to push this ship to the very edge of the known world."

Simon Pickman glared at the old man. "And turn around. Don't forget that part. Lining ourselves up with the Sunken Crown will give us our best chance to catch the wind."

"What makes you so sure the lighthouses will be on? That the keepers are still there?" Kuranes demanded. "Randolph Carter's forces may have already taken over. Hell, he may have even destroyed them."

Ellen pictured the floodlights back in Arkham winking out one by one. She could only imagine what the darkness would bring here.

"Do you have a better idea?" Simon Pickman exploded. "Because unless you can climb inside that maniac's head and find out what he's done, what he's planning to do, we have nothing."

Ellen's fingers brushed the ring.

"I know . . ."

The two men looked at her. "What?" they asked simultaneously.

"I know a way to get inside Randolph Carter's head."

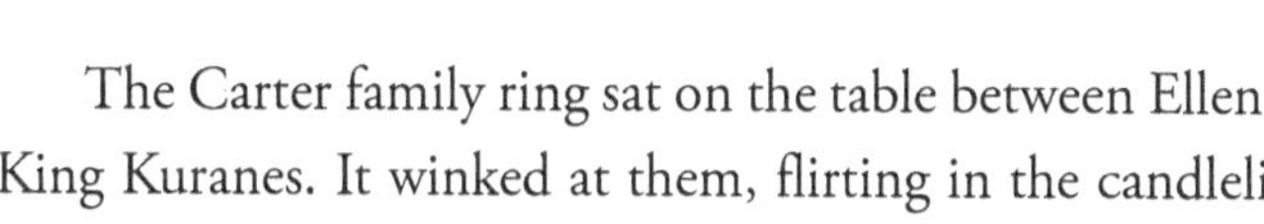

The Carter family ring sat on the table between Ellen and King Kuranes. It winked at them, flirting in the candlelight. When she brought it out, Simon Pickman beat a hasty retreat, mumbling about witchcraft and fool's errands. Ellen didn't blame him. She would much rather battle the forces of nature than . . . whatever this was.

King Kuranes broke the silence. "I thought it was lost. You had it all this time?"

"No," she replied. "When I realized what it was, I passed the ring on to Andrew Carter."

The old man's eyebrow spiked. "And he let you borrow it?"

Ellen looked at the floor.

"I took it."

"Took it?"

Her cheeks flared. "I stole it, okay?"

Thief, a voice hissed. *No better than your uncle Joshua.*

"Why did you take it?" Kuranes asked her in a gentle voice. "Did you think it was dangerous to leave it with Andrew?"

"No," she replied. "I knew what the painting would do. I knew where it would take me. And. And . . ." Tears sprang into her eyes, sudden and fierce. "Every time I've been in the

Dreamlands, Randolph Carter has been here. To help. To guide me. I didn't want to get lost." She nodded at the ring on the table. "This was the only way I knew to find him."

King Kuranes continued to stare at the ring.

"That's what it does, right? Takes me to him?" she asked.

Kuranes sat back, rubbing his face. "I've made a terrible mistake, my dear. I thought bringing the two of you together would help. That it would make things better."

Ellen frowned. "Make things better? Are you talking about his wife?"

"Olivia? You think this is about Olivia?" He laughed. "God, if it was only that simple! When I brought you together, I knew you would give him something special. Something he hasn't had in a very long time. And when I took that away, when I sent you back to the waking world . . ." His face clouded. "I broke him. The human side of him, at least."

Something dark stirred in Ellen's brain. "What are you talking about?"

"Remember when you asked if Randolph Carter was like me? An eminence?"

Uneasiness spread through her like a bruise. "You said he wasn't."

He studied her with dead eyes. "I said nothing of the sort."

The atmosphere between them suddenly grew thin. Ellen found herself struggling to breathe.

King Kuranes tilted his head. "Did you really think a mere human could imprison me? That he could pursue me like this? Did you think that making love to an ordinary mortal would be enough to save you from a demon like Solomon Reye?"

Ellen sat back, her hands curling in her lap. The news shocked her, but deep down, she knew. The moment she met Randolph Carter, Ellen knew he was different. She wrote it off as a generation gap. *Generations,* she corrected herself. Eighty years separated them—nearly a century of cultural drift. But there was more to it than that. Sometimes, when she looked into his eyes, she saw emptiness. Detachment. PTSD. That's what she'd thought at the time. Randolph Carter fought in the trenches of World War I, had seen humanity at its worst. Ellen assumed his alienation from the world reflected the horrors he'd endured.

It goes deeper than that. Way deeper.

Dear God, who . . . What *did I make love to?*

Kuranes continued to talk. "Hybrid creatures are delicate. They need balance. And balance was the last thing Randolph Carter had. Even as a child, he escaped into this world. To get away from a dead home ruled by tyrannical parents. He found meaning in the Dreamlands. Purpose. He indulged in endless flights of fancy. Explored forbidden places. Randy achieved great things, but his human side suffered."

She thought of her own diagnosis—the slow, stealthy spread of schizophrenia. *Supposed* schizophrenia, she corrected herself.

"Whatever problems you have in the waking world, you bring here," Kuranes said. "He told you that about me, but he didn't mention his problems, did he?"

Ellen blushed. She remembered her conversation with Randolph Carter the last time they were together. He told her about Kuranes's affliction: the memory lapses, "absences" severe enough to threaten parts of Celephaïs. He portrayed King Kuranes as an unstable dictator, holding a city hostage to his ego.

A childhood mantra popped into her head. *I'm rubber. You're glue.*

"Randolph Carter has pushed the boundaries of time and space more than anyone else in the Dreamlands," Kuranes continued. "He spent years, *years*, in an alien form. But those amazing adventures came at a price. He's . . . vulnerable. Easily influenced by others."

He fell silent, his eyes settling on the ring.

Ellen peered into the stone's ruby depths. She'd offered to get inside Randolph Carter's head. Now, she wasn't so sure. She imagined his mind snapping shut on her. Being trapped with a man who was . . . what?

"I don't know if I can do it," she admitted. "I don't even know if it's worth doing. What chance do I have if he's turned against all humanity?"

"Randy is a complicated man. He was at war with himself long before he saw a battlefield. But when he thinks about you . . ." Kuranes looked up from the ring. "You calm him."

"You make him sound like a wild animal."

"In a way, he is." Kuranes sighed and shook his head. "Look, I don't know what will happen. You might get some valuable information. He might shut down and give you nothing. The only thing I know for sure is that Randolph Carter would never hurt you."

Her hand dropped to her bandaged leg. "Could have fooled me," she grumbled.

"I'll be watching you the whole time," he promised. "And if you look like you're in trouble, I'll pull you back."

Ellen stared at the exhausted old man. *Could he react quickly if things went wrong?* she wondered. She decided it didn't matter. She needed to do this, even if it meant losing herself.

"Okay," she agreed, more to encourage herself than him. "Let's do this."

✦ ✦ ✦ ✦ ✦ ✦

Ellen watched as King Kuranes roamed around the cabin, gathering the things he needed for the ritual. She expected something elaborate: The burning of incense. The chanting of spells. The drawing of a pentagram. She longed for theatrics. For something, anything to delay the moment she'd slip on the ring. All Kuranes did was pull out a dusty bottle from a shelf and pour green liquid into a glass.

"What is it?" she asked when he set the drink in front of her.

"Absinthe. The fuel of dreamers."

Ellen had heard about it. It was a spirit favored by artists and writers. *Visionaries. Fellow travelers.* Her eyes watered as she downed the liquid. The sharp tang of licorice bloomed in her mouth. Kuranes guided her to a high-back chair and helped her get settled. As he arranged pillows around her, he smirked.

"What's so funny?"

"I was just thinking about rings. When you married Randolph Carter, you didn't exchange rings, did you?"

"We didn't have much time to plan the wedding," she quipped.

He took her left hand.

"Allow me."

Alarm bells rang in her head. Ellen didn't want to be reminded of her connection with Randolph Carter, her union with someone she now knew was only part human. She considered breaking free, running up to the deck, and throwing herself into the sea. Her lips twitched in amusement. *Virgin sacrifice,* her mind quipped. *A little too late for that.*

He slipped the ring on her finger before she could resist.

The metal felt unnaturally cold against her skin. Ellen expected it to be a bad fit—it was large and bulky, like a high school class ring. But when Kuranes slid it on her finger, it constricted, curling around her finger like a snake.

Ellen blinked.

Absinthe, she thought. *It must be the absinthe.*

"Relax, my dear," Kuranes said. "What do they say? Just go with the flow."

"Go with the flow?" She snorted. "Get with the times, you old—"

The words froze in her mouth.

Her body jerked.

The ring tore her away from the warmth of Kuranes's cabin and hurled her across the raging Twilight Sea, toward a ship as black as the city she'd escaped. The vessel's bow materialized out of the gloom, approaching with alarming speed. Searing heat spread through her as she melted through wood and metal. Ellen closed her eyes, forcing down a wave of nausea. She hit a barrier, then juddered to a stop. The first thing she saw were bodies. Lots and lots of bodies. Panic shot through her.

The basement. Oh God, I'm in the serial killer's basement again.

A figure stirred and grunted in its sleep. As her eyes swept the floor, she realized she was surrounded by Randolph Carter's ghoul crew. The creatures occupied every square foot of space.

At the end of the hall, she spotted a closed door with a familiar symbol. She looked down at the matching pattern on the ring that gripped her finger. "The only way out is through," she whispered.

She drifted through Randolph Carter's crew like a ghost. Some of them shifted in their slumber, their doglike snouts twitching. Ellen wondered what they were dreaming, whether they sensed her presence as she glided by them.

And what about him? she wondered. *Does he know I'm here?*

The ring flared when she reached Carter's cabin, and the door opened on silent hinges.

"Guess so," she muttered. Ellen paused at the threshold, her mind chanting warnings. *Trap, trap . . . it's a trap.*

A strangled cry pierced the stillness of the ship. Ellen recognized the sound of Randolph Carter's pain. She rescued him from a nightmare once, pulled him out of his bad dreams and into her arms. This was a different kind of agony. When she rushed into the room, she found him sprawled naked on a bed, his eyes staring blindly at the ceiling. His hands were extended, his fingers plucking the air. Strange sounds bubbled from his throat. Every few beats, his body stiffened and jerked. The seizures were strong enough to rock the bed.

Ellen looked away, biting down on her lip hard enough to taste blood. Out of the corner of her eye, something moved. All around the bed, thick vines dangled. They swayed with the motion of the ship. One of them brushed her neck, skittering feather-like across her skin.

Not vines, she thought with a chill. *Tentacles.*

They covered the ship like a malignant growth. Randolph Carter's outstretched hands were tangled in them. A few were lodged deep in his body. He twisted and turned, trying to free himself. Every time he resisted, the tentacles tightened their grip. He stiffened, and the veins on his neck corded. He shouted words in a language she couldn't understand.

Ellen dropped to her knees and tried to free him. She hissed as her hands passed through the tentacles.

You're not here, remember? she reminded herself. *Not in physical form.*

"Randolph," she called out, peering deep into his vacant eyes. "Randolph Carter, wake up!"

The tentacles jerked, startled by the intrusion.

The ship lurched in response, throwing Ellen to the floor. She scrambled to her feet and quickly returned to his side.

"Randolph, can you hear me? It's me!"

A flicker of recognition sparked in his eyes, then died.

She knew what she had to do. She'd threatened him with it the last time she found him fighting a nightmare.

"All right. I'm coming in there," she murmured in his ear.

Ellen climbed on top of him and let her spectral form pass through his body. This time, the journey was easier. Even though she still tumbled through space, there was no burning sensation or agonizing passage through solid material. It reminded Ellen of being on a fun-house slide. Out of control but moving in a set direction, she traveled in a way her mind could grasp. Reaching the end of the ride, she landed hard. The spongy ground, wet and thick with the taste of salt, cushioned her fall. When she raised her head, tiny granules clung to her hair.

Sand, she thought. She looked out at a beach that curved before her like a scythe. A short distance away, Randolph Carter stood, his eyes fixed on the horizon. He clutched a peacoat to his body. His dark hair whipped wildly in the wind.

"This isn't real," he said as she approached. "You're not really here."

The voice that greeted her was so soft, so different from the maniac on stage that Ellen wondered whether he was the same person.

"This was the only way I could reach you," she murmured.

Randolph Carter favored her with a glance. "You destroyed my city," he said as if they were discussing nothing more than the weather.

"Yes and no."

"What do you mean?"

"It wasn't really me. And that's not your city. It hasn't been for a long time."

A ghost of a smile tickled his lips. "It's always complicated with us, isn't it?" In an instant, his expression darkened.

"What is it?" she whispered.

He raised his arm and pointed to the sea. On the distant curve of the bay, his ship sliced through the whitecapped waters. The fog reached out from the Plateau of Leng to the *Olivia*, wrapping its long tendrils around the vessel. The spidery fingers pulled the ship forward like a tractor beam toward the jagged jewels of the Sunken Crown.

A familiar cloud loomed over the rocks, oily and black.

It was the same thing she saw in the city. The menacing presence that hovered over him. It lurked behind the lighthouse, using the fog to mask its presence.

"You see it, don't you?" he said softly, and when she nodded, he relaxed a little. "Not many do. Especially those who've been in the Dreamlands for a long time."

"Like King Kuranes," Ellen offered.

"I didn't notice it until it was too late. Until it . . . attached to me." He glanced at her, pain seeping into his cold blue eyes. "I used to take my son along on adventures like these. For that very reason. I couldn't trust my senses. He was my eyes and ears. My lookout."

"The canary in the coal mine," she murmured, and Randolph Carter's pain morphed into anger.

"No. Never. He was never a sacrifice!" he hissed at her.

Ellen looked out at the water and said nothing. Her thoughts turned to Robert Carter living alone in Edgewood. Living in the Witch House because it was the only way he knew to get closer to his father.

"How long has this . . . creature been with you?" she asked after a long silence.

"I don't know, but I think it started in the trenches."

Ellen shivered as she remembered the nightmare he had the last time she was with him. Its tidal pull had been so strong that it dragged her into the trenches of World War I, where she found Randolph Carter wounded, struggling, and trying to pry off . . .

Tentacles, she thought numbly. *He was trying to pull off tentacles.*

"What does it want?" she asked.

"A foothold, a way to worm into the waking world."

Randolph Carter cried out, doubling over in pain.

Ellen moved to his side. "What is it? What's wrong?"

"You've seen enough. I can't hold it back anymore," he gasped. "Get out!"

"I'm not leaving you," she insisted. "You need help!"

He looked up at her, his eyes inky pools of nothingness.

"I said *get out!*"

She felt a sharp tug around her middle. Randolph Carter and the beach retreated. King Kuranes popped back into view. She groaned at the glass of clear liquid he offered her. "What are you dosing me with now, old man?"

"A little vodka. To calm your nerves."

It was only then that Ellen realized she was shaking. She tossed back the drink, welcoming the warmth that coursed through her body.

"What happened?" he demanded once she settled.

Ellen frowned. "You didn't see it? You mean you weren't there?"

King Kuranes made a sour face. "He blocked me. I tried to follow you, but he blocked me. He kept me out."

She shook her head. "He didn't block you. He only had enough energy to let one of us in."

The old man snorted. "Please, Randy has more than enough power to—"

"Randolph Carter isn't Randolph Carter anymore. He's possessed."

"What?"

"He's possessed," Ellen repeated.

"That's impossible! He can't be—"

"He's possessed!" she insisted, her mind drifting to the sleeping ghouls at her feet. "It's not just him; his entire crew is affected. And . . ."

Whatever is pulling his ship is taking us with him. Luring us to the jagged points of the Sunken Crown.

Ellen jumped to her feet and sprinted up the stairs.

When she reached the deck, the Abbot's Howl slammed into her, trying to hurl her back into the ship. Now that she knew what was behind it, the wind took on a different form.

"Sacrifice," it hissed as she fought her way to Simon Pickman, who was piloting the ship. "You're nothing but a sacrifice."

It doesn't have to be this way, the alien voice sizzled in her head. *Don't fight it. There are other paths for you . . .*

"Binoculars!" she bellowed when she reached Simon Pickman at the helm. "I need binoculars!"

Simon turned to one of his crew, who slapped a spyglass into her hand.

Thanks to Randolph, she knew where the lighthouse was relative to the ship, but the fog was too thick to see anything.

"Randolph, help me," she whispered as she scanned the coastline. "Let me see what I need to see."

A ghoul rested its claws on her shoulders. Ellen jumped, startled as her vision deepened. She didn't know that ghouls could share their night vision, but the lighthouse came into sharp focus. Its thin, circular body punched into the night sky, looming defiantly over the Plateau of Leng. At the top of the tower was the beacon. The light should have been clearly visible, but it flickered weakly across the Twilight Sea. As Ellen peered through the spyglass, she soon saw the reason why. The fire in the lighthouse had dwindled to mere embers. The glowing points of light flickered, in danger of being smothered by the approaching darkness.

"Oh, God," she breathed. She looked again to be sure. "The fire is dying," she said as King Kuranes reached her.

"What?"

"The fire in the lighthouse. The beacon. It's going out."

Simon Pickman threw up his hands. "Then it's over. If we don't have the light, we might as well crash the ship into the rocks and be done with it."

"I'll relight it," Kuranes offered.

"You can't go. You're needed in Celephaïs," Pickman insisted.

"One of the crew, then," Ellen suggested.

Simon Pickman shook his head. "They won't go near the Sunken Crown. They're afraid of it."

Ellen looked down at the ring on her finger.

I need to do whatever I can to stop this. "I'll go," she volunteered.

The two men looked at her, astonished.

"Oh no! Oh, no, no, no! I absolutely forbid it!" King Kuranes insisted.

Ellen glared at him.

"You can't *forbid* me from doing anything, old man."

"If you leave this ship, you might get stuck here," Simon Pickman warned her. "You may never be able to return to the waking world."

"I know," she breathed, keeping her eyes fixed on Kuranes. "But the needs of the many outweigh the needs of a few."

"I hate that saying," King Kuranes grumbled.

A strange calm washed over Ellen. "This is what I'm meant to do. It's why you brought me here," she reminded him. She pursed her lips and gazed out at the dark, churning water. "Now, I just need to find a way to get to the island without dying first."

"I can help with that," King Kuranes said. He plopped onto the deck, tucking his legs under his body. Ellen had seen Kuranes go into trances before, but those flights had always been involuntary, the product of his declining faculties. Now, as he slipped away, oblivious to the howling wind, she saw his strength—the sheer force of will.

Eminence. An important person. *But didn't it mean something else? To jut, project?* At that moment, Ellen had a vision of Kuranes using the Pickman painting, ringing it like a bell and sounding an alarm that reached across worlds.

Kuranes was the one who reached out to me and sent me a message. Through Michael Sloane, through Edgewood. He summoned me. Here.

She shifted nervously in place. The thought of anyone, even an ally, having that kind of power over her . . .

"Not good," she breathed.

A low thrum filled the air, more sensation than sound. It vibrated Ellen's sternum, pushing the air out of her lungs.

Two figures appeared, inky black on gray. They twisted and tumbled like kites in the sky.

"What is the old man doing?" Simon Pickman asked.

Ellen barely heard him. Her ears popped loud enough to make them ring. Off the bow of the ship, the shadowy shapes took form. They had long, barbed tails; talons; and huge, bat-like wings. The sleek, humanoid creatures landed on the ship, sending a flurry of excitement through the ghoul crew.

"Nightgaunts," Ellen breathed.

The hybrid creatures were the gatekeepers of the Dreamlands, capable of passing through dimensions. They snatched up travelers who strayed too far from the waking world. Ellen wasn't afraid of them. The last time she was here, they helped her. They rescued her just as Solomon Reye's forces attacked Randolph Carter's ship. They plucked her off the *Olivia*, delivering her to the safety of King Kuranes.

Looks like I'm going on another trip, she thought as one of them approached.

The creature had no eyes, ears, or mouth, but Ellen recognized the curve of the horns on its head and the pattern that decorated its tail. "Mr. Poe?"

"I thought you might appreciate seeing a familiar face," Kuranes offered.

Ellen scowled at him. "Are you trying to be funny?"

"Am I trying . . . Oh!" he exclaimed, looking at the creature as if he had just noticed it was faceless. "I'm sorry, my dear. I've been around them so much I forget how they look to Flatlanders."

Flatlanders. Ellen gritted her teeth but ignored the insult.

"Why did you call *two* nightgaunts?" Simon Pickman asked.

"One is a decoy. I want to make Randy"—Kuranes stopped and considered Ellen—"or whatever's controlling Randy, think I'm headed to the lighthouse with you. Hopefully, he'll change course—"

"And stop chasing us," Pickman finished the thought.

Kuranes continued to study Ellen. "There's one thing."

"What?" she asked when the silence became unbearable.

"You have to let Mr. Poe sting you."

"Excuse me?"

"If you're conscious during the trip, Randy might see where you're going and figure out what we're doing. We can't risk that."

Ellen glanced nervously at Mr. Poe. She had been stung by a nightgaunt before. It was a light tap, only a hint of what the creature could do, but the pain, the psychic agony of it, left deep scars.

King Kuranes sensed her distress. "I'll tell Mr. Poe to be gentle. It won't be any worse than the absinthe."

"'Quaff, oh quaff, this kind nepenthe,'" she whispered, quoting the human Poe.

Kuranes stepped forward. "I'm asking a lot, Ellen. I know that."

"I'll do it if you promise me one thing."

His eyes narrowed. "And what would that be?"

"If I'm right and Randolph Carter *is* possessed, be kind to him. Show mercy."

"Mercy?" He spat out the word like a curse. "You want me to show mercy after everything he—"

"If he's possessed, he's not the one behind this," she pointed out. "Your time would be better spent figuring out who or what is responsible."

King Kuranes stepped forward and pulled her into a sudden, fierce hug. "You are a wise woman," he whispered in her ear. "If things were different, you would rule Celephaïs by my side."

By my side. The words unnerved her. She thought again of this man's power, his ability to reach across worlds. Ellen withdrew, a polite smile frozen on her face.

Simon Pickman stepped forward and pressed something into her hands. "A flare gun and some extra cartridges. To feed the fire."

"Thanks," she murmured, stuffing the weapon into her pocket.

"*Fiat lux*," Kuranes murmured. "If you forget everything else, my dear, remember. "*Fiat lux*."

"Let there be light," she whispered as Mr. Poe approached.

The nightgaunt unfurled its wings, exposing its shimmering, membranous skin. Bright, flashing colors danced across its surface.

Ellen moved toward the creature, hypnotized by the rich display.

She never felt the barb that sank into her skin.

Chapter Twenty-Three

Klick, klick, klang. Klick, klick, klang.

The sound drew Ellen to the strange, coffin-shaped clock. It had been part of the house for as long as she could remember. She had been scolded when she tried to go near it, sternly lectured it wasn't a toy. But there was no one left to stop her now. She had been lulled out of a deep sleep by the front door being kicked in. A flurry of voices erupted as she snuck out of her room, clutching her teddy bear, Winston. Below her, shadowy figures circled the adults like sharks. She knew the people being threatened looked after her. But she felt no connection to them, no sense they were her "real" family. Still, when she saw their bodies hit the floor, an anguished cry escaped from her throat. One of the intruders peered into the darkness, searching for the source of the sound. Ellen knew she needed to move. She needed to get out of the house.

That's when the clock on the ground floor started to chime. *Klick, klick, klang. Klick, klick, klang.*

She had never heard it make a sound before. It had always been a silent presence, keeping her company while she ate her lunches alone in the kitchen, read for endless hours in the Victorian parlor, played with her toys in the empty halls. Every so often, when the afternoon sun seeped through the curtains, the light hit its silvery face, and the strange markings on the clock danced. Ellen would stop whatever she was doing and run over to it, giggling and bouncing. Trying to get it to come to life. To be her friend.

And now, it called out to her.

"Get the girl!" one of the voices bellowed from below. "We need her. We need her for the . . ."

Ellen didn't wait to find out why these strangers needed her. She scurried to the servant staircase. She crept down the long, narrow passage, her heart thundering in her chest. One of the family members used to be in the military. Whenever she got upset with something and started to melt down, he always stopped her temper tantrum with a chant.

"Slow is smooth and smooth is fast. Slow is smooth and smooth is fast," she whispered as she made her way down the steep stairs, avoiding the steps she knew would creak. Her mind flashed on a movie she saw when the rest of the family thought she was asleep. She remembered the scene now: a boy hiding from a madman by covering his tracks in a snowy maze.

"Slow is smooth and smooth is fast," she said one last time.

The hidden staircase deposited her in the kitchen. A storm had just moved in, plunging the world into inky twilight. Rain sheeted down the picture window as Ellen tiptoed through the house, passing familiar objects made sinister by flashes of lightning. Normally, the sounds of a storm would have frightened her. Ellen didn't mind the noise. It kept her movements hidden from the intruders. She could hear them storming up the stairs, heading to her last known location.

That's not very smart, she thought, remembering the lessons she learned playing hide-and-seek. *One of them should have stayed down here. Kept an eye on things. Made sure I didn't run out of the house while the others looked for me.*

Her eyes drifted to the front door, which dangled from its hinges like a loose tooth. She ran for the exit, even though she knew the family locked the gates at night. If she wanted to escape, she would have to climb over the wrought-iron fence to get out.

She skidded to a stop.

Wait a minute, if the gates were locked, how did these guys get—

"And where do you think you're going, little miss?"

A man stepped into the doorway, dripping rain onto the polished wood floor. Even though his face was obscured by a hood, she could see his mouth curled in a smug little smile.

"Hey, guys! She's—"

A sharp object punched through the man's chest, cutting short his gloating. The intruder groped for the weapon, trying to pull it out. But it was attached to something. As Ellen watched in disbelief, a huge faceless creature emerged from behind the intruder. A pair of bat-like wings unfurled around the man and wrapped him in a tight embrace. The man's screams were muffled by the membranous skin, but they were loud enough for his partners to hear them.

"Hey, Neil! What's the hell is going on down there?"

Klick, klick, klang.

The door to the clock popped open. Ellen expected to see the guts of the clock, its chains and gears and bells. All she saw was a black hole, a rectangle of pure darkness. Her eyes returned to the entombed man, whose body twitched in the leathery cocoon of the creature. She was so entranced by the sight, she didn't hear the approaching footsteps.

"Jesus, we give you one thing to do . . ." the man started to complain but froze on a step that creaked loudly under his weight.

The creature's featureless head pivoted. It pulled what Ellen now realized was a tail from the first man's body and launched it at the second intruder. It whipped around the man's neck like a lasso. His eyes bulged, and he collapsed onto the floor, spluttering and choking, his face turning blue. Ellen screamed, dropping her teddy bear, and ran to the only place she could hide.

The clock door slammed shut behind her. As she burrowed into the tight space, she heard a humming. It masked the sounds of the struggle, the screaming, lulling her into a deep—

A sharp, snapping sound jolted Ellen out of her dream. She groaned and curled into a tight ball. All she wanted to do was huddle under the warm blanket and finish the scene. To find out what happened next. But an angry buzzing filled her head, and the blanket lifted, letting in a whistling sound that made sleep impossible.

A dark creature loomed over her. *Protecting her from the priest's . . . pope's . . .*

Scream. Shout. Yell. The words refused to take form. Ellen felt unmoored, lost in a fog. Her first thought was that she was back in the mind of the woman with Alzheimer's she had explored so long ago. Panic shot through her body.

Maybe I never left, she thought. *Maybe I've been trapped all this time. Tangled up in tentacles, just like . . .*

"Randolph Carter," she whispered.

A figure stepped out from behind the nightgaunt, spewing curses.

"I'll make him pay. I swear to God, I'll make the bastard pay for this!" Randolph Carter ranted as he approached.

Ellen scrambled away from him, as far as she could in the enclosed space.

Questions tumbled out of her.

"What did you—? How did you—? Why are you . . . ?"

"Here? Why am I here?" he replied, latching on to one of her questions. "Actually, I'm not really here."

Ellen frowned. "What do you mean?"

"I've split myself. My physical form is still on my ship, but my spirit is here. With you. I need to be here. I want revenge. That thing"—he paused, his blue eyes burning as he gestured at the dark cloud approaching the lighthouse that loomed above them—"that thing destroyed me. Destroyed my city. My reputation. Everything I've managed to build since . . ."

Ellen cut him off mid-rant.

"How did you manage to find me?" she asked.

His mouth split into a broad, Cheshire cat grin.

"Well, Kuranes summoned two nightgaunts, and I had no problem recognizing our old friend Mr. Poe. And with this"—he nodded at his hand—"my odds went up even more."

It took Ellen a moment to recognize his wedding ring. The glowing stone pulsed on his finger. She held up her own hand and stared at her matching piece. It seethed with the same strange energy. She expected it to burn, to bite, to mark her in some way, but she felt nothing.

"You used it to connect with me," she said softly.

Randolph Carter chuckled, a grim, humorless sound.

"Tell Kuranes the next time he wants to play hide-and-seek, the ring works both ways. If you can see me, I can see you."

Hide-and-seek.

Ellen's mind flitted back to the strange dream she had, of being chased by intruders and hiding in a clock.

Was it a dream or a memory? she wondered, groaning as she sat up in the small tentlike space.

"Are you okay?" Randolph Carter asked.

"Are you?" Ellen shot back.

His eyes narrowed.

"What do you mean?"

"The last time I saw you, you were possessed," she replied, shivering as she remembered the tentacles attached to his body.

"I'm still fighting that thing, but I think I'm gaining the upper hand."

Ellen looked at the ground, hiding a smile.

"It's always complicated with us, isn't it?"

The nightgaunt, hearing their conversation, lifted its wing and gave her a better glimpse of their surroundings. It was only then that Ellen's mind snapped into focus, that she realized she had made it to the island.

The Tiara—what King Kuranes called this place—had nothing shiny about it, nothing the least bit alluring. The island was a jagged rock—a shark fin that rose out of the sea, threatening anyone who dared approach. Scrub brush clung stubbornly to its sides. At its peak, where the jewel would have been, sat a lighthouse, its surface worn smooth by the elements. It had been carved out of the same rust-colored rock as the island. Thin strands of fog licked the top, obscuring the light.

"Light," she murmured. "I need to tend to the light. To feed the fire."

"*We* need to tend the light. You and I are a team, remember? The ones who guard the borderlands." Randolph Carter said, giving her a quick glance. "The only question is how we get up there."

He looked hopefully at Mr. Poe, but the nightgaunt extended its taloned hand, drawing their attention to an opening in the cliff face. A set of stairs descended into the dark rock.

"Basement," she sighed, remembering her friend Greg's words. "Why does it always have to be in the basement?"

"What?"

She waved Randolph Carter off. "Nothing."

Heading underground did have one unexpected advantage. The moment they headed down the stairs, the thick stone walls silenced the shrieking wind. Ellen didn't realize how much the Abbot's Howl crept into her senses until it was no longer there. Almost immediately, her thoughts cleared. The oppressive feeling that had been with her for most of the journey lifted. Ellen's eyes wandered across the walls of the cave, over rich colors that glowed silver and blue. The vibrant hues reminded her of the oily feathers of a bird.

She moved forward and touched the stone, marveling at its buttery coldness.

"Labradorite," she murmured, remembering what she learned at Mote It Be. "The stone of protection and psychic boundaries."

"Each of the stones in the Tiara is different," Randolph Carter explained. "Celestite, moldavite, azurite, prehnite. But they all serve a single purpose."

"To enhance psychic abilities and facilitate astral travel," Ellen offered, imagining the Sunken Crown guiding dreamers to their destinations.

Carter snorted. "Does this place look like a bus terminal to you? No, the monks built a wall here. A psychic boundary to keep people out."

"And stop other things from coming in," Ellen murmured, shivering as she remembered seeing the Plateau of Leng.

That dark land, she thought. *It's so close. Just across the water . . .*

When they reached the large, cavernous space that formed the heart of the island, the defensive nature of the Tiara made itself clear. Their path dead-ended at the entrance of a huge stone labyrinth. In the center, a thin, circular tower loomed over the maze, reaching for the ceiling of the cave. Ellen assumed the tower led to the lighthouse where the monks dwelled.

"Where's Ariadne when you need her?" Randolph Carter grumbled, filling Ellen's head with unwanted visions of a monster lurking in the maze.

"No one here but us Persephones, I'm afraid," Ellen said, wondering if the goddess of the Underworld had any sway with minotaurs.

His eyebrow arched.

"You remember that? The whole Persephone thing?"

"Kind of hard to forget."

"Most people forget. It's better that way."

"That's what my psychiatrist keeps telling me."

He shot her a sideways look. "Have they institutionalized you?"

"Not yet. For now, I'm just one of the walking wounded."

"Aren't we all," Randolph Carter muttered as his eyes drifted to the tower. He lapsed into a long, uncomfortable silence.

PTSD, she thought before she remembered what Kuranes told her.

Either that or something happening on his ship.

"So, how are we going to get through the maze?" she blurted to keep her mind off her troubling thoughts. "Do you know the way?"

"I don't, but my spirit does."

Ellen scowled. "What do you mean?"

Randolph Carter headed to the entrance of the labyrinth and pointed at what Ellen thought was an imperfection in the stone. She squinted at the surface, trying to figure out what he was trying to show her. She was just about to ask when he stepped forward, moving closer to the wall. The black strands she thought were veins in the rock came alive, roiling and writhing, reaching out to him. Carter closed his eyes, and the filaments shifted like metal filings reacting to a magnet, forming . . .

"An arrow," Ellen said as the growth pointed in a clear direction.

"You ever heard of dowsing?" Carter asked.

"You mean those guys who find underground water using sticks and rods?"

"The very same," he replied. "My entire body is a divination tool. I've been that way ever since . . ."

He cut off his words and stared into the maze, his jaw tensing.

"Since that day in the trenches, when that thing attacked you," she offered.

He gave her a flat stare, and his form flickered. For one breathless moment, Ellen thought Randolph Carter was going to disappear.

"It didn't attack me. I invited it in," he admitted.

Ellen's first reaction was denial. She had been in his nightmare; she had seen how frantically he resisted the tentacles trying to pierce his body. But then she remembered she had only been in part of Randolph Carter's dream. She didn't see what happened before the thing appeared.

Did Carter summon it? Light some candles or etch symbols into the ground?

She tried to remember whether she had seen signs of a ritual scattered around him but came up blank.

"Why would you do that? Invite that thing into you?" she demanded. "Why would you sacrifice part of your humanity?"

"You did it with that worm creature. Why did you let it possess you?" he snapped, but just as quickly, his anger evaporated. "I was in the middle of a war. The *First* World War, as I later found out," he said, shooting her a pointed look. "I thought if I summoned something powerful, if I could control it . . ."

"You could change history. Save lives," Ellen said.

He shook his head. "No good deed goes unpunished, does it?"

"And it's been inside you ever since."

"Yes," he replied.

"Is something like that inside me, too?" she asked in a hushed whisper.

"I don't know," he replied. "It wasn't in you the last time, when you and I . . ."

Made love, she thought, her mind drifting to their one-time liaison. *When Randolph Carter and I made love.*

Ellen snorted. "I wasn't aware that could be a divination device. Gives thinking with your dick a whole new meaning."

His laughter startled her. It was intense, like a sudden summer storm. It was also completely out of character. Ellen glanced at Randolph Carter, wondering how much the darkness stained his soul.

Enough to make the walls dance, she thought.

"You don't trust me," he said quietly.

"Why do you sound surprised? You've been the bad guy for most of this journey," she pointed out, but as Ellen's eyes wandered the cold stone of the labyrinth, she realized she didn't feel like he was her enemy anymore. The strings that bound him to the creature had been cut. Or were in the process of being cut.

Loose ends, her mind warned her. *Be careful of the loose ends.*

"What I don't trust is this," she murmured, nodding at the filament that swayed on the walls. "What did you say about the ring? If you can see me, I can see you. I think the same might be true about this stuff. Have you ever heard of mycelium networks?"

Randolph Carter shook his head.

"Scientists have discovered that fungi are interconnected. Mushrooms have underground networks that can stretch for hundreds of miles. And they can communicate with each other. They can even alter their patterns in response to other organisms."

His gaze drifted to the living wall.

"An early warning system," he said as he scanned the tower. "You're worried that whatever is up there is already tracking us."

Whatever is up there.

Kuranes mentioned the lighthouse was run by monks. He never said they were human.

Ellen shivered, rubbing at the gooseflesh on her arms.

"That's exactly what I'm afraid of," she whispered.

Randolph Carter turned to confer with Mr. Poe. She leaned in, trying to pick up on their psychic communication, but all Ellen heard was white noise. She wondered whether night-gaunts could only communicate with one human at a time.

Like magic items in D&D, she thought, *they need to be attuned to the person who uses them.*

Whatever the nightgaunt said bothered Randolph Carter. He let out a frustrated hiss.

"There's no other way. We must follow their path if we want to get up there," he informed her.

Ellen glanced at the creature. "He couldn't just fly us to the tower?" she asked, half joking, half hoping.

"He can't," Carter replied. "The monks put up barriers that nonhuman creatures can't cross. This is where we part ways with Mr. Poe."

She stared at the tower, dread seeping into her body.

"What the hell is going on up there?" she murmured.

"We won't know that until we reach the tower." He sighed and shot her a resigned look. "Come on. We're wasting time."

They headed deeper into the maze. The walls around them emitted enough light for them to see their way. The black filament in the stone that Randolph pointed out rustled as they passed, making a raspy sound that reminded Ellen of the tightening of a rope.

Or the tightening of a noose . . .

He stopped and glared at her.

"Tread lightly with your thoughts," he commanded.

"It would help if we could talk," she grumbled.

"So, talk. To be honest, I don't think it matters. It's not like these things have ears."

They might, Ellen couldn't help but think.

"I met your son," she blurted. "Robert."

Randolph snorted. "Is he still mad at me?"

"Yep," she replied. "He's a grumpy old man now. Lives in Edgewood Manor. Might even have an in-house girlfriend if he plays his cards—"

Randolph skidded to a stop so suddenly, Ellen almost ran into him.

"Wait a minute. Did you just say my son lives in Edgewood Manor?"

"It's a retirement home now," she offered, and when he stiffened, she asked the question that burned in her mind. "It *is* the Witch House, isn't it? The one Lovecraft wrote about."

"I can't say for sure. I wasn't directly involved with that case," he insisted, but Ellen could see the real answer in his eyes.

"A portal opened there. That's how I reached the Dreamlands. That's the way other things got through to the waking world." She paused, then added softly, "He misses you."

"Who?"

"Your son," she replied. "In fact, I think he would love it if you paid him a visit."

"Are you kidding? If I showed up, he'd probably drop dead!"

"He's stronger than you think," Ellen insisted.

Randolph Carter gave her a long look.

"You admire him."

"I admire all Carters," she replied, her mouth twisting into a smile. "For all the good it's done me."

"What about me?"

"What *about* you?" she countered.

"Did you miss me?"

"Yes," she admitted, and if there were any doubt the Randolph Carter she knew was with her, the heat of his stare erased it.

They lapsed into silence as they negotiated the labyrinth. On and on they went, threading through the maze, turning this way and that, always looking to the writhing walls for guidance. Ellen soon fell into a meditative trance. Her thoughts drifted to Andrew Carter fighting the shadow zone that opened in the waking world. She wondered whether he was okay, whether Miskatonic University's emergency team was making headway. She hoped the darkness that invaded Randolph Carter hadn't reached Andrew.

Is it possible for this stuff to make it to the waking world? she wondered. *To survive and inhabit people like—*

Tread lightly with your thoughts, she reminded herself.

After what seemed like an eternity of narrow passages, they reached the center of the maze. The path dead-ended, opening into a large circular space. The tower sat in the center, its spire punching through the ceiling of the cave. The structure was made of the same material as the labyrinth. A humming filled her ears, and a weight settled on her chest. By the time they reached the entrance to the tower, the pressure was so intense, her entire body felt like it was being squeezed like a tube of toothpaste.

Randolph Carter closed his eyes, his lids fluttering.

"I think you're right," he said in a distant voice. "I think that stuff in the maze alerted the monks. They're trying to keep us out."

Ellen stepped forward, ignoring the pain that threatened to split her in two.

"Let us in. We're here to help," she said as she laid her hand on the door, her fingers caressing the weather-beaten wood. "This is our purpose."

The door sprung open, creaking as it yielded to her. It was a classic haunted-house sound, a cliché that normally would have made Ellen roll her eyes. But here, on the edge of the human Dreamlands, the wooden groan soothed her. It reminded her of the waking world she left behind.

Each step in this journey takes you farther away from home, a voice whispered in her head.

"You can't go back to a world if it's gone," she reminded herself.

A dank, vegetal smell greeted them as they crossed the threshold. The stench was so overpowering, Ellen half expected to see a malarious mist rising around them.

"What the hell?" Randolph Carter blurted.

It took her a moment to locate the source of the light that blazed in the cavern. The stone walls glowed fiercely in the gloom, bathing Ellen in a rich blue hue that made her feel like she was underwater. The light was strongest on a dais. She moved toward the platform and studied the egg-shaped object resting on it. As she got closer, she realized it was the source of the hum and the pressure in her body. Ellen didn't recognize the rock it was made of. It was black and irregular and threaded with golden highlights. A ring of eyes covered the surface of the stone. Not all of them looked human.

She let out a breath she didn't know she was holding.

"No. It can't be," Randolph Carter whispered in wonder.

When he moved closer to the object, his image flickered again.

"What is it?" she asked, and he snapped into sharp, almost painful focus.

He blinked as if she had woken him from a deep sleep.

"It's the eye of Nephren-Ka."

"The eye of Nephren-who?" Ellen echoed.

"It's an otherworldly relic rumored to be in the Boy King's possession. A relative of mine unearthed it when he opened the tomb."

A jolt of recognition shot through Ellen.

"Wait a minute. The Boy King? Are you talking about King Tut?"

"And Howard Carter. He was a distant relation," he offered, his face darkening. "And the source of all our misfortune."

"The curse? Are you talking about the famous curse?" she asked, remembering the tragic stories of the people who opened King Tut's tomb.

Randolph Carter made a sour face. "Howard thought it was all 'superstitious mumbo-jumbo,' but the eye of Nephren-Ka's power made itself known soon enough. When it started affecting my family, I broke into his house and stole it. I brought it here, to the Dreamlands. I thought the monks would be able to handle it, keep it from falling into the wrong hands."

"And keep it from tainting you," Ellen added.

"I assumed the monks would hide it, not make it the central relic in their goddamn monastery."

"What does it do?" Ellen asked as she circled the object.

"It's a portal, a way of looking into Leng. Into all the places untouched by humanity," he replied. "The monks must be using it to keep an eye on things, to know what is happening in the distant parts of the Dreamlands. The only problem is—"

"If you gaze long into an abyss, the abyss gazes into you," Ellen murmured, quoting Friedrich Nietzsche.

"They looked a little too long," he offered with a sigh. "All the corruption. The stuff that got into me, the creatures that invaded your world . . . this is where it all comes from. Something is trying to get through. To reach out from Leng and *influence* things."

Ellen stared at the alien stone. "We need to destroy it."

He shook his head.

"We can't destroy the eye. The best we can do is sever the connection," he insisted as he stepped closer to the wall. It was only when the surface roiled that Ellen realized the black stuff coated everything around them. Thick, cobweb-like tendrils dangled from the stone; its long strands connected to the stairs that wound up the inside of the tower.

"God, there's no escaping it," she said, her voice trembling. *Iä O. Iä O.*

The monk's chanting drifted down from above, settling damply on Ellen's skin. At first, she thought the words were what caused the sensation. But as they crept up the stone stairway that ringed the tower, she saw a mist swirling above them. When they reached the point where the tower punched through the ceiling of the cave, they found themselves deep in a cloud. Ellen noticed open notches in the walls—porthole-shaped windows with metal apertures. Each opening was adjusted to a different width, allowing the storm outside to seep in.

Iä O. Iä O.

The words slithered into Ellen's brain, making it hard to think. The wind, that dreaded Abbot's Howl, shrieked in response, rising and falling in pitch as it passed through the narrow openings.

"This is what they do. Their sacred mission," Randolph Carter informed her. "Whenever the Abbot's Howl blows, they listen. This place is an instrument that gives the Abbot's Howl a voice."

You are not worthy.

A stormy voice rocked the tower. Its roar gained strength as it passed through the building, shaking the foundations of the ancient stone structure. Ellen had heard nothing like it before. She could only grasp it in biblical terms. Gabriel and his horn. The walls of Jericho being blown down.

She turned to Randolph Carter, who stared at her, wide-eyed.

His image began to falter again.

"Is that what you're talking about? The—"

You are not worthy, the wind-blown voice boomed. *You do not belong here. Two half breeds. Good for nothing but sacrifice.*

A vision bled into Ellen's brain, of being held down as a man in robes waved a knife over her. The hilt of the weapon had the same strange markings as the egg-shaped object, a row of eyes that seemed to wink at her. She strained against the ropes that held her in place but only managed to knock her teddy bear, Winston, to the floor. The man with the knife chuckled and kicked her stuffed animal into a corner. Seeing her beloved companion so abused infuriated Ellen. A white-hot ball of rage shot through her body, spreading through her limbs, erupting from her eyes. The man with the knife hesitated as a low animal growl escaped from Ellen's gagged mouth. Like the Abbot's Howl, words emerged from the noise.

"I am a *kore memagmeni*. Daughter of the twilight. And we are the dwellers of the in-between places," she rasped, her voice rising with each word. "You will respect us. You will release us both. *Now!*"

The image shattered the moment she spoke the words. Ellen found herself slumped on the staircase, holding her head in her hands. Randolph Carter knelt beside her. He looked whole again.

"You're back," he said when their eyes met.

"Yeah," she replied vaguely as she rubbed her neck. "At least I think I am."

"They launched a powerful attack on us. I'm surprised you were able to resist it."

"The monks did that?"

"Let's just say they don't like unexpected visitors." He stood and offered her his hand. "Come on. We have promises to keep."

"And miles to go before we sleep," she murmured, supplying the next line of the Robert Frost poem.

Randolph Carter arched his eyebrow.

"Robert Frost *and* Nietzsche? I'm impressed."

"Not bad for a Flatlander, eh?" Ellen blurted as she looked away, trying to hide the fact that his praise pleased her.

The clouds thinned as they neared the top. Fiery orange light trickled down from the tower. Ellen felt like a creature rising from the depths of the ocean. Starting in inky darkness, making her way through the blue twilight, then seeing dappled sunlight as she neared the surface.

Iä O. Iä O.

The monks continued their endless chant. Now that she was closer, she realized that their voices sounded wheezy. Congested.

"Dear God," Randolph Carter murmured when he reached the tower of the lighthouse.

"What is it?" Ellen tried to peer around him, but he was solid enough to block her view.

"I don't think this is something you should . . ."

"Let me *see!*" she hissed, and he obliged, stepping aside.

At first, Ellen couldn't make sense of the scene in front of her. She had taken her time climbing the stairs, so her eyes had adjusted to the light. It was her mind that couldn't process what she was seeing. In the center of the room, slumped around a dying fire, were two large figures Ellen assumed were the monks. She knew immediately they weren't human. The Abbot's Howl blew across their fallen forms, and their robes billowed in the wind, exposing extra limbs. Joints that bent the wrong way. Feet that just looked . . . wrong.

Ellen's stomach knotted.

Carter whispered in her ear. "Look closer," he commanded.

She peered at the gruesome creatures, not sure what he was pointing out. Then the monk's bodies swelled, and Ellen noticed long tentacles snaking out of their robes. The appendages flexed and relaxed, working the creatures like bellows.

With every exhale came the dreadful chant.

Iä O. Iä O.

"They're being used," she breathed. "Their bodies are being played like an instrument."

"Just like I was." Randolph Carter shook his head. "I'm sure you don't need me to tell you this, but this is bad."

The two monks rose like puppets on strings. One of them launched itself at Randolph Carter, hitting him squarely in the chest. The two figures pinwheeled backward, twisting and turning, grappling with each other. The creature smashed Randolph Carter into the glass of the lighthouse, and he dissolved, exploding in a burst of light.

"Randy!" she shrieked at the window, empty except for the fog pouring into the lighthouse.

The creature that tackled Randolph Carter turned to sneer at Ellen. The veil that covered its face had been ripped away, the fabric dangling from its ears like shredded skin. All Ellen could do was stare in shock at the riot of features.

The monk resembled a ghoul, with its humanoid body and long, lanky limbs. But its head was bat-like. The creature had huge pointy ears, a squashed nose, and jet-black eyes. Its lips were stretched thin, curled in a grimace that exposed a row of razor-sharp teeth. On its head was a set of ram horns.

Satyrs. It was the closest Ellen could come to describing the things in front of her, to give her mind something "normal" to grasp.

Ellen stepped back, her mind skipping. "Umm, umm, umm . . ."

The creature lunged for her. This time, it didn't have the element of surprise. Ellen easily evaded its grasping claws. She ducked under the massive creature, scurrying around the mountain of flesh. As she dodged the hostile monk, she noticed the other one struggling against the tentacles that bound it, tugging at the appendages lodged in its body. Ellen thought of Randolph Carter on his ship, trapped in a web, his fingers yanking at invisible strings.

A voice filled her head as the creature reached out to her, broadcasting in several human languages.

La Luz.

Khafifa.

La Lumiere.

Cbet.

"The light. The light," she muttered.

The "friendly" monk had done most of the work. Piles of wood were stacked in the corner, fuel gathered from the scrubby bushes that dotted the island. She grabbed armfuls of branches and tossed them into the cauldron. The embers latched on to the dry wood. New flames sprang from the tinder. The blaze lit up the surrounding space, but Ellen knew it needed to be stronger to drive back the darkness and guide Kuranes and the others to safety.

She reached into her bag and pulled out the flare gun Simon Pickman had given her. The hostile monk tried to grab her again, but she scurried around him.

She fired a flare into the cauldron.

A bright flash filled the lighthouse as flames erupted. The tentacles that controlled the "friendly" monk flexed and burst him like a balloon, showering Ellen in gore. Some of his blood splashed into her mouth. Ellen screamed, the sound scorching her throat, ripping through her vocal cords. Stars exploded against her closed eyelids while the blood of the dead monk trickled down her throat. Ellen tried to spit it out but couldn't get rid of it. The hot liquid spread inside her. Her voice dropped to an impossibly low register. Every organ in her body, every nerve, every sinew vibrated.

She growled at the hostile creature as she dug into her pockets, retrieving the extra flares she'd been given.

The creature hesitated, unnerved by the change in her. It gave her the time she needed to reload the gun.

"*Fiat lux*, you bastard," she whispered as she fired.

The flare hit the thing's body with a satisfying thump. The world around Ellen erupted in a blaze of red. Tendrils of light shot through the monk and into the clouds, revealing the shape connected to the monk, to the ships, to . . . everything. Ellen stared at the monstrosity. It was an entity bigger than the lighthouse, than the island, than the entire Plateau of Leng. It swirled around her, a tornado of protoplasm desperate to touch down. The flare's heat disrupted the thing's attempt to take form. A cry split the air above her, and Ellen knew she was hearing the true voice behind the Abbot's Howl. The ghost of the "friendly" monk appeared beside her, tilted its head, and bellowed a deep-throated challenge. The ground vibrated beneath her feet as the building hummed with the frequency.

Ellen grabbed the lighthouse railing and held on for dear life. It felt like she was standing on top of a rocket about to lift off.

The form in the fog curdled, retreating from the wall of sound.

"Look at his lies! Look at his deception!" the ghost monk said through her, his eyes blazing as the massive entity collapsed in on itself. "Serve as a witness. *See!*"

The fog on the Twilight Sea cleared. Ellen saw two ships on a collision course with the reefs ringing the island. The crews boiled across the decks, adjusting sails, trimming lines, doing everything they could to avoid crashing into the rocks. At the helm of one of them was Randolph Carter.

A mixture of relief and outrage shot through her body as she watched the ships steer clear of the Sunken Crown. Kuranes and Simon Pickman had warned her they might have to leave her behind, but she didn't truly believe it until she saw the ships turn and start to sail away.

"Shit," she spat, plucking nervously at her lip. "Shit, shit, *shit!*"

Out of the corner of her eye, Ellen saw the charred husk of the hostile monk crumble to the floor, leaving a thick residue of ashes.

A heavy silence descended on the lighthouse. Even the Abbot's Howl was quieter than it had been only a few moments before.

"I did what I needed to do," she whispered to the weapon still clutched in her hand. "Now I need to find a way out of here."

Before she headed back to the lighthouse stairs, Ellen glanced down at the point where the lighthouse base met the stone of the island. A dark tentacle clung to the foot of the building. The amputated limb twitched and slithered, blindly groping for something to grab. Something it could use to re-generate. Gather strength.

A wave of dread shot through her.

It's not over yet, she thought. *That thing is like cancer. You need to root out every little bit or else . . .*

She dug into her pocket with shaking hands and fished out her last flare. She fired a thousand degrees of heat into the shadowy mass. The thing seethed and exploded, splitting open like a ripe fruit. Black liquid splashed onto the wall of the lighthouse, emitting a hiss as the substance hit the stone. A fine mist rose from the spatter.

Ellen groaned, her heart sinking as she watched an oily cloud form.

A cynical voice sounded in her head.

Did you really think that would work? That destroying it would be easy?

The vapor wasn't the only problem. The flare had started a fire in the bushes. Gusts of wind fanned the flames, sending up a plume of smoke.

If that thing gets behind another cloud . . .

"In the darkness, multitudes," she whispered.

The saying sounded familiar. She wasn't sure where she'd heard it. Maybe in the Bible, in the part about demons.

"No," she croaked as she backed away from the inky form. "No, no, no."

Ellen fled from the darkness that climbed the lighthouse, her feet thundering down the long spiral staircase. She had no idea where she was going, where she *could* go to escape what was forming outside. Halfway down the stairs, she skidded to a stop. The dark mist poured through the openings below, gathering in a thick pool. Ellen reversed direction, only to discover the smoke from the wildfire seeping into the tower of the lighthouse.

"Not good," she muttered to herself. "Oh, this is not good."

Stuck, she thought. *You're stuck, and you have nowhere left to go.*

Her mind flashed to a scene from *Star Wars*, when Luke and the others were stuck in a trash compactor with the walls closing in on them.

Ellen straightened.

Call for help.

That's what Luke did.

He called for help.

She pressed her head against the wall of the lighthouse and tapped out the signal she and Robert Carter agreed on before she crossed over.

She banged out the standard SOS.

Three fast knocks, three slow, then three fast.

Stony silence greeted her call.

Ellen crept down the stairs, ear pressed to the stone, and pounded out the SOS signal again.

It occurred to her she was in the same position Michael Sloane was when she first saw him in Edgewood—searching the walls, desperate for a way out. She wasn't sure what she was listening for. A hollow thump? A vibration? All she knew was that she had to keep trying to cling to the shrinking space between mist and smoke.

SOS.

The crawling mist reached the stair she was on. Like an eager cat, it curled around her legs.

They left you behind, a disembodied voice taunted her. *You're a sacrifice. You and all the Persephones. Nothing but meat.*

"Come on, damn it! Come on!" Ellen cursed through clenched teeth. "Where are you, Robert? Where the *fuck* are you?"

The ring on her finger burned in the darkness. She pounded on the stone hard enough to skin her knuckles.

A square space appeared on the wall, and a familiar face peered through the opening.

"Robert!" Ellen yelled as she lunged for the passage to the waking world.

The old man stared past her, eyes wide with fear.

A tendril whipped around her ankle. Icy cold branded her skin. Ellen looked down at the shadowy form wrapped around her foot.

Chaos. It was the only word to describe what she saw.

What you think you're seeing, her rational mind corrected her.

The mist changed from inky black to a sickly yellow. Faces struggled to emerge from the boiling mass. Most burst before fully forming, their shapes dissolving into the pus-colored pool. But a few . . . a few . . .

A wave of nausea rose in her throat.

Joshua. Greg. Lily. Tom. It cycled through friends and family as if deciding what mask to wear, what facade would lure Ellen into its darkness. Her entire body stiffened in defense, but it wasn't enough to protect her from the thoughts that churned in her head.

He's back.

Solomon Reye.

Dear God, Solomon Reye is back.

Cold laughter boomed in her head.

"Foolish girl," it chortled. "I am that and so much more. Solomon Reye is only one of my incarnations."

The words hit her like a blow, and she slumped, letting her mind slip away from her body.

"That's it," the voice cooed as she went under. "Just give in. Once you surrender, you can rest."

She heard a sound, what sounded like a thump on the stairs above her. Her body jerked, and she stared up at the tower, trying to find the source of the disturbance.

"Don't worry about that, my child. Just close your eyes. Relax. Rest. Don't you want to rest?"

"No, she doesn't," a voice answered for her.

Randolph Carter emerged from the mist, wielding a fiery sword. He plunged the weapon deep into the bubbling cloud. A shriek pierced the air as lightning streaked through it. The creature released Ellen and turned inward, trying to fight the blaze that raced through it.

She felt a tug on her body as Robert Carter grabbed her and started to pull her back into the waking world.

She locked eyes with Randolph Carter. With his weapon gleaming fiercely in the gloom, he reminded her of a holy warrior.

Not just a warrior, she thought. *My partner.* "Thank you," she mouthed as she slipped through the portal between the two worlds.

Ellen landed in a pile on the hardwood floor. She stared at the ceiling, eyes soft and unfocused. Around her, shadowy forms flitted and twirled like dervishes. At first, Ellen thought the monks were back, to help her stop things from crossing over into the waking world. Then she saw the flash of a badge. Heard handcuffs jingle on a belt.

Robert's pale face appeared in the gloom.

"The painting," he wheezed at her. "Get the fucking painting off the wall!"

Ellen stared at the Pickman, into the glowing red eyes of the lead ghoul. She knew it was a sign that the portal was still open. She also knew taking down the painting wouldn't be enough. If she took it off the wall, she had to put it somewhere. On the floor, against the table.

No matter what surface it's on, something could still come through.

She rolled onto her side. The hammer she used to hang the picture poked into her. Ellen grabbed it and leaped to her feet.

A police officer spun in her direction.

"What the . . ." the man spluttered, caught off guard. He jumped out of the way as she charged the painting, striking the ghoul with the hammer's claw and ripping into its face.

An inhuman scream sounded in the distance.

The light in the ghoul's eyes fluttered and went out.

It wasn't enough for Ellen.

THUNK, THUNK, THUNK.

She hammered the creature repeatedly until its face was obliterated. Until she could be sure no one could ever use the Pickman again.

The click of drawn guns snapped her out of her trance.

"Drop the weapon *now*!"

Weapon.

Only then did she return to the reality of the waking world. The walls of Edgewood Manor popped up around her, locking her into physical space. White light pinned her shadow to the mangled canvas.

I'm back, she thought as relief coursed through her body. *I did what I needed to do.*

Now I can rest.

The hammer slipped from her hand and tumbled to the floor.

Ellen fell with it.

Chapter Twenty-Four

5 150.

For the next three days, these numbers ruled Ellen Logan's life. They weren't part of a hidden equation or the secret language of mathematicians. The meaning behind the numbers was clear. "When a person, as a result of a mental health disorder, is a danger to others or himself or herself . . ." The incantation landed her in Arkham Asylum for seventy-two hours of psychiatric evaluation. Ellen didn't mind. It gave her time to transition, to relax and adjust to the waking world. Her first night there wasn't as peaceful as she hoped it would be. The entire asylum was alive. The turbulence in the Dreamlands seeped through the walls, scrambling the inmates' delicate senses. They shouted and gibbered, charging the air with their frantic cries. Some pled, bargaining with invisible forces.

Ellen thought about the shadow that swirled around the lighthouse. The familiar faces that had emerged from the bubbling ooze to entice her.

A voice tickled her ear. *I am that and so much more.*

She stuffed her head under a thin, institutional pillow. She wasn't interested in talking to anyone. Or anything.

News trickled in from the outside world slowly, through a TV in the dayroom.

"Radiation Leak at Miskatonic University Lab Kills Six," the headline blared.

She snickered and crossed her arms. "Radiation leak? In the math department? *Seriously?*"

"Seriously, seriously?" the man on the couch in front of her chirped, mimicking her.

Ellen watched workers in hazmat suits scurry in and out of Mandelbrot Hall. The place had been sealed off in the interest of public safety. According to the reporters, the building had been ground zero for the toxic leak, which investigators, using the language of arson, called "the point of origin."

Most fatalities occurred within its walls. Kyle Donovan, the man so desperate to keep Michael Sloane's note, was among the dead.

"Andrew," Ellen breathed as she watched the paramedics wheel out the body bags. "What about Andrew?"

Her fingers twitched, longing for her cell phone. They had taken away all her belongings when they'd admitted her.

She had no way of reaching Andrew Carter, of knowing if he was alive.

Unless . . .

Ellen plopped onto the threadbare couch in the dayroom. She closed her eyes and imagined the ring, that mysterious object that bound her to the Carters. Burnished metal flared in her mind. Its ruby gem burned bright. Her mind traced the sigils etched into its surface.

A glimmer.

A flash of movement.

Randolph Carter's impatient voice pierced the stillness. *What do you want?*

Ellen leaned forward, trying to form words, but the sedatives they had given her were too strong.

A shadow stepped in front of her. "Miss Logan?"

Ellen blinked, squinting against the flood of sunlight. Her eyes darted to the television. Miskatonic was holding a press conference to contain the furor that had erupted about the dangers the school posed to the community. Looking cool and impeccably coiffed, Miss Strauss stood beside the university president. And behind the first row of officials, a face tight with anger and impatience . . .

"Andrew!"

"Miss Logan?" the nurse in front of her waited for a response.

"I'm sorry. What?"

"It's time to see the doctor."

Ellen glanced at the television one last time to be sure. Relief coursed through her body.

Andrew Carter is alive.

"Thank you," she whispered to no one in particular.

Ellen learned a new language during her short stay in Arkham Asylum. She toyed with it before, right after she returned from Calvin Leonard's house of horror. Now, confronted by doctors who could keep her locked up, she dedicated herself to mastering the native tongue. Ellen still told the impossible tale. She had no choice. Not sharing her experience hindered her "progress." But Ellen recast the story using the language of trauma. She peppered her accounts with therapeutic words like "flashbacks" and "triggers." She even voiced her genuine fear she may have hurt someone when she escaped from Calvin Leonard's lair.

Her psychiatrist, Dr. Knowles, nodded sagely. "Survivor's guilt," he pronounced.

Ellen's eyes dropped to the floor. *Reduced to a label. Just like that . . .*

"You went through a terrible experience only a few months ago," he reminded her. "You survived, but you were forced to make extreme decisions. Decisions that didn't sit well with you. So, when you heard there were problems where your friend was living . . ."

Ellen looked up. "I saw an opportunity to be a hero. To redeem myself," she offered.

The doctor flipped through her files.

"Actually, you *are* a hero," he said. "You discovered a hidden passage under Edgewood right around the time it started to collapse. When the building started to shift, you realized what was happening and convinced the staff to evacuate the residents. You saved lives."

"Collapse?"

Dr. Knowles glanced up from his paperwork. "Edgewood's been condemned. Deemed unsafe for human habitation. And not a moment too soon, if you ask me," he said, muttering the last words.

Ellen pictured the Pickman painting. The ghoul's red eye buried under tons of rubble.

Is that the end of it? she wondered. *Is that enough to stop what's trying to get through?*

Ellen felt the weight of the doctor's stare and settled on a more rational question.

"What about the residents? What's going to happen to them?"

Her psychiatrist peered at her over the top of his glasses. "Why don't we focus on you first, Miss Logan?"

✦✦✦✦✦

Hero.

The title sat uneasily on Ellen's shoulders, but it made things happen. When news broke about what she did at Edgewood ("In the Middle of Crisis, Final Girl Rescues Neglected Seniors," one headline trumpeted), officials at the retirement home decided not to prosecute her for trespassing. The Arkham PD also dropped their more serious charge: assault with a deadly weapon. She and Robert Carter were still indicted for resisting arrest, but the judge dismissed the case. Far worse crimes had been committed on that chaotic night. Ellen was already getting professional help. And Robert Carter had been transferred to the care of his son until other arrangements could be made.

That was good enough for the powers that be.

When Ellen Logan was released from the asylum after serving her three days, a summer storm had just swept through Arkham. The smell of ozone and damp earth hung thick in the air. Trees pattered tears onto the asphalt parking lot. Ellen stood at the entrance for a long time and stared at the freshly washed world. Her cell phone bloomed with messages—most from reporters wanting her side of what happened at Edgewood.

It was the silences she noticed the most.

Andrew Carter?

Nothing.

Robert Carter?

His lawyer left a message the day their case went to court.

Uncle Joshua?

Ellen didn't expect to hear from him. The moment the Pickman entered her life, he disappeared, which would have worried her if she hadn't heard the recording of his conversation with Robert Carter. And when she went back to the house and discovered his suitcase and passport were missing, it only strengthened her conviction that he had vanished of his own free will. She assumed he was hiding, at least until things settled down.

When that will be is anyone's guess, she thought.

PING!

She glanced down at her cell phone. "Speak of the devil," she said.

The message was short and businesslike.

Joshua Logan: I see they've finally discharged you.
A man named Owen Cartwright is coming to pick you up.
He is with the Athenaein Association.
Trust him.

Ellen's fingers flew across the keyboard of her phone.
Where are you?
Are you okay?
How do you know where I am?
She didn't expect an immediate reply, so she was surprised when the phone chimed again.
A winking smiley face, followed by a message.
Joshua Logan: We put stalker-ware on your phone, remember?
Ellen smiled, blinking away tears. She remembered the argument they had over the tracking app. He had demanded she install it so that he'd know where she was, "just in case." She balked at the prospect of surveillance, but Joshua insisted. He wouldn't let her attend Miskatonic University without an electronic tether. And since he was paying for her education, she had no choice but to agree. Besides, she reasoned, she *was* attending a university with a high student death rate. And he depended on her for his care.

So she kept the app active, disabling it only when she went to her secret room.

Her only regret? That she didn't insist on tracking him.

Where are you? she typed again.

No reply.

> I know everything, old man. Robert Carter
> and I have been working together.

The winking face reappeared on the screen.

> **Joshua Logan**: And how does Andrew feel
> about that?

Ellen looked up at the storm clouds fleeing to the west. Of all the variables in her life, Andrew Carter was the biggest unknown. Ever since she'd returned from the Dreamlands, he had been a ghostly presence, a fleeting glimpse on the television. She had no idea what he had gone through, what his side of the shadow zone looked like. Several people had died. Had he been there? Had he watched them die? She remembered their first adventure together, when he'd killed a man whose soul had been ripped apart by demons.

"Even your enemies deserve mercy," he had told her.

Had Andrew Carter been forced to dispense more "mercy"?

She didn't want to think about it. Not yet.

> I have no idea how Andrew Carter "feels"
> about anything, she messaged her uncle.

Oh, I think you do, came Joshua's teasing response. Or are you still pretending to be blind?

Ellen's lips throbbed with the memory of Andrew's kiss. It had been the only good thing to come out of the whole mess. When Carter had pulled her into his arms, she'd felt like she had passed through the wall of a hurricane. The world raged around them, but she was safe, nestled in the calm heart of the storm. For a few magical moments, Ellen had entertained the thought that they might have a future together.

Now?

"No way," she whispered to the phone.

A silver Mercedes pulled up to the curb, and a man climbed out.

Ellen recognized him as the suave stranger who'd visited Joshua right after the thin place opened in Edgewood.

She'd almost emptied a can of mace into his face.

"I'm sorry I'm late, Miss Logan. Traffic out of Boston was a nightmare," he apologized as he approached her.

"Are you Owen Cartwright?"

He looked at her, surprised. "Why, yes! How did you—"

"May I see some ID, please?"

He presented her with a driver's license.

Ellen studied it carefully.

"Thanks," she replied, grinning as she handed him back his ID. "You can't be too careful. There are a lot of crazy people around here, you know."

The man burst into delighted laughter and opened the passenger door for her.

"Well, then, let's find someplace to hide, shall we?"

Chapter Twenty-Five

Owen Cartwright had thought of everything. He booked Ellen a room at The Five Eaves, the luxury hotel in downtown Arkham. A pair of tuxedo pants, a white silk blouse, and ballet flats lay on the bed. Everything, even the underwear, was in her size. Not just her size. Her style. This man didn't expect her to play dress-up like King Kuranes or Norm at Mote It Be. The clothes were things she would have chosen, dressy but comfortable. The room was dotted with other thoughtful touches. A bathroom was stocked with a toothbrush and an assortment of toiletries. A bottle of wine and a cheese plate waited for her on the table.

A Post-it note clung to the plastic wrap.

> *Enjoy the spread, but make sure to save your appetite.*
> *We have dinner reservations.*
> *Meet me in the lobby at 8 p.m.*

Ellen glanced at the clock on the nightstand.

Three-thirty. Enough time to indulge. She wolfed down the food and drink and liberated some chocolate from the minibar. After that, she surrendered to a hot bath and a long nap. When she emerged from her room, rested and fed, in brand-new clothes, Ellen felt normal again. More than that. She felt reborn.

Owen Cartwright rose from a leather couch in the lobby. "I see you approve of my choices," he said, nodding at her outfit.

"I feel like Cinderella."

He offered her a courtly bow. "Then I've done my job," he insisted.

"And what exactly is your job?"

He glanced at his watch. "Why don't we talk about that over dinner? We're due at Brezza Fresca."

✦✦✦✦✦

Brezza Fresca was one of the fanciest restaurants in Arkham, where students took their parents when they were in town. Ellen had been there a few times with Joshua, but it had been years since she set foot in the place. Nothing had changed. The dining room was suffused with soft light, and its walls were decorated with tapestries that muted the voices of other diners.

The perfect place for a discreet conversation, she thought as a maître d' escorted them to a table in the corner of the room.

The prices shocked Ellen. Despite her hunger, she began to map out a strategy that involved splitting entrees or making a salad the main course.

"Order what you want. It's my treat," Owen Cartwright said without looking up.

She smiled at the menu. "You're going to regret saying that. I am a starving student, you know."

He smiled and fell silent as she weighed her options. Ellen appreciated the quiet. On the rare occasions Joshua took her on a business dinner, conversation always took center stage. The menus lay ignored on the table as Joshua chatted with a client—all while Ellen's stomach rumbled and the waiter circled the table like a pilot waiting for clearance to land. A half hour often passed before decisions were made.

Owen Cartwright didn't play that game. The moment the waiter appeared, he was ready with his complete order, down to the chocolate soufflé that took an hour to prepare. When he selected a bottle of wine that was more than what Ellen earned in a week, she decided he was serious about ordering what she wanted. She rattled off her choices with the same thoroughness. They engaged in small talk while the wine was opened and poured.

Owen Cartwright raised his glass. "To fresh breezes."

"Excuse me?"

"The name of this establishment. Brezza Fresca. Italian for 'fresh breeze.' Appropriate, don't you think?"

Her eyes narrowed. "Who *are* you?"

"Please, drink," he urged her. "I'm very superstitious about toasts."

She would have suspected he had slipped something into her drink if she hadn't seen the waiter open the wine.

"To fresh breezes." She lifted her glass and took a sip. The red wine trickled down her throat, soft and silky.

"So, how do you know Joshua?" she asked.

He unfurled his napkin and smoothed it in his lap. "I'm the one who set up your adoption."

A jolt shot through Ellen.

Set up.

Like Brezza Fresca, the choice of words was deliberate. Ellen remembered the way Joshua Logan blew into her life, as sudden as he was unexpected. At the very least, it implied shortcuts had been made. At the very most—

Owen interrupted the thought before it had a chance to form. "I've dealt with unusual business partners in my day, but Joshua's been one of the most challenging," he admitted. "I've smoothed his path on more than a few occasions."

The waiter arrived with bread. Ellen plucked a warm roll out of the basket and pondered it.

"If this is about the painting, I don't have it. It's—"

"I already have the painting, Miss Logan. Or what's left of it." He leaned forward, eyes dancing. "You did a lot of damage before the police arrested you."

Ellen bit into her roll to hide her surprise. The bread melted in her mouth. Its velvety texture took her mind off the situation for the split second she needed to recover.

"I know who you remind me of," she announced. "I was struggling to place you the first time we met."

Owen Cartwright blinked, obviously caught off guard.

Good, she thought. "I'm a movie nut, so I have a habit of thinking in film," she explained. "You remind me of the Nazi in that Quentin Tarantino film."

She expected him to take offense, to balk at the comparison.

His smile deepened. "You're talking about Christoph Waltz. The opening scene of *Inglourious Basterds,*" he said, humming his approval. "I take that as a supreme compliment."

Ellen took another bite of her roll and studied the man in front of her. She wasn't sure she trusted him, but she was glad the Pickman was out of her hands. "That painting is dangerous, Mr. Cartwright. Be very careful with it."

"Is that why you attacked it?"

"Yes."

They fell silent as their first course arrived.

She waited until the waiter left before she dug in.

"This organization you work for. The Athenaein Association. Named after Athena? The goddess of wisdom?"

"The goddess of wisdom *and* headaches," he added. "Miss Logan, do you know the difference between a library and an athenaeum?"

"Educate me."

"Most people think *athenaeum* is another word for *library,* but they were originally temples, where knowledge was squirreled away and access to materials was controlled."

"So, you're a private research organization?"

He made a face. "You make us sound so corporate. We are independent professionals who have dedicated our lives to pursuing sensitive material."

"Like that sounds less corporate," she teased.

"Fair enough," he replied as he picked at his salad. "You talk in film. At the risk of bringing up Nazis again, have you seen *The Monuments Men*? About the Allied group that recovered stolen art during World War II?"

Ellen remembered it well. Joshua wasn't usually the type to sit down and watch a movie, but he insisted on joining her. Observing Joshua watch a film about the group he idolized had been a rare treat.

"We're like the Monuments, Fine Arts, and Archives section, except we liberate art from the Eldritch Market. Keep sensitive material from falling into the wrong hands. Joshua has been an agent of ours for years."

"Agent?" she echoed. "Wait a minute. Are you telling me Joshua is a Monuments man?"

"In a way, yes. Mind you, he doesn't do it out of pure generosity. We offer a finder's fee for any art that's recovered. It can be quite substantial."

Ellen sat back in her chair and let the wave of information wash over her.

Joshua Logan. Secret agent. She wanted to believe it. *Much better than art thief.*

And the same pieces that made him a thief made Joshua a secret agent. His recent withdrawal from her life, his insistence on keeping his study locked, his squirrelly reaction when she asked him about the robbery at the art gallery. Ellen shivered as she realized how deep the rabbit hole might go.

"Oh, that reminds me." Owen Cartwright reached into his jacket pocket and slid a small booklet across the table. "I was supposed to give you this when you turned twenty-one, but . . ." He paused and studied her with his foxlike eyes. "You'd already been through so much with the serial killer. I didn't want to disturb you until you recovered."

She eyed the object suspiciously. "What is it?"

"Your inheritance. Joshua's been putting money aside since he adopted you. He's done an excellent job managing your funds."

She continued to stare at the object. After a few moments, she grabbed it, her fingers tracing the Athenaein Association's ornate logo on the cover.

When Ellen opened the book, she saw a spreadsheet with an account number and a temporary password. A number leaped out at her in bold print: $15,322,451.63.

Ellen blinked at the jumble of numbers. She was convinced she was seeing double. *Not double. Triple. Quadruple.* Her mind needed to spell it out.

Fifteen million dollars. This says you have fifteen million dollars.

A fierce blush spread across her face.

"Are you all right?" Owen Cartwright asked.

"Is this . . . are you . . ." She glared at him. "This is a joke, right?"

Out of the corner of her eye, she saw someone heading toward their table.

Okay, here it comes, she thought. *The moment people jump out and say I've been pranked.*

"What are you doing here?" Miss Strauss demanded.

The sudden appearance of the Miskatonic bureaucrat only deepened Ellen's confusion. When she said nothing, Miss Strauss scowled at her.

"Are you stalking Dr. Carter?"

At the mention of his name, Ellen turned.

Andrew Carter sat on the far side of the restaurant, trying his best to blend in with the tapestries.

Joy flooded through her.

She lurched to her feet, her voice piercing the quiet of the restaurant.

"Andrew!"

The other diners stopped midmeal to look at her.

All Ellen wanted to do was run to him, to throw her arms around Andrew and feel the warmth of his body, to feel that he was there.

Owen Cartwright laid a hand on her arm, keeping her from running across the restaurant. It was only then that she made the connection. Andrew Carter was here. Miss Strauss was here. He was having dinner with the bureaucrat who despised her.

Ellen sank back into her seat.

What's he doing here? With her? she wondered.

Owen Cartwright fixed the woman with a cool gaze. "Excuse me? Who are you, and why are you interrupting a confidential conversation with my client?"

Client.

The word drained the color from Miss Strauss's face. Ellen remembered threatening to sue the woman the last time they were together. It seemed like a lifetime ago. She would have enjoyed the moment more if she hadn't been so addled by the fifteen million dollars.

Her companion reached into his pocket and set his phone on the table.

"I think we need to record this," he said to Ellen as he pressed record. "I will repeat my question. Who are you, and why are you interrupting a confidential conversation with my client? A client who came here at *my* invitation?"

Miss Strauss's mouth opened and closed, but no sounds came out. Like a fish out of water, she gulped the cold, hostile air, then abruptly turned and headed back to her table.

"I despise bullies, don't you?" Owen Cartwright quipped as he reclaimed his phone.

"That. Was. Awesome," Ellen marveled. "You really saved my bacon, Mr. Cartwright."

"Owen." He beamed. "And I'm pleased to be of service." He tapped the booklet that lay untouched on the table. "Surprised?"

Ellen snorted. "To put it mildly."

"May I offer you some advice?"

"Please."

"Inheriting money is a life-changing event. It takes time to process. Use the money you need to pay off any outstanding debts, then don't touch it for at least a year. Put off making big purchases."

"There goes my Porsche," she joked before she realized it wasn't a joke. *You really could buy a Porsche,* her mind whispered.

"I can put you in touch with someone to help you manage your money. But that can wait until later." He held up his glass and offered a toast. "To your newfound prosperity."

"Can I ask you something?"

"Of course."

"Is this money . . . dirty?"

He peered at her over his glass.

"What money isn't?"

Chapter Twenty-Six

Morning light poured through the leaded glass window of The Five Eaves, dappling the bedspread with diamond-shaped patterns. Ellen kicked off the covers and stretched, letting the golden light bathe her naked body.

She glanced at the clock.

Ten.

She couldn't remember the last time she'd slept in. Arkham Asylum certainly didn't give its residents the luxury.

Arkham Asylum.

Only twenty-four hours ago, she had been an inmate in a mental institution. "What a difference a day makes," she croaked as she reached for a glass of water.

She had been out late, celebrating her newfound wealth with Owen Cartwright. Cocktails had followed dinner. Afterward, they retired to a cigar bar, where he introduced her to a fine (almost certainly illegal) Cuban. Smoking wasn't something she particularly liked, but she appreciated the pace it imposed. She and Owen lingered on the patio, enjoying the cool summer night. Before he returned to Boston, he encouraged her to spend another day relaxing at the hotel, courtesy of the Athenaein Association.

After taking a shower and slipping into a cozy hotel robe, she ordered room service. As she munched on her croissant, her eyes darted to the booklet on the nightstand. "Fifteen million dollars."

Saying it didn't make it any more real. As soon as she finished breakfast, Ellen logged into her account using the information Owen Cartwright had given her: $15,628,900.66.

She looked at the new number several times before her rational mind took over.

Yesterday must have been a good day on the stock market.

The stock market.

Interest.

Taxes.

You need to start thinking about these things now.

A startled sound escaped her throat. Ellen slumped in her chair and gazed at the courtyard below. She once read that positive life events were as stressful as negative ones. She had blown off the idea at the time. *Give me a big helping of positive stress, please!* she joked with her friends. Now she was in a five-star hotel, staring down the barrel of a first world problem. The freedom her new wealth gave her was staggering. Mind-boggling. She felt like she had been cut loose, left to drift in a void.

Ellen was seized by a sudden desire to move.

After locking her account information in the wall safe, she changed into last night's clothes and gathered her things.

Old Arkham had cooled overnight, but heat still clung to the buildings. As Ellen navigated the shadowy lanes, the morning sun pierced the trees, blinding her with light. She slipped free of the tight confines and walked along the riverbank. The summer storms had left the Miskatonic swollen and unhappy. Water roared by her, its frothy waves bearing tree branches and other debris.

She paused on the bridge that connected the two parts of the city and stared at the uninhabited island in the middle of the river.

Ellen shivered and kept walking.

Her body knew where it was going, even if she didn't. The suburbs where Andrew Carter lived seemed to appear suddenly, like a mystical city. All around her, children played, taking advantage of the cool summer morning. Parents watched their activity from kitchen windows and front porches. A few of them scowled at her. Ever since the "gas leak," strangers in New Arkham were viewed with renewed suspicion. Impromptu neighborhood watches had been established to protect the community.

Ellen was glad she wasn't wearing anything identifying her as a student. Even so, hostile eyes followed her. She held her head high as she walked by them. But the moment she saw Andrew Carter's Range Rover in the driveway, her brave facade crumbled.

What am I going to say? What could I possibly say to . . .

To what? she asked herself. *What is it you're trying to do?*

The front door to Andrew Carter's house flew open before she could answer her own questions, and he emerged. He looked different. It took Ellen a moment to realize what had changed.

"You shaved," Ellen announced as she approached him.

Andrew looked at her like she'd sprouted another head. "What?"

"You shaved off your beard."

Really? A voice taunted her. *You came all this way to say that?* The weight of her bag reminded Ellen of the reason for her visit.

"I'm here to return your things. What you gave me in Edgewood when the shadow zone opened," she offered.

Andrew blanched when she mentioned the shadow zone, but he stepped aside and let her pass. The house was refrigerator cold. Ellen rubbed her arms as he appraised her with a stare as icy as the room.

"What are you supposed to be this time?" he grunted.

"Excuse me?"

"Your getup. What's Norm dressed you up as this time?"

She looked down at last night's outfit.

"I . . . this isn't a costume. This is me. Just me."

A quavering voice called out. "Andrew, who is it? Is it her?"

"Robert?" Ellen ran past Andrew and into the kitchen.

Robert Carter sat at the table drinking coffee. His left arm was in a cast that was strapped tightly to his body. A blotchy network of bruises crisscrossed his face. When he saw her, his battered face came to life. "It *is* you," he marveled.

Ellen rushed to the old man's side. "Oh my God, what happened?"

"The police happened." Andrew offered as he followed her into the room. "Let's just say they don't take it easy on people who violate martial law. Even if they are harmless idiots."

Robert Carter patted her with his good hand. "It's not so bad," he reassured her.

"At his age, a broken bone can be a death sentence," his son pointed out.

Her stomach dropped. "Broken?" she whispered.

Robert ignored her concern. He stared at her with big, innocent eyes.

"*Kore memagmeni*," he breathed, his hand tightening around hers. "Daughter of twilight," he intoned. "The girl who walks through walls."

An oily sensation trickled down the nape of Ellen's neck.

"I saw you with my father. Fighting the darkness, side by side," he continued in a dreamy voice. "You made him look brave. Noble. You *changed* him." The old man slid off his chair and dropped to his knees.

Ellen cringed as he pressed his dry lips to her skin.

Just like King Kuranes, she thought with a shudder.

For the second time that morning, the boundaries of physical space seemed to collapse, trapping her. This time, it wasn't as easy as slipping out of a hotel room. Robert Carter clutched her hand as if she was the only thing holding him together.

"My dad," the old man sobbed, his body shaking. "I want to see my daddy. Please."

Ellen knelt beside him and gathered him in her arms. Robert's bones creaked when she hugged him.

"You listen to me. Don't you kneel and beg to anyone," she whispered, her voice hot on the top of his head. "If you want to see him, you demand it. It's your right as a son. And his duty as a father."

Andrew Carter's hand landed on her. Ellen jumped, half expecting him to yank her away from his father. But the hand that gripped her shoulder was firm but gentle.

"I need to talk to you, Ellen," he murmured. "Privately."

Ellen slowly detached herself from Robert Carter. She stood, bringing the old man up with her. She helped him into his chair, then followed Andrew into the living room. As soon as she got there, she deposited his things on the coffee table.

Wallet. Car keys. House keys. Gun.

Her fingers brushed the cold metal of the Carter family ring.

She pulled it out of her pocket and set it next to his other belongings.

Andrew sighed when he saw it. "Goddamn it, Ellen." He shook his head.

"I know, and I'm sorry, but I really needed it." She paused before she remembered what he told her. *Don't censor yourself. Not with me.* "I really needed it to reach him."

"Randolph Carter?"

"Yes," she replied as she gazed into the dead stone. Now that it was in the waking world, it no longer flirted with the light. "Maybe Robert could use it. To get in touch with his—"

"I don't think that's a good idea," he cut her off. "Not in his state."

Ellen nodded and stared at the blond hardwood floor.

"I'm leaving Arkham," Andrew announced.

Ellen's head jerked up. "What?" she blurted.

"Miskatonic has put me on academic leave until a full investigation into the shadow zone is complete. And God only knows how long that will take."

Her mind flashed on seeing him in the restaurant. "That's why you were with Miss Strauss. Last night in the Italian place."

A bitter smile spread across his face. "I guess she thought she was being kind, breaking the news to me over dinner. Either that or she figured I wouldn't explode if I was in a public place."

Ellen's eyes flooded with tears. "Oh God, Andrew, I'm so sorry."

He shrugged. "I don't mind. It gives me time to attend to the other parts of my life. I need to find a new home for my father. Hell, once he's settled, maybe I'll even take a trip or two. Conduct some field research. I've never really liked teaching, to be honest. I hate being in front of an audience."

Her heart twisted with the news.

"That's a shame," she whispered. "You're a great teacher, Andrew. I've learned *so* much from you."

Now it was his turn to look down at the floor.

"They're coming after you, too," he murmured.

"What?"

"I think Miss Strauss is going to have you expelled from Miskatonic."

Expelled. The word should have stung her to the very core. All she ever wanted in her life was to attend Miskatonic University, to get into the special program and explore the mysteries of the universe. But when Andrew warned her of her potential exile, the only thing Ellen felt was relief. The missed summer school, the piles of books waiting to be read and digested, the papers she needed to write . . . all that weight suddenly lifted off her. None of it mattered anymore. With the money Joshua provided her, she could write her own ticket. Transfer to a new college. Take a year off and travel the world. She could do whatever she wanted. She was free. Still . . .

"Pretty shitty way to treat a couple of heroes, if you ask me," Ellen grumbled.

Andrew erupted in a peal of laughter, an outburst that sounded dangerously close to tears.

"Are you okay?" Ellen asked as she moved closer, ducking down to catch his eye. When he refused to look at her, she plucked the sleeve of his shirt. "Andrew?"

"I'm sorry I couldn't protect you," he said in a small voice. "From Miss Strauss. From Solomon Reye. From any of it."

"I never wanted you to protect me," she insisted. "I always wanted to be on equal footing with this thing of ours."

His mouth curled into a smile. "This thing of ours? You make us sound like the Mafia."

"I don't know what to call us," she admitted. "A partnership? A friendship? Something more?" she ventured, her lips tingling as she remembered their kiss.

Andrew Carter finally looked at her, and she saw the passion burning in his bright-blue eyes.

"Oh, we're definitely something more," he assured her. "But it's a dream, Ellen. It will never happen. Not as long as I'm a professor."

Words surged on Ellen's tongue, desperate to be unleashed. She wanted to argue, to insist that she was no longer his student, that the moment he gave her a grade, that part of their life was over. The pain in Andrew's eyes stopped her. She could see the difficulty he had setting boundaries. She could feel his turmoil. And his desire. It swirled like a living, breathing thing in the space between them. Ellen knew that if she chose to press him, if she insisted on being something more, he would give in. And the moment he yielded, something important inside Andrew Carter would die.

"You do understand, don't you?" he blurted, sounding astonished.

"Yes," she murmured as she looked around his living room at the peaceful place she had grown to love. "This really fucking sucks," she said with a sigh.

His sudden laughter startled her. Ellen reeled from the outburst, feeling like she had been slapped in the face.

"Oh, no. No, no, no. Don't take it that way," he scolded her as he pulled her into his arms.

Ellen didn't expect Andrew to hug her. Especially after everything he had just said. But here he was, sweeping her up, offering himself without hesitation. She pressed her face into his shirt, relishing the warmth of his body, the rich, exotic smell of his cologne.

He trusts me, she thought. *That's why he's letting this happen. He trusts me.*

"Yes, I do," Andrew murmured as he buried his face in her neck, sighing his desire into her skin. "You're an amazing woman, Ellen Logan," he whispered in her ear. "It was an honor to meet you."

Her hands clutched at the muscles in his back. "Will we ever see each other again?" she asked in a choked voice.

"I don't know, but I hope so."

She turned just enough to kiss him on the cheek.

"I meant what I said in Edgewood," she said as she pulled away, swiping at her tears. "If anything happens to you, I'll be pissed."

A sudden movement in the room broke the spell. Robert Carter hovered in the doorway, looking at them with a longing that rivaled their own.

"I really do wish you were my daughter-in-law," he said in a trembling voice.

A fresh batch of tears threatened to overwhelm Ellen.

"Thanks, old man," she croaked, pausing long enough to take one last look at the two men. "You take care of each other, okay?"

Ellen turned and ran out of Andrew Carter's house before they could respond. She rushed past the prying eyes of his neighbors and didn't stop until she was on the bridge back to Old Arkham. Only then did she stop and allow herself to break down.

The Miskatonic River absorbed her misery, masking the sound of her sobs. Sweeping her tears into its storm-addled waters.

Chapter Twenty-Seven

"So, you're rich? Tell me, Logan. How does it feel?"

Greg Linley hid a smirk as he took a sip of coffee. The espresso machine at Hallowed Grounds hissed behind them, spitting out caffeine for students racing off to finals.

Ellen watched them wistfully through the window. "It's been an experience, to say the least." She sat back, twisting a napkin in her hands. "I've learned some valuable lessons."

"Such as?"

"Money doesn't make everything better." She dug into her bag and pushed a letter across the table.

She had only received it a few days before, but the words were burned into her brain.

Dear Miss Logan,

We regret to inform you that due to violations of school policies and expectations, you are being dismissed from Miskatonic University, effective immediately.

The administration has been aware of your actions during the recent emergency, which resulted in your arrest and subsequent institutionalization in Arkham Asylum. This, coupled with previous questionable behavior, has led us to question your safety, as well as the safety of others, if you continue to attend the university.

Please contact the Registrar's office if you have any questions about your records and transcripts.

Dr. Charles Hayley
President of Miskatonic University

Her friend scowled. "This is bullshit!" he snapped, slapping the letter onto the table. "If they suspended everyone who engaged in questionable behavior or spent time in an asylum, no one would be left! And you're a hero! You saved lives! Jesus, Logan!"

"I know," Ellen said softly.

"You can fight this. With your money, you can get yourself a hell of a lawyer. And you've got reporters on your side. You could hold a press—"

She interrupted him. "I don't want to fight it."

"Don't want to fight it?" Greg echoed her words in disbelief. "Getting into Miskatonic's special program is all you ever talked about. It's what you've wanted ever since I met you. You busted your ass to get in. Now you're just going to give up?"

"I'm not giving up. Just giving into reality," she insisted. "Sure, I could stay here if I wanted. And I do have the money to fight my expulsion. But the appeal might take months. Even years. And if I won? I might get back into Miskatonic, but the powers that be would always be watching me. Waiting for me to screw up. Then the process would start all over again."

"It's not fair," Greg groused.

"No. It's not," she agreed.

"Do you think the Big Man was behind it?" he asked after a few moments of silence.

"Excuse me?"

"Dr. Carter. Do you think he was behind it?"

"No," she replied quickly. "He's the one who warned me about it."

Her friend snorted. "Warned you about it? The man should have *done* something about it."

"He couldn't."

"Why not?"

"He's in the doghouse, too. On administrative leave pending a formal investigation."

Greg slumped in his chair. "This place," he hissed before taking a swig of coffee.

Ellen's eyes drifted to the crutches perched against the table. "How's your foot?"

Greg shot her a knowing look.

"You're changing the subject."

"Yes, I am," she replied. "Seriously, how are you?"

"I still have a few more weeks on crutches, then some physical therapy. The doctors think I'll make a full recovery." He stopped and shot her a pointed look. "I'm lucky. Some victims of *dog* attacks don't fare so well."

Now, it was Ellen's turn to smirk and take a sip of coffee. "Dog attacks. Radiation leaks. Mass hallucinations. I'm certainly not going to miss all the lame explanations."

"What are you going to do?"

"That's what I brought you here to tell you. I'm leaving," she announced.

"Leaving?"

"It doesn't make sense staying in a college town if you've been thrown out of college."

"Where are you going?"

"New Orleans. My uncle Joshua told me it's where I should go if I want to learn more about my family."

She and Joshua had a long video chat after her visit with Owen Cartwright. During their conversation, he admitted what she already suspected. They weren't related, at least not by blood. Her eyes filled with tears as she remembered what Joshua said next.

That doesn't mean I don't love you.

Very much.

"I thought I'd chase some leads and see where they take me. Maybe continue my education down there. Thankfully, my credits aren't affected by being booted out of school, so I won't have to retake classes."

"I'm going to miss the *shit* out of you, Ellen."

Tears spilled onto her cheeks. "I'm going to miss you, too. And I better see you in New Orleans. Because if ghost hunting and barhopping don't lure you down for a visit, our entire friendship has been based on a lie."

As he raised his cup and they clinked on it, Greg's cell phone blared the opening bass line of Queen's "Another One Bites the Dust." He silenced it with a wince. "Time for me to go. Finals." He shot her an apologetic look.

She helped him gather his things.

Greg hugged her as soon as he was balanced on his crutches. "Go in peace."

"And may God be with you on the dangerous path you tread," she murmured, finishing the traditional Miskatonic blessing.

When Greg hobbled away, Ellen returned to her seat. She dug a richly embossed leather book out of her bag. She'd bought the journal on her last day of work at Mote It Be. Opening it, Ellen smoothed down the creamy white paper.

It was time to start a new journey.

What Comes Next?

Thank you for reading Shadow Zone.

While this chapter of Ellen Logan's journey has ended, the shadows are still moving.

There're more adventures to come in the **Shadows of Miskatonic** series.

Want to be the first to know when the next book arrives?
Join Barbara's reader list for exclusive updates, bonus content, and behind-the-scenes looks at the world of Miskatonic.
Sign up at: BarbaraCottrell.com/subscribe

Catch up on the rest of the series and explore character lore at BarbaraCottrell.com

Acknowledgments

Like my main character Ellen Logan, *Shadow Zone* marks a major transition in my life.

After almost ten years, I am now working with a new editor. As I delved deeper into the world, I realized I needed someone with a thorough understanding of the works of H. P. Lovecraft. My heartfelt thanks to Robbi Sommers Bryant, who started with me on this journey and shepherded the first two volumes of this series. I wouldn't have gotten this far without her guidance. And to John Palisano, my new editor, thank you for jumping so enthusiastically into the work. I appreciated a pair of fresh eyes on the series. I look forward to working with you on future books in the series.

I also wanted to thank one of my beta readers, fantasy writer Marion Deeds, who went above and beyond the call of duty. Not only did she read *Shadow Zone* in record time, but she helped me strengthen the areas where the story faltered. And she did this all for the price of a churro latte!

Thanks to authors James Chambers and Brian Hodge, who allowed me to use their Keziah Mason formulae and the fictional artist Cecil Conklin, respectively. One of the things I love about Lovecraft writers is how open people are to sharing their worlds. I hope to return the favor someday . . .

Speaking of sharing worlds, thank you to my brother-in-law, Dr. Seth Cottrell, for helping me understand the world of mathematicians and to Dr. Lauren Cottrell (yes, there are a lot of doctors in my family!) for diagnosing Ellen Logan. They gave me the information I needed to avoid embarrassing myself too much. I probably still got some things wrong, but any inaccuracies are mine and mine alone.

And last, I must thank my husband, Lance. He is my greatest supporter—lifting my spirits when I doubt my abilities, encouraging me to venture outside my comfort zone, always making sure I have everything I need to get the work done. He is also not afraid to offer me honest criticism. His feedback made *Shadow Zone* the book that it is.

I look forward to many more years of our partnership.

Teamwork makes the dream work!

Biography for Barbara Cottrell

Barbara Cottrell gave up her career as a professor to pursue her true passion: writing weird fiction. The first book in her series, *Darkness Below*, received Best First Book from IndieReader, three gold medals from the BookFest, and a silver medal from Readers' Favorite. The second novel, *Thin Places*, was also critically acclaimed, celebrated for its "powerful potion of cosmic horror, urban fantasy, and romantic tension."

When she's not exploring the darker corners of the imagination, she makes wine in Northern California with her husband, Lance.

To find out more about her and the world of Miskatonic University, visit www.barbaracottrell.com.